THE EVERLAND BAY SERIES | BOOK ONE

JOURNEY TO EVERLAND BAY

A NOVEL BY

LYNNE SHANER

Black Rose Writing | Texas

ISBN: 978-1-68513-404-4
LIBRARY OF CONGRESS CONTROL NUMBER: 2023949034
PUBLISHED BY BLACK ROSE WRITING
www.blackrosewriting.com

Printed in the United States of America
Suggested Retail Price (SRP) $20.95

Journey to Everland Bay is printed in Minion Pro

*As a planet-friendly publisher, Black Rose Writing does its best to eliminate unnecessary waste to reduce paper usage and energy costs, while never compromising the reading experience. As a result, the final word count vs. page count may not meet common expectations.

Acknowledgments

To my mother, who first read to me and encouraged my writing; I wish you could be here to hold this book in your hands. I will always be grateful for the ways you made reading and writing enchanted worlds. I am grateful, too, to so many others. To the amazing team at Black Rose Writing, from Reagan Rothe to the whole magical crew. How lucky I am to be with you as one of your authors. To the founder of the writing salon AllWriters' Workplace and Workshop, Kathie Giorgio, for her excellent coaching and her encouragement, as well as to all those in her Saturday novel writing group. To Carrie Newberry, wonderful writer and coach who loved this book from its beginning and made it so much better along the way. To mystery writer extraordinaire Patricia Skalka, who encouraged me to keep going with this book. Special thanks to my loving friends and family who cheered for me along the way, especially, Hayley, Eva, Jane, Elizabeth, Linda, Shelly, Sue, Pat, Kevin, Julie, Erin, and Brooke. And most of all, I am grateful for my wonderful husband, David Nelson, who just kept supporting me, encouraging me, and believing in me.

Praise for
The Everland Bay Series

"A beautifully engaging fantasy teeming with dragons, fae, magic, and the importance of family and friendship. A joy to read from beginning to end. I found myself rooting for our main heroine, Jemma, as she grew into a wonderful and powerful young woman. I am already looking forward to the next work in this thrilling series!"
–Julie Boglisch, author of the *Elifer Chronicles*, the *Requiem of Stones* series, and the standalone, *Ghost of a Mystery*

"I want a pocket fairy! And a scrying stone, and a grove of flutewood trees, and all the other tools and abilities that the mages here have at their command. What a wonderful—and credible—world Lynne Shaner has created. She makes magic seem the norm in this classic tale of good versus evil while weaving in parallels to the very real-world we humans inhabit. I shuddered at the politics and strife that so sadly reflect our society and delighted in the science she so deftly incorporates. A job well done, with the happy promise of more to come in this new series."
–Patricia Skalka, author of the *Dave Cubiak Door County* mysteries

"For those of us forced to accept that our Hogwarts letter is sadly never going to arrive, Lynne Shaner's new book, *Journey to Everland Bay*, is an opportunity to find magic in the everyday world again. And what magic it is! From knitting bags that transform into a wearable bracelet, to tiny pocket faeries, to a dragon that can scale her size down smaller than a teacup or up as large as a house. I want to sit and enjoy a cup of tea with so many of these characters. I'm just going to have to move to Everland Bay!"
–Carrie Newberry, author of *Pick Your Teeth with my Bones* and *Wolf is a Four-Letter Word*

"A magical journey full of whimsy, discovery, family drama, betrayal, and redemption. If you loved the magical world of Harry Potter and long for a new, enchanting place to call home, you should give *Journey to Everland Bay* a try."
–**Ross Hightower, author of *Spirit Sight***

"The prologue sets the reader up for a smooth ride into a new world where fae, elf, human, dragons, and magic dwell. So realistic I could relate immediately. As the story moves deeper, the blend of real world and magic is both exciting and comfortable. Magic appears, weaving in and out of characters and settings with astonishing ease, taking readers along for the ride."
–**Mary Ann Noe, author of *Water the Color of Slate***

"*Journey to Everland Bay* weaves the contemporary world into a magical world with originality and urgency. It is like a battle between fast moving steel and slowly falling rose petals, never forgetting the cost of progress or what true destruction looks like. It is iridescent at its core, a shimmering and ethereal reminder that sometimes, the old ways are best."
–**Del Blackwater, author of *Dead Egyptians***

JOURNEY
TO
EVERLAND
BAY

Prologue

Annalyn raised the shades and summer flowed into the bright, airy kitchen. Jars and vases of late peonies filled the air with the scent of summer in the countryside, and a soft scatter of petals fluttered down to the counter as they caught the breeze. Queen-Mab's Lace filled another row of vases, adorning the kitchen counter and table with living green-and-white lace. A very simple spell served to keep them upright, instead of wilting instantly. She nodded in satisfaction at the flowers, then turned toward the sound of her granddaughter coming down the stairs. A tangle of dark curls atop a long, lanky frame emerged from around the corner.

"Morning, Grandma!"

"Good morning, my sprite," said Annalyn, stretching out her arms and giving her beloved granddaughter a hug. She reached up and tucked a rogue curl behind one ear. "Heavens, how you've sprung up again this year! You're taller than I am now. But guess what day this is?"

"Story Day?"

"Yes! You always guess right!" They laughed together as they recited the familiar phrases. Jemma was fifteen now, well past the days when she curled up in her grandmother's lap and settled in to hear the story of Everland Bay. But Annalyn knew that she still enjoyed the ritual as much as she had as a little girl. Every year, Jemma visited Grandma Annalyn and spent the summer with her on her rambling, comfortable homeplace. Known as Borderlands, the large, sprawling property encompassed woods, streams, hills, and forestland, and even sported a lovely shoreline along Lake Michigan, a lake so large many assumed it was an inland sea.

The boundaries of Annalyn's property were irregular, having been created so long ago that the land itself had rippled and changed over time. One part of the land touched the grand and celebrated Everland Bay Institute, and another portion of the border ran along the outermost edges of the small hamlet nearby called Everland Bay Village, which had grown up around the needs of the great research institution. Annalyn thought back fondly to the time when her daughter Elise, son-in-law Agni, and toddler Jemma lived close by, within an easy drive. It used to be that Elise, Jemma, and Annalyn, "The Three Graces," as her son-in-law used to call them during happier times, spent summertime together. Berry-picking, reading in the worn, green-and-white striped hammock, catching frogs, finding sea glass and small, beautiful stones on the beach, were all part of the time they spent together. And story time.

This year, for the first time, Jemma was staying alone after her mother dropped her off. This year would be very different. The family moved to Verandalands a few years earlier. Despite Annalyn's warnings to her daughter about the dire consequences of living in a place that had come to hate and even begun to deny magic, Elise said she must stay with her husband. Annalyn suspected that he was discouraging the use of all magic, even in their home. She was seeing the inevitable signs of magical decline in her daughter, who was beginning to seem depressed, and was starting to emotionally recede and physically fade. The normal, subtle iridescence that usually brightened her face was dull, matte-looking, and sometimes not visible at all. Part elf, part fae, part human, Elise was both very sensitive and potentially very long-lived. Not quite immortal, but capable of living into the low hundreds. But only if she stayed true to herself and her magical nature. If she did not nurture that part of herself, Annalyn knew, Elise would become weak. Her delicately balanced immune system would suffer, which would mean that she would fade and succumb to illness and, possibly, an early death. Annalyn was distraught at what she was seeing in her daughter, but powerless to reverse the decisions that Elise made.

Annalyn thought back to the day before when Elise dropped Jemma off. "Mama, I'll need you to take her on her own this summer. This might be the last time I'll be strong enough to drive this far, and I need to go back to Verandalands, to Agni, to sort things out and turn things around before I lose more strength. Before I, well, before I fade further."

"Oh, honey, why? Being here with us, even if just for a few weeks, will help heal you, or at least keep you strong, and will help Jemma learn more of what she needs to know to be prepared."

"I can't. Verandalands is draining me. And Agni's insistence on keeping us there is also wearing me down, taking it away. My magic. It is fading. I am fading. I don't have the strength to make him stop."

"Why didn't you tell me it had gotten to this point? You will lose everything. Even your life. How can this happen? What is wrong with him? I thought you said he loved you. And Jemma. How could he do this to you if he loved you? You can leave him now, you know. You can come and live here." Annalyn wiped tears away and glanced around to make sure Jemma was out of earshot. Jemma was out in the meadow, far away from their voices.

"I kept wanting it to stop," said Elise. "But I grew weaker and weaker before I knew it. And now I am no longer strong enough. I can't leave him, not really. I still think he is really trying to do his best, in his own way. I believe he still loves me, loves Jemma. He thinks he has done what is right for us, financially, and therefore in every way, by taking us there. We live in the most mixed part of Verandalands. In D.C. There used to be a lot of magic in the area before it was discouraged, then actively discriminated against. There is some still, but most is fugitive, furtive. People make fun of us, so we hide it in public. I have a couple of good friends who are magical, so we are close. Agni believes that should be enough for me. For Jemma and me. And he earns so much more there because his skills in attracting, raising, and managing money are so much stronger than anyone around him. The money and the power that go along with it have become irresistible to him. Full humans adore him because he brings in and makes so much money. They don't understand why, but they love him for it. Because he brings in such incredible amounts, they never question it. They do not know of his, or our, magic. But now it seems that more and more he can no longer see beyond the power and money."

Annalyn could see how much the effort to speak of all of these difficulties had cost her daughter, whose breathing was now labored. Annalyn felt a chill wash over her; she was terrified.

"But how can this be happening? How can he not see how ill you are?" said Annalyn, feeling desperate, scrabbling inside her mind to find something to say that might sway Elise.

"Mama, he doesn't perceive the physical fading, the loss of iridescence. Remember that. He is a mix of dragon and human. He is also a man. Certainly, if he were to look closely, listen closely, to what I say, what I'm feeling, what I can no longer do, he would know. But the visual part of this is powerful; he cannot see the way you and I do. And in addition, he has never quite understood that my magic is necessary to me. His magic is so different. It is just baked in, needs no specific practicing. It just strengthens if he stays within his rules. This is my fault, too. I was full of pride and full of that sense of being invincible that comes when we are younger," said Elise.

"But you are nearly invincible, or you could be! You are partly immortal. You are losing your truest self in this marriage, Elise. Think of Jemma. Think of what will happen to her if you are unable or unwilling to take care of yourself for your own sake," said Annalyn.

"I know, Mama, I know. I know I should have done all of this earlier. I really thought I could be in Verandalands, keep my magic by practicing in private and visiting with you. But I was terribly, terribly wrong. I forgot, or maybe didn't want to remember, the innate weaknesses that can also come with the mix that I am. I forgot that I can't do this all alone. I need my magical community. My women friends. You. And now my strength is continuing to ebb, my will is softening. And as I fade, I grow so weak, Mama. It is difficult to even speak these words."

"You need to stay here then, even more than ever. We can get your strength restored. And at the end of the visit, if you are certain you must go back, I will go with you. I can help, even there, you know."

"No! I need to go back. And you can't come with me. I have to return to my home in Verandalands. But I am afraid for Jemma. I think he would strip away her magic if he could. And you know that would kill her. You know." Elise was whispering, and trembling. Tears flowed down her cheeks. "I must go back now. Maybe I can somehow make things better this summer. I keep hoping he will listen to me, change back to who he was when we were first together. He used to be so filled with love." She brushed away tears, took a deep breath. "I can try."

Jemma walked into view, and the two turned toward her.

"Jemma, sweetheart, come over here and say goodbye," said Elise.

Annalyn watched as Jemma came to join them. She longed to make things better for all of them but knew there was very little she could do. Her daughter was a woman grown, and Annalyn could not trail after her, insisting, when she was not welcome. Even if she did go, Annalyn knew she would only be turned away.

"You'll be staying here all summer on your own," said Elise. "Like we talked about on the way here; I'm going to go back home and take care of things there. Are you certain you'll be okay? Can you make sure to listen to your grandmother and be a good help to her?"

"Mom. I'll be fine." Jemma rolled her eyes, sighed, but with a small smile that dimpled one cheek. "And I promise to be a very good girl," she said, with an impish grin. She looked again at her mother and her brow folded into concern. "But why are you crying? Maybe you'll start to feel better, if you get more rest and don't have to worry about me." Jemma moved to be closer to her mother, reaching out to touch her hand.

Annalyn watched Elise hug Jemma and could see Jemma holding on tightly. She felt a great weight of sorrow yet to come, as she watched these two most beloved to her. How will we all bear this? She took a deep breath and hugged her daughter, whispering into her ear. "You can come right back here any time, okay? We can get all the help you need. Any time."

And with that, Annalyn stepped back, wiping her eyes with the back of her hand, taking another deep breath as she watched her daughter retreat and drive away.

"Grandma, are you crying, too?"

"We're just going to miss each other. We'll talk more about all of this in a little while. Your mother needs to sort things out at home," said Annalyn, waving still, though the drive was now empty.

Annalyn knew things were getting worse but didn't know Elise was in such danger. She always tried to look at the positive things in her daughter's life, despite her misgivings about Agni, who was so drawn to, and even ruled by, money and prestige. She wished she had spoken up more when he moved the family to Verandalands. And she did speak up. But she couldn't insist. She had no authority over her grown daughter and her husband. And what more could she have said? Whatever she voiced, Elise would have dug in even more. She could be very stubborn. At the time, Annalyn questioned the move, and Elise became defensive and prickly. They so rarely were in conflict, it was hard to know what to do. Annalyn didn't want to jeopardize her relationship with Elise or Jemma.

Annalyn came back from her musing and started breakfast for Jemma. "We'll have a bite to eat together and then start with our story," she said, turning toward the stove and heating up the oatmeal. She reached into the small kitchen drawer nearest the stove and drew out a very small knife, her favorite for cutting almonds, as its special properties, which allowed the blade to quickly sever energetic and molecular bonds, made the work go so quickly. Most mages used it for more elevated magic, but she enjoyed using tools like this in her ordinary life as well. She felt that keeping tools in her hands helped keep the magic fresh. She carefully wiped the knife before putting it away. Then she turned her attention again to Jemma, thinking things through and figuring out a next-steps plan.

Jemma came from a long line of powerful, magical humans. But some were mixed a bit. A little faery or elf here and there, sometimes a whisper of dragon in the misty past, and now, with the arrival of Agni in the family, an indisputable, significant portion of dragon. Many were still leery of admitting to dragon lineage, but Annalyn always welcomed the idea. She remembered how grateful she was for that perspective when Elise told her she was planning to marry Agni. Some still despised and vilified those of dragon heritage, not seeing the hypocrisy of assuming fae/elf/human mixes were normal but judging dragon as inferior. At one point, deep in the past, having many bloodlines, especially dragonblood, was considered an honor. Now the acceptance of the mixing was varied by region, custom, and even level of education. Most in the Great Waters Regions welcomed the notion. But even there, sometimes old biases remained, though it was considered inappropriate to admit to this. Fae, elf, and human all tended to forget that the weaving of backgrounds makes for stronger beings.

Dragonmarked humans were almost universally despised and even targeted for brutality and violence in the Verandalands. But throughout many other regions, things were changing; the younger generation loved all things dragon. Annalyn knew Jemma would one day need to fully understand and manage the various aspects of her mosaic background. She did her best to encourage Jemma's pride in her dragon self, celebrating the small, sparkly dot near the corner of her left eye. Indisputably a dragonmark, though they were becoming rare in recent generations. She encouraged Jemma's understanding of fae and elfin magic as well, which came from her own line. She worked hard to teach her that she was a special soul and would be with or without any magic at all.

Annalyn and Elise taught Jemma small magics from the time she was little, including turning on a little light in the evening, right inside her palm, knitting a small faery net to keep bugs away (this had to be refreshed in the event of rain, but Annalyn was always proud of the way Jemma caught on to spidersilk and flutewood silk knitting so quickly) and heating up tea without a fire. It worried and frustrated Annalyn that Jemma could no longer attend routine magic classes now that she was in the Verandalands. So Annalyn saw to it that Jemma could still perform basic magic, including general healing and defense, visualization, and manifestation. Annalyn also knew that Jemma was receiving nonmagical martial arts and self-defense with her father, which could be helpful, she knew, in the mix of topics for Jemma to learn. Annalyn tried to add to the magical complexity Jemma was learning each year, but it was difficult at such a distance. Jemma was not nearly as far along as she would have been if they stayed in the Great Waters Region.

But of all the magics, Annalyn loved story magic best, even as Jemma grew older. Loved the simple comfort of having Jemma curled against her when she was small. She loved the ritual of tea and settling in as Jemma asked for the story each year. Books that were chosen came to life in the telling and Story itself was a felt presence. Baking scenes were animated with flour that puffed up and out of the pages along with the tantalizing aromas of pies and cakes. Stories of princes and princesses fell open and rich fabrics—deep velvets and satin ribbons, fine buttons and fastenings of silver and gold—festooned the living room as the stories were read aloud. Each telling of the story was a little different. A tapestry might include a unicorn in one telling, leaping out of its small enclosure, and in another, a small fox might vault out of the book along with a rabbit or two, and tear around the room. Annalyn always kept an eye out for lost-looking bunnies and foxes afterward, in case they needed to be rounded up and ushered back into Storyland. She also made sure teacups were well out of the way during Story Time, lest they get upset by an exuberant creature.

The summertime visits were always framed as ways to simply spend time together. To help Grandma around the house and the garden. But Annalyn and Elise knew that these times were critically important in the shaping of a young mage, especially one who was so unusually interwoven among the magical lines. And with this new and awful knowledge from Elise, Annalyn knew that this summer might be the most important one she and Jemma would ever have together.

"Okay, Grandma, I think it's time. Can you tell me a story?" said Jemma, looking up from her now-clean oatmeal bowl, eyebrows raised and a smile on her face. "And shall I make us another cup of tea?"

"Tea would be lovely. And we'll start on the best story, though this year, we will have additions." Annalyn reached up to the bookshelf and before she could touch it, the storybook lifted itself off the shelf, floated down to Annalyn, riffling its pages a bit as if in eager anticipation, then settled into the couch. Many of the pages were worn in places, but still legible. "You know, my own grandmother read this to me every year when I was little. It tells the true story of Everland Bay," she said, opening the tooled-leather cover, turning the gold-edged pages, until she reached the first story. For now, she let the story sweep into the room and clear away their current worries.

"Long before anyone remembers, long before our grandmothers were mothers, there was a very special place for mages young and old to go to gain deep wisdom. Back then, there were hundreds of institutes and universities of magic of every level. Various countries and continents had their own, all of which existed in a spirit of pleasant community rivalry."

Annalyn turned the pages back to look at the contents page and thought of the various schools she knew of, most long gone. She flipped ahead again to the story and continued.

"Each of them claimed to be the best, but in the main, all knew that each was excellent in its own way. Respectable schools always graduated young mages, who went into the woven world; a world in which humans and many other creatures, including dragons, elves, and faeries, worked together.

"But at some point in the befogged past, humans began to assert themselves, driving away the good faeries and elves and dragons, and driving smaller schools out of business, for faeries and elves and dragons were helpful in running many places. Many humans were worried about this change, and they created, together, a different sort of place of magic and learning. So Everland Bay Institute was born. Older, expert mages of any sort could come to teach and finish their important work, both scholarly and applied, while younger mages in the beginnings of their work could apply for fellowships to come for a period of time to learn magecraft at a deeper level, and to live among the many creatures. Instead of simply learning the basics, these promising young scholar-mages could study with the best in the field, who were, by design, often those very wise and older mages who were finishing their big legacy works.

"Back then, some of the schools of magic had begun to decline, not only for the reasons noted earlier but also because humans in various parts of the known world began to decide magic was not something they wanted to fund in any way. True magic was often unpredictable and unexpectedly beautiful, as well as unexpectedly messy and inconvenient, and many humans found that frightening. So, some humans decreed it wasn't allowed, and cast doubts upon magic in general, pretending it wasn't real. They made rules against magic, punished those who practiced. Magic began to be discouraged in some parts of the world, particularly in the Verandalands, which, although it was beautiful and gracious and full of charm in many places, had become a refuge for frightened, angry, nonmagical humans. There were rumors of magic becoming illegal."

Jemma interrupted. "Grandma, I am scared about things at home. It has already gotten really bad there for Mom and me. And really, for Dad, though he doesn't see it, I think."

"I have been worrying about that, sweetheart. Can you tell me more?"

"Well. I am not supposed to talk about this. Dad says I should just ignore it and not talk about it. But kids make fun of me for my mark now. A lot. And whenever I do anything, even just a little mage light, I get in trouble. I'm not supposed to do anything magic. Not even heal anyone."

"Honey. Are you in danger?" Annalyn asked, setting the storybook aside.

"No. Well. I don't know. Maybe," Jemma said, looking down into her mug of tea. "One day, a while back, I was in art class, and we were weaving. Lame, but we were weaving baskets with some long grassy stuff. So, I just kind of invited some of my mini faery friends to help out. You know how they are."

"They are so good at weaving, and they love baskets, yes," Annalyn said, wondering where this was going.

"They were so happy. All giggly, like they can get. So, we all started weaving together. But the teacher couldn't see the faeries and it looked as if the basket was weaving itself. The teacher was angry and asked me what was happening, and I just said I was doing the basket. She got angrier. Other kids were laughing and pointing at me, though I'm not sure if they could see the faeries either. I was getting so upset. I asked the faeries to stop. The basket stopped being woven and sort of fell over. Then the teacher yelled at me. She said, 'No more of that, do you hear me? We will have none of that in my classroom. We don't allow that, that nonsense in my classroom. And you know it. You others, stop staring. There is nothing to see here. Jemma, take your little basket and weave it like you are supposed to, with your own hands. You will receive poor marks for unruliness for your little stunt.'"

Jemma stood up and walked over to the windows. She looked down and shook her head as she continued. "I didn't know what to do. I was crying and I just wanted to go home. I was so embarrassed. They were all laughing at me, and my faery friends were all upset, too. We were just so sad. I wasn't allowed to go home right then, but I wanted to. I tried to keep going on the basket, but it just wouldn't work. I could see a tiny faery curled up underneath the half-finished basket, crying. No one else could see her, but everything just was awful after that day. I mean, I know I'm not supposed to worry about what others say, but it is really bad there for me."

"Oh, sweetheart, I am so sorry to hear this." Annalyn got up went over to Jemma, hugged her. She gave her an extra squeeze, then let her go. "We need to talk about all of this. Let's go for a walk and get some fresh air."

Annalyn was deeply worried about her daughter and her granddaughter. Annalyn thought back to a time when she saw evidence of the deeper change in her son-in-law. She remembered how she called out to him, just last summer, when they were all visiting. They were all gathering things to go down by the lake for a picnic and Annalyn encouraged him to come with them all. He looked up, annoyed, as he was looking at his work phone, ignoring the beautiful day and buried in the messages on the tiny screen. Elise asked as well. He refused to go with them, and Annalyn remembered that he snapped sharply at Elise, not simply repudiating the request, but shaming her for asking in the first place. "What is wrong with you? You know I have to work. And I'm doing it for you, you know. Leave me alone!" he snarled.

Jemma's father was masterful in banking, as most human-dragon mixes were, but his success began to poison him, and he became more arrogant. And Annalyn knew he wanted more. Elise mentioned it to her, though just in passing. More power and more money. He decided to move them all to the Verandalands, despite the fact that dragonfolk were stigmatized and shunned there, and increasingly, denied altogether. And he made the move despite the first steps toward the denial of magic. Despite the rumors of the possible outlawing altogether. But the money was vastly better for him than it would be anywhere else.

Even after the move to Verandalands, Annalyn thought their usual summers together would continue for many years and would give her and Elise enough time to shape Jemma, and to teach her all that she would need. They assumed that Jemma would be able to take ongoing magical classes and one day apply for entrance into Everland Bay Institute if she wanted to. But things deteriorated more quickly than she imagined they could. And if Elise was to fade away and die, Annalyn knew, not only would her own heart break, but Jemma might not be able to come visit. Then Jemma would be in the same danger that Elise was in now. The stakes couldn't be higher and Annalyn was distraught.

"Let's walk to the lake," Annalyn said.

"Sounds good," Jemma said, jamming her feet into shoes and pulling a sweatshirt over her head, shaking out her curls. "These curls are a mess, as ever. But—let's go!"

"Here," said Annalyn, drawing Jemma toward herself. "Let me show you how to do that little braid, like we used to do when you were tiny." She quickly twisted and braided a small section from just above one ear, up over the crown, and over to the other side, allowing the curls to weave together and down Jemma's back. "Done, and that will stay all day!"

"Wow, thanks."

"If you forget how to do it, just ask your pocket faeries. They'll know.

Now. How much do you know about the other part of Everland Bay? The village itself?"

"Well, since we visit most summers, we've been in most of the shops, I think. And you know Mom always mentions the bookstore and we used to bring books back with us. What was the name of it?"

"Folio," Annalyn said, smiling at the thought of one of her favorite places.

"Yes, and of course, the frozen custard shop is a personal fave."

"Leroy's, yes. That stuff is really wonderful, even without a drop of magic. But there is a level of the Village that is deeper. You know it is quite magical in its own right.

"As you know, the Village is filled with shops and cafes and a library. Even a small museum. Over the years, each location, and the whole land on which everything stands, grew more magical. After hundreds and hundreds of years, it is as magical as the Institute itself, some say." They stopped at the bluff overlooking the lake. The lake was a thousand colors of blue. Aquamarine, indigo, sapphire, silvery blue, all glinting as the breeze whipped up whitecaps and the surf washed the shore.

"I never grow tired of looking at the lake," said Annalyn.

"Me neither. It always feels like I've come home when I see it again. Let's go down the bluff," said Jemma, leading the way. "Can you tell me more about the Village?" she said when they got down to the shoreline, filled with stones smoothed by millions of years of watery tumbling. "I knew it was special but mostly we were just in and out for quick visits.

I never stopped to think about any of this. How could it become magical?" Jemma asked, reaching down to pick up a small, smooth, flat speckled stone.

"The Village grew up around the Institute over generations. Mages were always coming and going, and some stayed in the Village instead of going further out into the woven world. There are tools and supplies of every sort; everything is available that a mage might need. Gear shops have scrying stones and bowls, rucksacks that can make your dinner and turn into a tent. Or a cave."

"Sound amazing," said Jemma, laughing. "We never had one of those."

"And the best knives."

"Like the one in your kitchen?" asked Jemma, tossing the stone, watching for the small splash.

"The very one! The Village also has a marvelous café, and we've talked about the bookstore. There's a vintage clothing shop and a wonderful yarn shop that has spidersilk yarns, flutewood silk yarns. The kind we use for those wraps we knit together. The Village grew into a place that specialized in magical offerings. Mages who decided to leave the Institute itself but loved the area stayed, raised families, and opened up businesses, which, of course, were magical. It all happened gradually."

"I remember the vintage shop; remember that time Mom and I went down on our own? We tried on hats, and they were definitely magical! I wish she had come this time so that we could go there again," said Jemma. "We never got around to going last year, though, and the last time we went, I think I was mainly interested the frozen custard. Can we go visit again this year?"

"That's a great idea. It's a little bit of a journey, but there's no reason we can't go there. I can show you all around and re-introduce you to everyone. Then one day, when you are older, maybe when you are on your way to the Institute yourself, you will know your way around a bit, from a more grown-up perspective."

Annalyn made a few calls to friends when they got back from their walk and arranged the trip.

"We'll just go over by house portal," said Annalyn. "We could walk, but it would take a while. And portal is better than the car for travel between enchanted places." The portal door, next to the pantry, looked like every other door in the house. But once it was opened, Annalyn only needed to touch the wall map that appeared on the wall above the banister to set their destination. By the time they walked down the steps and opened the door at the bottom, they would be exactly where she indicated on the map. Annalyn ran a finger over the top of the door. "It's been quite a while since I've visited anywhere by portal. I need to get out more. Look at this dust," she said.

"When can we go? Can we go now?"

"I need to let your mother know that we're going, but there's no reason we can't go right away. I've been in touch with my friends there, and we'd be welcome even today."

"I can't wait!"

Annalyn felt an answering delight as she saw the excitement on Jemma's face. She was so happy to be able to provide a little day trip. She knew it would help prepare Jemma for the future, but it was also going to be great fun. A very welcome break from this difficult time.

The phone rang. "I'll make the rest of our plans as soon as I see whose calling." Annalyn was smiling as she picked up the phone. "Agni? Hello! Perfect timing. We're planning a little trip to the Village, and—"

"Annalyn, it's about Elise," said Agni. Annalyn could hear the tension in his voice. Her smile faltered and disappeared. She sat down, slowly. "She's had some kind of a seizure. Jemma needs to come home right now. I don't have time to say more. I'm following the ambulance to the hospital. I've called for a car service to come get her. It will be at your place in about an hour. Please pack her up and for now, just have Jemma wait at home for me," said Agni.

"My god, Agni. This is terrifying," said Annalyn. She was filled with fear and felt a cold sliver of desperate worry slicing through her. She had a thousand questions but knew there was not time for those right now. "Okay. I will come with her. I can help out there, be there with Jemma now and later with Elise."

"No. You will not come here. This is not something for you to get involved in. I will handle it. Just get her packed up!" The line went dead. Annalyn was stunned, found herself staring at the phone. She could feel a river of anger churning through her. And now she had to collect herself as well as she could to make the most of the next few minutes.

"What's wrong? Grandma, what's wrong?"

Annalyn turned to Jemma, who was standing in the kitchen listening, forehead furrowed in worry.

"Honey. It's your mother. She had a seizure of some sort. Your father wants you home right away."

"Oh no. Oh, Grandma, I am so afraid. So afraid for Mom. So afraid that she is…that she might be dying. Is she?"

"Sweetheart. I don't know." Annalyn hugged her granddaughter and the two were in tears. "We have to get you home," she said, standing up and heading into Jemma's bedroom. "Your father is sending a car. It will be here soon. He prefers that I stay here. Let's pack as we talk. I need to tell you a thousand things, but we will start with some basics. You always have a home right here. No matter what. No matter what happens. Remember that your mother is a very strong and special woman. She may leave this earth soon. I don't know. But she will know that you are safe. It is a very small comfort, but it will mean a great deal to her."

"What do I do? Maybe she will get better. Maybe this will convince Dad to bring her back here."

"I don't know what is happening right now with her, and we won't know anything more until she is out of danger. You will be a great help to her once you are home. In the meantime, we can prepare you as much as we can now, and you can visit here anytime. And don't forget what I said about having a home here."

"I wish there were something more I could do. I wish I were a grownup and could bring her here."

"I know, honey. I wish I could bring her here, too. I can't force her or your father, though. Right now, this is beyond us both."

"You said I can prepare. How? What do I do?"

Annalyn could see the strength in Jemma's set expression. She knew her granddaughter had a depth and resilience that was continuing to reveal itself.

"You need to practice all of your magic, when you can, at home. And right now, I need to tell you more about the Village. The Village, and all the people in it, could be allies for you, in ways we can't imagine now. So, back to the storybook," Annalyn said, reaching again for the familiar book. She turned to the last chapter. "Here are all the places that you'll visit, or visit again, one day. As we were just saying, you've visited many of them already. Let me tell you just a bit more about them." Annalyn smiled at her granddaughter, and told the story of Folio, the bookstore; Time and Time Again, the second-hand shop; Heartwood, the outdoor gear shop; Enchantment, the chocolate shop; as well as the café, museum, the yarn shop, and the library. Each one had a place on the map and in her heart.

"I'll try to remember everything." Jemma said, looking at the map and again at the photographs of each place.

"You will. And remember the name Giselle Azule. She is a dear friend of mine and was your mother's favorite professor at the Institute. She's still a professor. Quite well known for her magic, but I know her and her mother both for their kindness and wisdom."

"I've heard of her. Dr. Azule came to visit once. Mom was so happy."

"She's a great mage and a good soul. And now, we must finish getting you packed and ready to go."

Annalyn and Jemma went upstairs, and Annalyn began to think through the problems ahead. For Elise. What happens if the hospital isn't magic-friendly? Will they know Elise is a fae/elf/human mix? There are only certain doctors in Verandalands able to treat mixed beings. Annalyn realized there was no way around it. No matter what

Agni wanted, she was going to go with Jemma and make sure Elise got into the right hands.

"I've decided that I need to come with you after all. Your mother needs special medical care, which isn't available in every hospital in the Verandalands," Annalyn said. "I need to contact some of my friends there."

Moments later, with everything packed and loaded into her car, they heard the hired car as the tires crunched on the gravel out front. The horn sounded. Annalyn went over and spoke to the driver. "Change of plans. I'm driving my granddaughter straight to the hospital. What we need you to do is go straight back, and intercept the ambulance if you can, have them go to Dumbarton Gardens East. I will also be telling Agni this. Please go on and even if you can't intercept the ambulance, inform Agni." She turned away and left the driver sputtering. Exasperated, he backed out. She could see him talking into an earpiece as he went.

Annalyn put her arm around Jemma's shoulders and gave her a little hug as they hurried over to her car. "Okay. In we go. Hang on while I make things go a bit faster than usual." Annalyn used the accelerator clutch, which allowed the car to cover ten times as much ground as usual.

"I am scared, Grandma."

"I won't say everything will be fine. This is going to be a tough time. But I am here, and I have strength, and I love you. And we are not alone. We have friends in the Village here and even in Verandalands. I will stay there as long I can. And perhaps we can get you back up here more often after that. In the meantime, I know you are strong and brave. And it's okay to be scared. One last thing." Annalyn reached behind her, where she had stowed a few last-minute things. She handed the Storybook to Jemma. "I think this needs to be with you now. It will give you strength and guidance."

Jemma gasped and began to cry as she reached for the book. "Are you sure?"

"I know it's not what we usually do. But the book will help you after I have gone. And it might help when it comes time to bring you back for good," said Annalyn. Quickly taking a deep breath, willing herself into steely determination, she pulled out of the drive with a squeal and sped to the nearest highway, not at all certain she could get there in time.

Chapter One
Jemma

Jemma blew through the ornate brass doors of the elegant Swain Museum of Art, held up her badge to the guard and glanced up as they smiled their usual morning greetings. She got to her cubicle and dropped her bag off at her desk, then headed down to the staff dining room to get a cup of coffee. And maybe a scone. Because they were so good, and they reminded her of the ones her grandmother made. Everland Bay cherry scones! If only she had some of the magic of that place, and those scones, here. Or better yet, just her grandmother's presence. She sighed, thinking of her grandmother, who still lived in her rambling house along the lake. I am overdue for a visit, she thought, and I should really bring the Storybook back with me this time—I keep forgetting when I visit. Probably because I really love having it here. She shook her head a little, smiling. And she pushed away the thoughts of her mother, who died ten years earlier, when she was just fifteen. That awful day when she brought the Storybook home with her from the visit that was cut short so painfully. How can it be that long ago? Sometimes it feels like yesterday, she thought, as the scenes flashed through her mind.

The fast drive back to her home in DC, the horror-strewn moments of rushing into the regular hospital, for they weren't there soon enough to send the ambulance to a specialized hospital for magical-being care. Jemma cringed inwardly, remembering the explosive argument between her father and her grandmother, as he tried to turn her grandmother away. Then watching helplessly as her grandmother found a nurse, too late then, who understood procedures for fae/elf/human care, and finally the look of deep sadness and exhaustion on her mother's face as she said goodbye.

Jemma shook her head again, trying to distract herself from the pain, wiping a tear away with the back of her hand. Back to work, Jemma, she said to herself, while glancing briefly at the galleries as she swiftly passed them on the way to coffee. History of the museum display, American art, tea ceremony display, Chinese porcelains. All those claws on all those Chinese dragons, she thought, reminding herself to check the special exhibition text again before they were silk-screened on the walls for the new show. Four claws? Five? Who cares, really? She found herself smiling again. The emperor cared once-upon-a-time and, today, the curator cares, that's who. And she always felt a special pull inside, looking at such exquisite dragons. Like long-lost, distant cousins. And really, the details about dragons *were* kind of interesting, on the whole. She loved the museum, and mostly liked her colleagues, each of whom specialized in some part of the complex system that allowed for the exhibition, study, and storage of so many beautiful objects.

"Hey, Jake," said Jemma, walking into the staff room, reaching for a cup and waiting for her colleague to fill his.

"Hey. You doing the Chinese cups and bowls show?"

"Yep. But, please. *Imperial Porcelains: Treasures of the Emperor.*"

"Suitably impressive," Jake said, with a serious nod that unfolded into a smile.

"Here's hoping our visitors think so. Or at least the director. And now, once I get my hands on one of those scones, back to work. We'll be finishing up soon."

"Sounds good. I'll be helping out on that show." Jake was an art handler, part of a small team seeing to the task of getting the artwork properly and safely displayed. "See you in the galleries sometime during walkthrough, no doubt."

"No doubt. Or maybe at your show. Did I see you had a flyer up?"

"Glad you saw it! I've got a few things in the Midland Galleries show. You know how we Midland/Great Waters artistes are exotic here in zee Verandalands," he said, with a faux French accent on *artistes*, and a raised eyebrow. "Sometimes that makes for a little extra interest. You should come to the opening if you can. They always have good treats."

"Plus, all that great work."

"That too. Also, we should get together soon for our other stuff."

"Definitely. I'm overdue for a practice session." Jemma waved a goodbye with her scone aloft and slipped out before anyone could overhear them. "Other stuff" was one of their code phrases for magical work, not outright forbidden, but discouraged now in this part of the country. They didn't think that anyone knew the two of them practiced. If they were found out, it could end their careers and put everything at risk. Jemma smiled, thinking of her friend Jake. He was a good guy. In addition to being a young mage and artist, he was on a temporary apprentice assignment from Everland Bay Institute, here for woven-world museum training. His work as an art handler would allow him to be in a museum setting permanently someday.

Museums the world over were often filled with portals to the magical realms, so it was a good bridge-between-worlds job for any artistically inclined mage. Even here, where magic was discouraged severely now, it was still very helpful to have mages like Jake trained to care for all the objects and be able to get from one place to the other via portals. Most people knew Jake as just an art handler; only the Swain's director knew of his true standing, besides Jemma and their group of mages. The director was one of the old-school mages, still in place in high leadership in the Verandalands museum world. The staff there had long ago forgotten this detail, and Jemma knew from Jake that the director kept this quiet now that magic was considered controversial.

Formerly, before the repression of magical power in the region, museum directors eagerly opened their doors and their staff rosters to mages from places like Everland Bay Institute and Village. This was still true throughout the parts of the world in which magic was welcomed.

Young mages loved these positions, and the Swain, as one of the top museums in the land, was highly sought after. The between-the-worlds jobs came with lots of travel perks, great for young artist mages. It was not an easy job, but it tended to attract bright, interesting people, many of whom were artists in their own right. Jake was getting toward the end of his apprenticeship.

Jemma made it back to her cube and opened up the digital text, proofing it again as she remembered earlier when she met Jake. She blew on her coffee to cool it, crumbled a piece off the cherry scone, and started scrolling through the text as she thought back.

She just started working at the museum. She was alone, she thought, in a gallery, doing the final walkthrough to check that all the text, labels, as they were called, were next to the correct objects and that the objects were accurately described. The gallery was particularly dark, since the exhibition lighting was not yet done. Jemma didn't know where the light control panels were and was hoping to do a quick check and then be on her way. She decided to risk a small light. It'll just be for a second, she thought. No one will see, and even if they did, they'd think it was the light on her phone or something. She flashed the tiniest of magelights, a pinpoint, playing it over an object and reading the label. Okay, everything is right, she thought, as she snapped the light off.

"Who is there?" A lanky young man stopped mid-stride in the hallway to turn and walk into the gallery.

Jemma flinched. She was startled, eyes wide. She started gathering her things, getting ready to flee. "Me. Jemma. Editor. Just doing final walkthrough."

"What was that light? I saw a flash."

"I, I sometimes need to use my phone light to see things in here."

"Wow. Must be an amazingly precise app—that was such a tiny light beam. I love new tech. Can I see it? I'm Jake, by the way. I'm one of the art handlers. Nice to meet you. Here, I can get the gallery lights on," he said, as he went around the corner to the hidden panel and flooded the rooms with light.

"Oh, thanks. I didn't know where those lights were. Or even whether I was allowed to turn them on if I did. I just started here. And, uh, hi. Nice to meet you, too." Jemma was terrified. She was barely breathing. She could feel her heart racing. All that she worked for was about to fall apart. If he found out that she used magelight and reported her as a magical suspect, she could be out of a job and maybe out of her apartment, too, if word got to her landlord. And it wouldn't matter for a moment that the director knew magical folk were on his staff. He didn't know Jemma was magical, and she was far too low on the staff roster for him to be aware of who she was, except generally. She would be fired and gone before word ever got to him, if it ever did. "I was startled when you came in. Must have dropped my phone back into my bottomless bag, which has now swallowed it up. Don't remember the name of the app but I'll get it to you when I find it."

Jake looked at her closely, as if searching her face for clues to an important question. "Ah. I see, I think. Sure," he said. "Well. On another topic—quick head's up. Museum rules. No totes or bags like that into the galleries. Just FYI."

"Oh. Sorry. I'm so new at all of this," Jemma said, trying not to let her relief show, trying not to be too obvious as she let out a deep breath.

He smiled, glanced around. "Hey, it's okay. I saw what you did," said Jake, gesturing toward the wall.

"Ah, I… I mean, what? What do you mean? I said I…" Jemma was back in an instant to feeling her heart galloping in fear, her breathing shallow.

"Here. I've started this badly. I didn't mean to scare you," Jake said as he stepped closer to the wall. An extremely narrow beam of light streamed from his palm, illuminating the words that were on the paper text taped up to the wall. "See?"

"You? You can do this?" said Jemma.

"I come from the Great Lakes Region originally. I'm with Everland Bay now. The research institute. This is basic stuff. But, yeah. I'm here for an apprentice rotation, then I'll go back."

"Oh, thank heavens. I'm so relieved." Jemma sat down heavily on a bench and took several deep breaths. She clutched the velvet upholstery as if it were a life preserver, holding her safely above uncertain seas. Her voice was shaky. "I thought I was the only one here, and I thought my new job ended, just then."

"Sorry. I really am. But I'm relieved, too. Thrilled, actually. Nice to have another one of us around here. There are not many, even though, technically, museums are supposed to be full of mages. Still true elsewhere in the world, but around here, we're now unofficially and pretty aggressively frowned upon, so most of us are in hiding or just gone. Scary times. But I'll introduce you to another mage I work with once I know it's safe," said Jake.

"How did you know for sure? About my light."

"I can see the colors inside some lights. My techie brother, Fletcher, tells me it's a wavelength. So, for me, magelights are a very specific color when I look at them. I knew the minute I saw it out of the corner of my eye. I don't see them around here much. Like I haven't seen one here at the Swain the whole time I've been here, other than my own."

Now, a year later, they had become good friends, and when they could, they practiced together and stayed up to date as much as possible on news in the magical underground. Lately, the news was unsettling. Something was amiss.

Jemma was continuing to work, checking off the objects one by one, including finding out definitively the correct number of claws on dragons (four, probably a gift to nobility, according to the curator), but she was also thinking of their other close magical friend, Rhiona, who worked at the Great Library, a few blocks away. She was the one Jake had mentioned. The three always worked together when possible. She sent a thoughtwave to Rhiona. "My place for practice soon? Basics and news." Jemma was quiet, sitting still as she waited. She let out a sigh of relief when she felt the internal mage ping from Rhiona, who was free soon. It was always good to get together and practice.

The three gathered a few days later at Jemma's. To anyone observing, they looked like three young professionals, planning to spend an evening together. Pizza was on the way. As Jemma welcomed Rhiona and Jake, she checked to make sure they were who they were supposed to be. "Everland Bay" was the prompt, and the response was to be "Folio" this time. They rolled their eyes, feeling a little silly. Who would even know they were there? But Jake was a stickler on protocol.

"You two haven't heard the things my brother says. It can be bad out here, and we wouldn't necessarily know," said Jake. "Plus, it's kind of fun, really." He grinned and shrugged.

Jemma brought drinks for everyone and set them down on the coffee table in her tiny apartment. "Well, good to be cautious, right? And it's fun to think of Folio, that bookstore in Everland Bay Village. I love that place. Anyway, here you go. So, where are we? Do we know what is going on? I was talking with my dad the other day, and he, well, he was yelling at me as usual, and he was saying that magic was going to be shut down even more here."

"How can it be more shut down? We're already in real trouble if we get caught," said Rhiona, standing up and walking over to the window, which overlooked the street. Beyond, the trees lining the parkway were visible in the fading light. "I mean, I know it's not officially outlawed, but people in this region are so afraid of it and hateful that they are making things unofficially awful. Kind of the way racism works, you know? Okay if I close the shutters?" she asked, not waiting for a reply, fastening and closing up the old shutters.

"I'm not sure we'll be safe for long, really. Jake, what are you hearing?" said Jemma. She glanced around her apartment, filled with treasures of her own: the paintings by her mother, her soothing and softly shimmering knitting, with one of the magical wraps in progress on her needles. And her piano. Her favorite books were here, including her grandmother's storybook. Photographs, too, she noticed, glancing around, some of the only ones showing her mother and father during happier times. So much to leave, if it came to it.

"Well, we're in danger, but some of us also need to stay here to keep the communications lines open between the worlds. If we all leave, this whole region could plummet into an isolated, magicless void, which would lead pretty quickly to the possibility of authoritarianism, or worse, and even violence. There are already signs of authoritarianism. One-party rule, arrogant, ignorant jerks in leadership. It would get even worse here without any magic at all. So. I'm here for a little while yet. I'll be helping stabilize things," said Jake.

"But not all that long, really," said Jemma. "You go back at the end of your apprenticeship, which is, what, in a few months?"

"Yeah. But that's better than nothing. And someone else will be taking my place, so the slot will be filled by one of us. Another young mage," said Jake. "No doubt another starving artist, like me." He smiled, and Jemma knew he was trying to lighten the mood a bit.

"Well, I am here for the duration," said Rhiona, playing absentmindedly with magelight, allowing little points of light to float around her fingers, like a strand of small, incandescent pearls. "Some of my family, like my cousin Keltie, lives there in Everland Bay Village now, but I have to stay here with my immediate family, my mom and dad, so I want this to all work somehow. They are solid mages, both of them, and our whole clan is part of the magical stability here. But they are getting a little older and I may need to be here to take care of them one day. They can't go back and forth to the Village much anymore—travel between magical and nonmagical lands has gotten too difficult," she said, reaching for her drink, a sparkling water. "Nothing buzzy for me, since we're practicing. Also, you know, one thimbleful can be way too much. Remember, my mom's elfin, my dad's magic, though human. What a Heinz-57 lot we are in our family!" With a flick of her wrist, the lights lined up and fastened themselves around her neck, a beautiful, illuminated necklace. She patted it.

"Ooh, very pretty. I need to get you to teach me how to make one of those. And, yeah, I get it. Nothing buzzy for me, like, ever," said Jemma. "Too much mixed blood in this body of mine to risk anything at all." She smiled. "I never serve buzzy stuff, really, you know. Way too risky for all of us mixed folk."

"How is your dad, speaking of?" asked Jake.

"He's really upset with me, which is usual, lately, but he's getting even more into his very dragony obsession with gold, in the form of money. In the form of his work at the bank. I mean, humans love the gold, too, don't get me wrong. But the dragon in him is truly magnetic around the stuff, so he's really valuable to the bank, and he is convinced that this is the only place for him to be. And he thinks that goes for me, too." The phone rang once. "Front desk calling. That's the pizza. Hang on. I've got this one, and they still take cash!" Jemma said, holding some bills aloft then reaching to pick up the receiver in her kitchen. "Hey, Bill. Right. Send him up. Thanks. Okay, anyone want to pitch in for the tip?"

They pulled out straggly bills, and Jemma gave the box to Rhiona and Jake while she paid the delivery guy. They set the pizza box on the table, got everything ready.

"Nice! This is from that place in the Palisades, yes?" Jake said, reading the pizza box.

"Yep, that's the place. Love it," said Jemma, handing around paper plates and napkins.

"Oh, this stuff is good—you'd almost think they baked with some kind of magic, yes?" They all nodded and dug in.

Chapter Two

"Okay, back to my dad. He wants me to eliminate or hide my magic 'stuff,' as he puts it. Not possible, really, but he seems to think it's something I can just tone down a bit. Not put on view anywhere at all. As if I'm parading it around. Anyway, he says there's a move to shut down mixed people like us, or even just human but magical. The last time I was at my dad's, it was pretty bad." She remembered back to her last visit. It was a few weeks earlier. He invited her over to dinner, which was not unusual, but was becoming a little less frequent over the last several months. Takeout Indian was always their go-to choice. The boxes were jumbled in the elegant kitchen. The evening started out with a wonderful feast but spiraled into anger and frustration as their talk got more heated.

"Dad, I love magic. I've been practicing since before I can remember. You know that! Before I even knew it had a name. What is wrong with it? Grandma and Mom taught me, remember? You know Mom loved it too, and she always wanted me to follow her to Everland Bay to study someday. Also, you're magical, remember? Our whole family is magical!"

"I don't want to hear about it!" said her father. "Your mother was another type of being altogether and I wish to the heavens we never told you about your magical background. You would be better off not knowing at all."

"But it's who I am. It's who we are, in our family. Even you. Especially you! You are the most powerful of all of us," Jemma said. She felt jolted by her anger. Clashes with her father had rumbled over the years, but intensified recently, as she challenged his ideas about what she was doing with her life. She felt her strength growing along with her practice sessions.

"No," said her father. "You are the most powerful. You have a little of your mother and me and you have the most power, really. Also, the most risk. If I have power, a lot of it comes from the human world's love of control and treasure. Gold and the power that comes with wealth. It is what keeps us safe here. Period. I want you to be safe. I want you to find something you excel at and can do well in this world. Something nonmagical. Non flighty. This is the world that will last. Not the unstable, frivolous land of magic and marvels. I want you to stay with me! Here. In the Verandalands," he shouted, then bowed his head, breathing hard.

Jemma could see the redness of his face, his clenched jaw, even maybe a tear, though she knew he'd deny that. She knew he was thinking of her mother. Her mother faded away, dying young, her magic and strength seeping away over time. He was never going to heal from that loss. Jemma thought she might never heal from it, either. And how was it that he saw what had happened to her mother but now wanted her to deny her own magic? Jemma reached toward him. "Dad, I…"

"No! You don't understand," he said, turning away, staring out at the darkened skies that filled the windows of his gracious home in Georgetown, a short drive away from Dupont Circle, the quirky neighborhood in downtown D.C. where Jemma lived. D.C. was right on the line between the Verandalands and the magical north and, further west, the Great Midlands, Northwoods, and Great Waters Regions, the magical community's name for the Great Lakes.

Washington, D.C., known simply as "the District" to its inhabitants, was home to a vast collection of museums and repositories, along with the government. Young people, artists, intellectuals, scientists, were drawn there from all over the world. But nonmagical leadership had slowly and incrementally taken over most of the levers of power, hence the policies in museums and schools and throughout the area unofficially discouraging magic. The Swain was one of the last that had a functioning mage-apprentice program, and even that was administered in secret.

"Jemma. I am hearing rumors. At the office. I don't think this is necessarily real. It could be just exaggeration, or paranoia. Probably is. But in the hallways at work, there is some talk of large corporate takeovers and movements. Halcyon corporation, a huge Verandalands company that dominates, well, this whole area, wants to get bigger. It started decades ago as a bootlegging distillery and grew into a many-headed-gorgon of a company, all with links to the magic-hating world. It's pretty aggressive. A big, bullying company."

"What does this have to do with us?" Jemma said, trying to follow.

"They are trying to take over banks. Originally their goal was to just sell more of all their alcohol products. Pretty standard. But now Halcyon wants to grow by taking over banks and buying up land. It seems far-fetched, but they may have organized crime links, including drugs, gambling, and God knows what. That last part is probably just rumor though, very sensational and wild. But even without that, they are aggressive and hostile. And they may be coming for my bank. My bank has always had very high standards, high ethics, so I don't think it is a real problem. But I need to be there to keep my bank free of them, in case they get more aggressive, or infiltrate banks like mine. And that means playing by the rules in Verandalands right now. No magic. No cause for anyone to question my, well, my standing."

Jemma stepped back, turning to wipe tears from her eyes. She glanced around at his comfortable living room, where they had moved with their tea after dinner. Books lined one wall, large canvasses adorned the walls, one featuring a dragon, hidden within an abstract painting of flamelike forms, purples, fuchsias, and glimmering golds. It had been one of the last things her mother painted, Jemma knew. A small, framed picture of the three of them from a happy summer many years ago stood on his desk. She reached for the photo. "I wish she was here."

"I have wished that every single day since the day she died," her father said. "And it won't change a thing. Nothing really matters now, and I long ago knew that since she was fading, dying, I had to take charge. The only way I knew how to do that was to make all this happen," said her father, gesturing toward the luxurious surroundings. "This, I know. This comes by playing by the rules. Their rules."

"But Dad, I can't be who I am not. I can't pretend I have no magic," said Jemma. Also, she thought, how could he not know that it could kill me to stay?

"No? No. You have to be an idealist like your mother," said her father. "Well, you know what? It could hurt you here. I have tried to protect you, all these years. To teach you to hide it and go along with the ways of Verandalands. You can still be special. Just private about your other talents, and private about your origins."

"Private? But it means I can't be my true self. You have got to know that. I mean, private is one thing. But being completely dishonest about my mixed blood and magic is a whole betrayal. Of me, of Mom. Of us all." Jemma was breathing hard, felt heated and charged up. "I've got to go. I love you, Dad, but this is killing me. Seriously. Staying here could be killing me. Like it did…you know. Like it did with Mom." Jemma left in a rush, but not before turning to hug her father. She felt his solid arms around her as they both held tight for a moment. Jemma brushed angrily at tears as she left.

Rhiona's voice brought Jemma back into her apartment. "Jemma? Hey. You there? You've disappeared."

"Yeah, sorry. Just, well, it was an awful scene with my dad the last time we were together."

"Sorry. That must have been hard," said Jake. "Things are getting worse for him, no doubt, as the nonmagical world continues to gain power, even here in D.C. People stay in denial and outrage about any tiny bit of magic they perceive," said Jake. "But let's get to work here.

We need to go through basic stuff: lights, appearing/disappearing, quick glamour, simple manifestation, mostly for safety right now."

"Right," said Jemma, shaking herself, shaking her hands, loosening up to get ready to train. "Also, it would be great to have an update on where things are in the magical worlds, or at least Everland Bay, and what is next. Can I think about going to Everland Bay, ever? I'm supposed to be training later in the summer to start the application process. How bad are things? Maybe I should be thinking of moving in with my grandmother? But then I'd have to let go of my job at the museum. I'm feeling really lost right now."

"Yeah. Ditto. All of that. Though I'll be staying here. We each need to figure out the what's next phase," said Rhiona. "Okay. Let's get going."

They sat in unison, closed their eyes, and began their breath work. Ten minutes passed. As one, they rose, snapped on their magelights, and began their drill.

"We're getting good with that coordination," said Jemma, shaking out her hands again as she shifted into her stance. "I'm still not very good with the breathing/sitting part though. Still think we should just go straight into our real drills."

"Well, when you get into the Bay, you'll be very happy that we've done this. Trust me on this," said Jake.

"I'll have to, won't I?" Jemma grumbled, but softened it with a smile. She always heard from her grandmother that quiet sitting and breathing, meditation, was important. She just couldn't settle into it, though, and had mostly managed to duck it during her visits over the years.

"Listen, I've heard from Fletcher," said Jake, as they moved through their routine.

"How is he doing and what is going on with that brother of yours?" said Jemma, pivoting as they went into the quick-glamour phase of the drill, and in a flash, becoming a hunched, elderly man.

"Whoa, that always gets me," said Jake, frowning as he struggled with his own glamour overlay, his favorite aunt, complete with an apron and wooden spoon. She was an avid baker.

"It is always a little odd, but we have to keep straight faces," said Jemma in her guise. Her voice had already shifted down an octave and was a little wheezy. "I think my elderly man self has a touch of a cold!"

"My aunt has a nice voice," said Jake, "but it is weird when I'm speaking it!"

They all laughed, enjoying for the moment the simple delight of quick-glamour shifting. Rhiona chimed in from her teenaged boy self. "Whatever," she said, with a shrug. Then, grinning sheepishly, "I am *loving* this! No wonder teenagers are so uncontrollable. I forgot about this amazing high-voltage energy!"

"Just make sure you stay focused! We all must try for convincing outer forms, but consistent inner selves so that we don't take on the not-so-helpful aspects of whatever we've glamoured into," said Jake, wielding his wooden spoon like a pointer.

Jake, owing to his extensive training, as well as his experience living in Everland Bay Village and being an intern at Everland Bay Institute, generally led their training sessions. Jemma and Rhiona were both becoming good practical mages but didn't have more specialized experience and training. Jemma was counting on receiving much more of that in the near future. Jemma had been home-trained by her mother and her grandmother, and then with Jake and Rhiona during her recent time at the museum.

Rhiona came to the Great Library in D.C. as a mage and woven world go-between, as well as an entry level writer-editor. She grew up in the area, part of a large family of mages. Her family was firmly rooted and committed to staying in Verandalands to keep magic alive while staying in close touch with family in Everland Bay Village and other parts of the magical regions. She trained some on and off throughout her life, but it hadn't seemed all that urgent to add a lot of skill sets to her magical basics until recently, when the Verandalands increased its reputation as a refuge for magic denialists, threatening the many centuries of woven-world stability and cooperation. Others had given up on the region, assuming the woven human-and-magic world could only exist in other parts of the world. It now was very dangerous to be magical at all there; laws forbidding magic were threatened by those in nonmagical circles, and areas that were previously mixed and safe were now uncertain.

"Right. So, what's going on there?" said Jemma, melting out of her older-man glamour and into her nine-year-old guise.

"Fletch says that things have gotten strange," said Jake. "Soon, new leadership is stepping into place, which is normal, but there is a movement of ultra-crazy, destructive mages of despair and chaos—rogue mages—who want to tear things apart. It really sounds nuts, and, like, I don't get this, but there is some chatter about their not allowing the new leadership to begin. There is some really crazy talk of takeover of Everland Bay Institute and using it as a base for infiltrating other institutes, magic and nonmagic."

"What? How can they prevent new leadership from starting? I never heard of any of this! And I just talked with my grandmother recently; she didn't say anything about this. Surely this is just fringe craziness, right? There can't be, like, a takeover, right?" said Jemma, snapping back into her normal self, shaken at the news.

"The rumor is that they want to destroy the soul of the magic there, and make it into a base for evil magic, which they think of as pure magic, technomagic, synthetic, chemical magic. They've twisted it all around; it is not pure, it is dirty, demeaning, and rancid, it is not new and helpful. Their magic is degenerate, based on harm and fear and ignorance," said Jake, shifting back to his regular self.

"How is this even happening? Didn't anyone notice?" said Rhiona, who had shifted from teenage boy to her middle-aged CEO self, looking snappy in pinstripes and an updo, with gold-wire half-moon reading glasses glinting on the bridge of her nose.

"My brother says that on the surface, things are still really pretty normal right now, and that most of the staff think it is just chatter. Normal activities like research, skills workshops, magical tourism, all that, are still going on. But he thinks they have been ignoring the extremists for a while, and it's possible that someone of their own has succumbed to bribery and a desire for power. What are you hearing, Rhiona?" said Jake.

"Yeah, there's always been the crazy fringe. But my family and contacts haven't said anything specific. That's not necessarily good news though; they can be pretty unaware," said Rhiona, morphing back into her regular self. "There's so much to deal with right here that they don't tend to spend much time worrying about the Bay or the other magical regions much. But I am very concerned about this, the way you're putting it. I will talk with Keltie. As I mentioned, she lives right in Everland Bay Village and should be up on things. She was going to be starting her first term as a junior magefellow in the fall, I think, so she might have a lot of information," said Rhiona.

"Any chance Fletcher's information could just be somehow off? Like maybe he is getting news from a bad source?" said Jemma.

"I guess it's possible. He always says that some of the places he hears from are kind of nutty. Fringy. He and his colleagues are working with a wide field, though. He's been saying signs have been pointing to this kind of extremism for a while, but because he's still so junior, no one pays much attention to him. Also, the mages who are in charge of Everland Bay Institute have sort of a blind spot about other mages. They think that mages wouldn't do evil things. Not true mages, as they put it. So, if there are evil mages among them, they could be operating without much interference, simply because no one takes the threat seriously," said Jake, reaching for his glass and taking a sip.

"Who do you believe?" said Jemma, stopping to take a sip of sparkling water.

"I believe my brother. This can't go beyond us right now but said something about the rogue mages approaching him. Like to, you know, recruit him."

"To become one of them?" said Jemma. "That's crazy. Well, I don't know him, but…"

"No, it's definitely crazy. But he's in high demand anywhere, because of his skills. So, they wanted him. He said no, but not before he let them go on about what they are up to," said Jake.

"His information comes from a lot of other places, though, too," he continued as he paced the room. "He also has contacts in the Institute and the Village, which of course are completely connected and interrelated—the Village has been noticing problems for a while, but they are not taken seriously. They've been reporting bad behavior and have been threatened by a handful of fringy Institute mages on and off, but when they complain or try to alert anyone, excuses are made for the bad mages. That they are just kidding around, that they are just a handful in the ultra-fringe that nobody pays attention to, or that they are just a few and are mentally disturbed. Nothing to worry about, the leadership says. So, no one is really doing anything about the threats, or taking them seriously."

"I wonder if there's anything we can do, even from here. I think we need to be able to identify them. Can we train in some kind of enhanced seeing? Or in scanning for negative energy?" Jemma said, trying to imagine how to help. She stretched, wiggled her fingers, continued to shake off the lingering effects of her glamour.

"From what Fletch says, we need to listen and pay attention, then continue to strengthen our group here, as well as our connections with the more nimble and forward-thinking part of Everland Bay Village—Fletcher's group. Also, Rhiona's cousin, Keltie. Nothing very high-tech right now. Because these mages always talk about their hatred, their twisted ideology. They are not even bothering to hide their extremism. It's just that no one takes them seriously."

"Interesting. That happens here in Verandalands, too, only it's the top non-magicians who excuse all the other nonmagical terrorist behavior. Like really sick stuff. Racism, attacks on women, anyone who doesn't look and think like them, basically. I'm the wrong color, of course, with all the dragon in me, so I get flack for that. Plus, I have to hide my mark all the time, now," Jemma said, reaching up to her dragonmark and rubbing it as it pulsed and sparkled. "You two are probably fine here. But I'm so sick of this. There's got to be something more that we can do to be part of the solution," said Jemma.

"Here, here. Like you, Jemma, I'm mixed," said Rhiona. "My family is all mixed and have been for, like, millennia. Some of us, like me, have lighter tones, but a lot of us have that more usual dark oak tone—we call it 'lovely golden brown' in our family—the default," she continued, flashing a small smile, which faded quickly. "No problem in the magical lands and used to be not a problem in the woven world and, like, just ordinary or maybe quirky-but-okay even in some of the savvier parts of the Verandalands. But now, people here, especially in the suburbs, like, pull their purses close if I am walking with some of my family. Or they shove some of us, or call names, or even worse. It seems to be getting worse, not better."

"Yeah, this is getting scary here. We're all in dangerous territory, don't forget, just for our magic. And even though I'm not any of those more normal tones that dragonfolk or elfin/fey mixes sport, I've, you know, got these ears!" Jake pulled back his slightly shaggy hair to show off his ears, which came to neat points, in the way of most elvish folk. "I get the side-eye all the time! And sometimes more," Jake said, looking away for a moment. Jemma was about to ask him to tell them more, but he continued. "Anyway, we'll have to really get our strategy together. Let's do a little more practice and then break."

"Sounds good," said Jemma. "While we're at it, want to try something different? Like maybe bring Keltie in with us? Can we use a scrying screen to do that remotely?'

"It's kind of out there, but why not?" said Rhiona. "Let me get her coordinates into this thing," she said, digging into her bag and setting up a portable scrying stone.

"You are a whiz at that," said Jemma.

"Yeah, this is something my family taught me ages ago. The portable stones are a little small, but…there! Kelt? You there?" said Rhiona.

"I'm here. Hey thanks for the no notice. What's up?" Said an animated face, filled with freckles and grinning up at them from the small scrying stone.

"I know. Sorry to put you on the spot like this but we needed you to be part of our training. Kelt, this is Jemma, and this is Jake."

The three talked, trained a little more.

"Listen you all, I have to go—no offence, but it is late for me, and I wasn't expecting a training session." Said Keltie.

"I'm so glad we've all met," said Jemma. "So now, why don't we each go back to our own sources and meet again very soon. Maybe this sounds too paranoid, but I'd feel better if we'd meet again tomorrow after work."

"Yeah, me too. Something is really off, and it isn't getting better," said Jake.

The three went through their paces, with more focus than usual on far-seeing, cloaking, and landscape visualization, moving the contours of Jemma's tiny apartment around by imagining them differently.

Jemma was jolted by the news and worked harder than ever. She concentrated and could feel energy building within her. She opened her hands, directing beams of energy toward the center of the room. The velvet wing-back chair folded into a snappy-looking mid-century model, the couch morphed from its upright self down, down, down, changing before their eyes into a hand-hooked Persian rug, rich in deep maroons, iridescent mallard greens, and deep midnight blues. A tiny ottoman grew before their eyes and unfolded into an elegant gray velvety couch, complete with tapestry pillows, one sporting a unicorn, one with a princess sporting a train, pearls, and a chiffon scarf unfurling right out of the pillow from the tip of a pointed hat. "Early mage hat!" Jemma said, laughing, nearly out of breath. "One last thing I've been wanting to try," she said, raising her hands and directing her gaze toward the newly created couch. The center morphed into a hilly landscape, complete with miniature trees and flowers. Out of the center, a rocky point grew, and grew into a perfect, miniature replica of the castle at Everland Bay. A small pennant snapped cheerfully in an unseen breeze.

"Wow, Jem, you've been holding out on us. You're kind of scary-good at that!" said Jake.

"Uh, yeah, you are kind of amazing at that," said Rhiona. "I can make one of those coasters move a bit, but you, like, made a whole new mini-sitting area, complete with tapestry accent pillows. Which, I see, the faeries are enjoying. And then the castle! Sheesh, why haven't we noticed this budding talent before?" Rhiona stopped, her work, put her hands on her knees as she paused, breathing hard and reaching for her glass. "Phew! I'm done!"

"Oh, I love this stuff," said Jemma, pausing to catch her breath, but I'm beat, too! "Visualization and manifestation. My grandmother always just called it Viz and Mani, for short. I've been doing this since forever. My mom was really good at this. Way better than me. Practicing always makes me feel closer to her. When I was little-little, I didn't understand, and just made whatever occurred to me. Tiny, sparkling castles, little faery homes, all kinds of things. Lots and lots of sparkles everywhere! It has always been such fun. I was even allowed to make a piece or two of candy or sweets every once in a while. But not more than that. I hated that rule back then but I'm grateful now, really. Much more fun to learn to bake it for real! But anyway, somehow, this kind of magic seems so easy that it doesn't seem all that useful, really, but it is fun. My mother taught me how she did it and then my grandmother kept working on it with me," Jemma finished, reaching for her glass and taking a long drink.

"It shows!" said Rhiona.

Jemma smiled, shrugged a little, still breathing hard. "Now to put it all back," she said, with a sweep of her hand that caused things to move, contort, fold, and go quietly back to normal. The pillows were a trifle reluctant; the tiny unicorn bolted rather awkwardly out of one pillow and galloped around the room for a moment or two before Jemma reached out and touched its neck lightly, bringing it to a halt. It then leapt straight up and plunged back into the now-shrinking pillow, managing to wriggle in between some ragged threads. Before Jemma could relax, however, the chiffon headscarf left the other pillow entirely for a zippy flight around the room prior to diving back into the tidying whirlwind. "Show-offs," muttered Jemma under her breath. The castle, which had detached from the couch and was levitating just about an inch above it went last, flowing gracefully into the whirlwind, the pennant twirling away and out of sight.

Back in the living room, the faeries fluttered up and settled back to their usual places. After everything was back in place, they packed up. "I'll sleep well tonight after all that," Jemma said. "Even though I've done viz and mani for ages, it can still be tiring after a long practice session. This would be a piece of cake for my grandmother, but it's still tricky for me. Thank goodness we're done for the night." She swept a tangle of curls away from her forehead.

"So true. Okay. I'm outta here and will talk to my people," said Rhiona. "And here I thought we were just going to have a fun little magic exercise tonight. I'm going to try to stay hopeful, otherwise I'll be too scared to move."

"Right. See you all tomorrow. Maybe someone else's place, just to stay safe?" said Jemma.

"My place is fine," said Jake. "See you tomorrow."

Once everyone left, Jemma made a cup of tea, then curled up in her window seat, watching the street below. She reached automatically for her knitting. The gossamer-light wrap she was working on was complex and beautiful. The yarn alone, a micro-ply of the flutewood silk, spidersilk, and the silk of bearded mussels, was as dazzling as jewels and stronger than titanium. It unfolded itself, floating up out of the knitting bag, and remaining slightly aloft, suspended a little above her lap as she began to knit.

The tiny faeries who lived with her loved these shawls particularly, and often nestled in her knitting bag, wrapped up in the shimmering strands. It would look complicated to anyone who hadn't been knitting similar things since childhood, as Jemma had. She had knitted such wraps ever since she was a little girl, her tiny fingers following her grandmother's and her mother's as the three knitted together. She knew that her grandmother always had one of these on the needles. It helped make Jemma feel connected to her now.

Usually, knitting relaxed her completely, but tonight, it wasn't working as well. Still, she knew that at least she'd be adding to her grandmother's stock; these wraps were much sought after in Everland Bay Village and the wider magical world. She wasn't quite sure of their purpose; they were always around but somehow, her grandmother never got around to the technical details. But Jemma knew their magic was powerful and protective, and she also knew that she helped with her grandmother's income by knitting these. Her grandmother always said they were important for her work. She and her grandmother were, she knew, some of the only ones who knew how to knit these special wraps.

Jemma looked absently out the window as her fingers flew along with her thoughts. Her plans all felt so useless now, so up in the air. She was planning to stay at the museum for as long as need be until she was fully prepared to apply for a junior mage fellowship at Everland Bay Institute.

She worked on her application and her magical demonstrations in the last couple of years with the help of her grandmother, and they planned for a long visit in the coming summer so that Jemma could take vacation and do an in-depth training retreat there. Her grandmother was lining things up even then, and Jemma had begun to prepare, trying not to get her hopes up too high as she thought about the people and creatures, all of them magically accomplished, who would be training her in preparation for her final application. She wouldn't have the advantage of being in the magical lands and studying the standard magic curriculum all her life or going to elite private academies, like most of the other applicants, but she hoped she would have a decent chance with this plan.

Everland Bay Institute was an unusual place. It was a research institute, not a school. Magical schooling, usually at very well-known academies, was already long in the past of all those there. The junior mages who were invited to the Institute were generally beginning their adult careers in particular magical fields. They were paired up with senior mages. The senior magefellows were generally wrapping up long, magical careers, and used their time at the Institute to put the finishing touches on their final projects. The young ones worked or studied in the fields led by these mages and were given the opportunity to specialize by being under the guidance and supervision of the well-known senior mages.

The system brought delight to all around, and in addition, the setting was beautiful. There was the main castle house, small outbuildings, offices for all the residents, homes for everyone right on the expansive grounds. The juniors lived in an apartment house, beautifully crafted of stone, tile, and brick, which was often very helpful when the youngest and somewhat more rambunctious junior mages got overly enthusiastic and cooked up experiments in their rooms, igniting the occasional explosion.

The faculty and senior magefellows lived in quieter cottages and charming mews; the cottages were scattered here and there, the mews were smallish houses connected on to the next, each home slightly different, but similar in design and crafted of hand-hewn timber, cream brick, and butter-colored stone, as if a small, stonework village from long ago fitted itself together and landed on the Everland Bay Institute grounds.

Gardens, spilling over with bright blue delphiniums, flamingo-hued hollyhocks, shell-pink climbing roses, nodding canary-colored poppies, and iridescent green maidenhair ferns, flowed endlessly around each outside room. Musicians were forever spotted toting their basses, violins, piccolos, and keyboards around to the various tiny outdoor amphitheaters and gathering spots to join in on the chamber music, jazz, and other live musical concerts that were often performed. And the vivacious gatherings! Parties on the terraces in the summertime were legendary, with all the landscape adorned with tiny magelights; luminous pinpricks floating throughout the grounds, as if the stars themselves had grown tiny and hung low in the branches of the trees and bushes. Jemma's pocket faeries were terribly excited about that part of things; they believed that there must be some of their friends among the crowds of faeries, adding to the lights and amplifying the enchantment.

Most of all, Jemma longed to spend a few weeks with her grandmother. She began to hatch a plan for living with her grandmother full time. Or maybe even just nearby. Because she knew that she might not get into the Institute, and then what? There were mixed-magical cities all around that region, and surely, they had museums. Maybe she could work there? Maybe somewhere in Everland Bay Village, though more were discovering its charms and she had heard from her grandmother that it was becoming difficult to rent or find work there. But it wasn't what she really wanted, since she hoped all her life to be at the Institute, not the Village.

But now, with the news of things going so unexpectedly badly at the Institute, it sounded as if all could be lost, even before she tried. That no matter what she wanted, it was already too late. She took a shaky breath and found herself tearing up a little as she continued to take in the reality of the situation. She grew cold in the window seat and stood up to get ready for bed, gently folding her knitting and tucking it into her knitting bag, which then folded again, on its own, into a soft cloth band that she wrapped around her wrist, like a fabric bracelet, hidden in plain sight with all the contents secure. If she wanted to, she could use it to put her hair up. Even the faeries could stay inside if they wished. Despite her worries, she couldn't help but smile a little as she tucked the faeries in while admiring the shapeshifting knitting bag, a gift from her grandmother. She stopped at her bookcase and reached for the Everland Bay Storybook. She hugged it to herself, hoping for comfort.

Chapter Three
Agni

Agni Avalon, Jemma's father, glanced out the enormous windows of his office, looking down at the river below, one hand up to shield his eyes from the bright sun ricocheting from the water to the silver-blue steel and glass of the newest buildings. It was a beautiful view, but it barely registered as he turned his attention back to his screen and checked his calendar. His assistant came in with a cup of coffee and he glanced up, barely nodding as he accepted the cup. "Can you clear an hour or so for me at lunch? I want to have lunch with my daughter."

"Certainly. Tony and Roy's?"

Agni loved the rough-and-tumble atmosphere of Tony and Roy's, along with its mostly seared-meat menu, but he knew Jemma's tastes were different from his. "How about the Blue Wren? I think she likes that place better. More greens, less grease."

"Yes, sir. You'll call Jemma?"

"Yes. Let's say noon."

"Consider it done, sir. I'll arrange for a car," said the young man.

Agni nodded absently. He didn't normally arrange lunch with his daughter on such short notice. He used to; they used to enjoy last-minute lunch together all the time. But now, he knew better than that. Her schedule was always so busy. Today, though, he was feeling a sense of urgency he didn't quite understand himself. He was hoping she would come, even though he wasn't yet sure what he would say to her.

He decided to keep things casual by using the phone, and not resorting to a magical contact.

"Jemma? Dad here."

"Dad! Hi. Uh, how are you?"

"Jemma, I am sorry about our last, ah, our difficulty last time we were together. Can you come this way? Lunch at the Blue Wren?"

"I, well. Sure. I can make that work. What time?"

"Noon. Take a cab if you need to, my treat."

"Dad. I can afford a cab. But okay, see you then."

Agni let out a breath he didn't know he was holding. His only child. He loved her but didn't know how to be close. Elise always knew how to do all of that, even as Jemma turned into a teen. Talk about magic. Ability to communicate with a very particular former teen, now a young woman, was the magic he really needed. He sighed. He wished, yet again, for his wife's guidance. For his wife. He loved Elise to distraction but managed to allow harm to come to her without understanding how or why. He just had no idea how it all had happened, how it went so badly. It seemed to him that her decline and death occurred in an instant. He was still devastated and without a clue. He wanted to do the right things for Jemma. He wanted to try to make things better, even though he really had no idea what to do, other than try to convince her to adopt his own wiser and more mature, more practical way of navigating this land. This would be another attempt in that direction, and he hoped things would improve.

As the car got close to the Blue Wren, Agni spoke up. "No need to get the door for me; I'll just get out—here is good, right here," he said. Too pretentious, he felt, to have the driver open the door for him for a lunch with Jemma. He walked the last half block to the restaurant, more of a bistro, really, he thought, as he ducked under the breezy yellow-and-white striped awning over the cornflower-blue-painted door. The large blackboard proclaimed, "Very Veggie Spinach Wraps," an "It's the Berries" salad, and "Mystical Chocolate Ginger Cake." He tried not to roll his eyes at the light, chatty fare, glanced around and saw his daughter down the street a little. "Jemma, over here," he called out at her. He signaled to the hostess that he was ready for a table and waved in Jemma's direction.

"Dad, hello. This is a surprise," Jemma said, shrugging off her coat and walking toward the table, after the hostess.

"I, well, I wanted to see you," he said, giving her a quick hug, then settling into his chair, picking up the menu.

They spent a moment on the familiar menu, then ordered, deciding on the specials, including a slice of the chocolate ginger cake, with two forks.

"Honey. How are you? It has been a while."

"I'm fine, Dad. I didn't really think you wanted to see me much, so I've been scarce." Jemma was not meeting his eyes, glancing instead around the room as she spoke.

Agni could feel a prickle of irritation starting at Jemma's comment about his not wanting to see her. He glanced sharply at his daughter, then blew out a breath. "Well, that's probably my fault. I know it is. This is so hard." He knew he wanted things to be better, and that they just seemed to fight in recent months. He knew, too, he wasn't all that great about noticing what was happening inside of himself but that he had a tendency to snap when he was crossed.

"How do I make things right? I want what is best for you. I even think, this might sound a little surprising, but hear me out, I think the place I work could be a good fit for you, with some training. I hear that there may be some sort of new and beautiful development, somewhere in the Great Lakes, Great Waters area, possibly not too far from your grandmother, and…" He trailed off, noticing that she didn't seem enthusiastic.

"Oh, Dad. I don't know what to say. I want to be myself, which includes being my mother's daughter and your daughter, and all the, well, all the abilities that come with that. Nothing against banking, but I don't want to be part of that. Not here in Verandalands, even if we are in D.C, which is more, well, you know." Jemma glanced around the room.

"This place is secure," said Agni. "We're fine if we keep our voices low. And I know, I know. I know D.C. is more mixed, more friendly to people like us. But it has become more, well, more challenging. And you could be hurt if you are open about your special talents." Even though he believed that the place was safe, he worried that his daughter would draw too much attention to them. She just didn't understand how the real world works here, he thought, even after all these years.

"Dad. I know. It's not even safe to let anyone know at work, remember? Even here at the Blue Wren, they've changed the name of their cake to 'Mystical' Chocolate Ginger Cake, instead of 'Magical,' which is what it always was. Grandma Annalyn's recipe, by the way. They know her here, you know. But—back to the point. Magical people are just worried everywhere even here in the District about getting caught, harassed. Maybe one day arrested. Anyway, let's hope it is secure here. Actually, I've been thinking. I haven't wanted to say anything before, but since we're kind of on the topic, maybe it's time for me to really get serious about moving. Going back to the Great Waters region. I can be with Grandma, maybe. I am so, so tired of hiding who I am. Maybe Everland Bay Institute will take me as a junior magefellow, even without much formal training."

"That's not real, Jemma, that was your mother's dream," said Agni. "Not yours. If you just temper things a little, you could have a good, rich life here. Like we have always had here. And you know this part of the world, D.C. and even some of the close-in areas, are still somewhat mixed. Friendly. A little willing to overlook your, you know, unusual abilities."

"I don't *want* my—abilities, as you call them—to be overlooked! I am working to get even better, in fact. Oh, Dad. We're right back to where we were. You know, I wanted things to get better between us, but all you do is say that I should basically become who you are. How is that right? How is that supposed to work for me?" she said, leaving her just-served food untouched.

"Oh, honey. If I could just make you see things from my perspective," he said. "You are so like your mother."

"Right. Well. I think that's a good thing," said Jemma.

"Oh, honey. It is. It is a good thing. I just…" Agni felt himself starting to lose his way in the conversation, spiraling into their ongoing argument. He took in the steely set to her jaw and her exasperated expression.

"How did you two even exist together, really?" said Jemma. "She was so delicate yet so strong, and so completely, you know, talented in that special way of hers. Her magical nature glimmered everywhere."

Agni felt himself smiling, remembering. He paused, let himself think back, remembering. "Yes. She was exactly that. And I loved all those things about her. You know, you *are* a lot like her. And you're absolutely right; it *is* a good thing. How did we exist together? We were so idealistic. We said we would be extra-special together. My fiery dragon self and her gossamer-and-fey self would be a wonderful, if unlikely, blend, we said. We thought we would make a perfect team. And we made each other laugh so hard. Your mother was so witty. I get so serious sometimes, you know."

"Ha. No kidding. Hadn't noticed!" said Jemma, raising her eyebrows.

"Yes, well. Life is serious," he said, with a frown. Then a smile creased his face and he could feel its warmth inside. "But she made me see the other parts of life. And we wanted to make a beautiful life for our daughter. For you." He could feel his emotions swirl up, and he was embarrassed to sense tears. "You know, some told us that because we were so far apart, what with my being part dragon and her being part faerie and elfin, we could not have children. That it would be simply not possible. Or if we could, we should not. That our child would be too different, or maybe disabled. We were so astonished by our joy when we knew your mother was pregnant. And then, as you grew up, you continued to bring us so much…" He cleared his throat, swallowed.

After a pause, Jemma said, "I didn't know any of this. I guess it doesn't matter now, but I wish I had known. But Dad, why did you come here? To D.C. Even if it is the most northern, mixed part of the Verandalands. I know it used to be more, you know, more tolerant, but wasn't it always mostly bad for people like us? You've never told me, not really. Why did she agree? Did she? You knew she would hate it. And she did, right?"

"Did she tell you that? That one summer?" said Agni.

"No! She never said it outright. But she just…she became less and less of herself. She was fading, Dad. I could see it, but I had no idea of what was happening to her. How serious it was. I always thought you had my same vision and could see everything that I saw. I was just a kid, though, remember? I didn't know how to even put words around what I was seeing and feeling," said Jemma.

"I was so stubborn. I thought, and still think, this place is the best place for someone like me. Someone like us, since you have my nature in you, too. But I didn't fully understand about your mother. I knew her as being so very strong, and I didn't know she would literally wither here. I didn't really think it was even possible. I don't have the sight you have, so I couldn't see the fading the way you did. I thought she was overstating it. Maybe being melodramatic. I thought she was just overdoing things in general and was tired, or that she wasn't trying hard enough to like it here. I didn't listen. I'm just like a lot of fully human men that way, I guess." His shoulders sagged; his head bowed. He felt his throat close again. What was happening to him? This was not the way he wanted this lunch to go. He took a deep breath. "Enough of my wallowing. The past is the past. I will always be looking out for you and hoping to give you direction. I will always protect you. I will probably always think my opinions are right," he said.

"Oh, really?" Jemma said.

Agni felt his heart lift at the rueful smile that lifted corners of Jemma's lips and felt a glimmer of hope. Maybe they could agree to disagree, and he could keep her close, and just, somehow, ignore what she was up to. Just not worry about any of it. Didn't most parents of grown children do that? But most parents of young adults didn't have to worry about them being arrested, or fired, or homeless just for being different, for being magical. He tried to set those thoughts aside.

"Truce, then? I will stop mentioning your career and your, you know, your other talents."

"Oh, Dad. Okay. I'd rather you were happy about what I am, what I'm doing," said Jemma, with that very direct gaze of hers.

"I will try. Okay? I will try." Agni turned back to his meal, then looked up. "I'm always here for you. I might be a hot-headed old thing, but I am going to try to do better at, at all of this," he said, with a gesture that indicated the two of them.

"Okay. I will try, too. But I may still need to get out of here someday. Maybe someday soon. I may need to go to Everland Bay Village, or Grandma's."

Agni bowed his head, took a deep breath. "But we just said truce, right? How can you do this?"

"I am not doing anything wrong. I'm an adult, I can consider possibilities, remember?"

"Well, yes. But I don't think you're really trying. We said truce. I wanted to you to take a pause from all this." He gestured quickly, dismissing imaginary irritants. "I wanted you to come around a bit, rethink things." Agni felt his anger boiling and realized that really, he didn't want just to agree to disagree. He really did think he had things right and that Jemma was going to regret her choices, that he felt were so narrow-minded and juvenile.

"Oh, Dad, we are just going in circles. *Truce* does not equal *your way,*" Jemma said.

"This is not going the way I wanted it to," said Agni. "I'm not trying to be unreasonable. I really think the better, more responsible path for you is for you to stay here, in this area, near me. Not go running off to your grandmother's. Who is getting very old and can't do much anyway, I'm sure, by now. Never could," said Agni, furious and now annoyed with himself for losing his temper. Why couldn't he just let it go? He believed he was right, that's why. He also knew that he had not spoken the truth about Jemma's grandmother, Annalyn. He felt a wrenching inside at his lie. Annalyn, he knew, was a great mage, and was not old at all by fae/elf standards, though her human side gave her mortality. He also knew with an interior wince that he had probably just made things much worse. But he was feeling desperate. He just couldn't bear the thought of losing Jemma to that other world, one that would probably no longer welcome him.

"I love you, but no. I have to live my own life. I have been trying to make things work here for a long time and you keep wanting me to be exactly like you. You are not listening to me at all!" The small votive candle in the middle of the table burst into a bright pink flame as Jemma got up, grabbed her coat, and turned to leave. "I need to get back to work."

"Sir!" called the waiter, rushing over to the table. "Sir, I'm sorry, we don't have the candles on during the day. Not sure what happened here, but I'll just put this one out."

Agni reached over before the waiter could douse the candle and pinched the flame out, welcoming the small, sharp burn. Just like Jemma to set things on fire. It was a wonder she hadn't been caught before now. He sat there, head bowed. Defeated. He felt a sharp pang of anger and grief mixed together. He looked down at his now cold and unappetizing meal, grimaced. He watched Jemma leave and tried to master his emotions. He looked up, signaled to the waiter. The bill would be sent to his office. He left and knew his face was an angry mask. He swiped at a tear that threatened to betray his fury. How could things have gone so far wrong, so quickly? Didn't she care at all? He felt a sense of wronged self-righteousness. Maybe she was just too far gone into the faerie-elfin spectrum to listen to sense. Maybe she didn't have much of his dragon strength and fire. Maybe he should just give up.

As he left, he was startled to hear a snatch of conversation behind him "…a glimmer near his eye. Did you see?"

Immediately, Agni knew his mark must be showing. His angry tears washed away the covering cream he used every day. He decided to forego the car, hoping that a walk back would help him calm down. He walked swiftly, dabbing concealer on his dragonmark as surreptitiously as he could. He always kept a small vial of it in his pocket. He took a deep breath, squaring his shoulders as he strode through the doors to his office and stepped into his more usual, confident self. The self he was no longer certain he was in alignment with.

Jemma

Jemma made it back to work and buried herself in her miles-long to-do list, trying to focus on the porcelains show. She took a deep breath, pulled up images from the show onto her screen. Seeing the beautiful objects always soothed her, one of the many reasons she loved this work so much. She searched for a particular bowl. Hmmm. Image not available, read the area in which the photo usually appeared. No way to check the accuracy of the text, which said the bowl was white and the dragons had four claws on each foot. Jemma knew the importance of this now-insignificant detail. But it was critical to scholars now and the people those many hundreds of years ago, when the number of claws on a small dragon determined who once owned the bowl. The emperor himself or another noble family? Maybe a gift? Four meant a gift from the emperor, then, to a long-ago dignitary or attendant. Jemma came back to the present moment. Well. This was a puzzle that meant a trip to collections storage. After a call to the curator, who approved her request, she set up a quick visit to collections storage so that she could see the bowl herself and count those dragony claws.

Normally, this was not done, but occasionally, there was a need. She signed in and chatted with the registrar, Amy, who assisted staff and scholars as the need arose to examine the objects in the collection. As with most museums, only a small portion of the collection was on view. Most things are stored out of sight in environmentally controlled, secure areas.

"Odd that there's no image," said Amy, turning to pull up the image with the object number on Jemma's text.

"Very! I thought that the whole collection was photographed ages ago. Can you flag it for Photography? I can leave you a copy of the label if you need it," said Jemma.

"Thanks, that'll work. I'll give Photography a call. This thing hasn't been on view in years, so it must have missed its closeup moment. Still. Gives me the jitters when something is missing, so I'll take care of this as soon as we're done here," said Amy.

"Perfect. I'll tell the curator, so she doesn't worry. In the meantime, let's see," said Jemma, as she examined the bowl. She knew not to touch it, as she was not authorized to do so, but she was able to see it clearly. Exquisite, white-on-white, with a beautiful crackle glaze. The tiny dragons chased each other around the inside of the bowl, circling endlessly in a journey that began hundreds of years ago. Four claws. Check.

"Okay. I've got what I need," said Jemma.

"Great. See you later. Maybe we can catch lunch sometime?" said Amy, turning away, beginning the process for putting the diminutive bowl back into its place in storage.

"Sounds good," said Jemma. But she stood there, riveted, as she saw something flickering in the bowl. Surely not an insect of some sort. She flinched as the flickering grew and in an eyeblink, one of the dragons on the bowl flew out and zoomed toward her head, then straight up, missing her by a hair. She ducked, then looked over at Amy, who was looking in another direction and didn't see what Jemma saw. Jemma's heart raced. She couldn't believe what she was seeing. Not here. She never saw magical creatures in the Woven World, even though they were at the northern borders of Verandalands. So, technically, of course there was still magic around, and probably some magical creatures here and there but they had been mostly driven out.

And even though she knew that her father was part dragon, and so was she, their line was a mixed one, one in which the human side had been dominant for generations. Jemma and her father looked entirely human, with just iridescent marks that revealed their dragon side. Jemma had some additional elfin and fae influences, a little webbing between her unusually long fingers, for example. But this dragon! Flying out of the bowl and around the room? She didn't know they could exist this far away from a full-on magical place like Everland Bay or elsewhere in the North. She was taught that real dragons were rare, and not necessarily able to travel across to nonmagical worlds. She always thought that was sad, but understandable.

When she first started working at the Swain and saw the dragons painted so perfectly on the sides of the bowls, it made her happy to think that at some point in the distant past, dragons lived everywhere. Now, in magic-fearful places, they lived on only in stories and fanciful artwork, like the delicate dragons incised on these tiny bowls. And right now, she was completely stunned by this one. Which had flown OUT OF THE BOWL! Didn't know that was even a possibility, she thought.

"What's wrong?" asked the registrar.

Immediately, Jemma knew she might be in danger. "Thought I saw something in the bowl." Jemma tried to sound offhand.

"Oh no, that couldn't be. You know we never put anything in these bowls!" said Amy, glancing at the bowl and reaching for it.

Jemma flinched a little, again, wondering whether there might be another dragon in there that might decide to escape the bowl. "Right. I know. Must just be my tired eyes. Too many pages of proofreading and editing," Jemma said, dividing her gaze between Amy, who was going about her registrarial routine, and the one very small dragon that just freed itself from the bowl. And was now enthusiastically flying up to the ceiling. "I, uh, I'm good to go. Thanks so much for getting this out for me," Jemma said hastily as she started to leave the room, pausing at the desk up front to sign out.

"Sure, no problem," Amy said. "You sure you're okay? You seem rushed all of a sudden."

"I'm fine. Just way behind on these labels. Thanks again. And definitely, lunch soon," Jemma said. Clearly, Amy could not see anything amiss. Jemma knew that if she flinched again or asked about the dragon, Amy would think she was either crazy or, worse, someone who harbored magical beliefs or was a mage herself. Given the dangers of magical knowledge in this area, Jemma never discussed the topic with colleagues, so she didn't know where they were on the magical spectrum. Amy seemed so unruffled that Jemma was certain she was the only one who was seeing the dragon.

She put her hand on the door as casually as possible, despite the tiny jewel-scaled creature now perched on her shoulder. Jemma could see it out of the corner of her eye, scales shimmering in tones of iridescent emerald, aquamarine, amethyst, and gold, turning its head this way and that, flicking its small tail with a flourish, and generally exuding an air of delight about its escape.

"What is going on? Who are you? Or have I just completely lost my mind?" Jemma hissed to the dragon as she hurried back to her office. She tried to sound stern, but found herself smiling at this small being, despite her skyrocketing fear of being observed with evidence of magic. Huge evidence of magic. Dragon-on-her-shoulder evidence of magic.

"No time for much detail. Your grandmother and others sent me. Well. Authorized me to be free. I'm your transport," said the dragon, whose voice sounded gravelly, yet melodic. Like wind chimes with a bit of a cold.

"Transport?" said Jemma.

"To Everland Bay Institute. Timetable was moved up. Something about an insurrection. I don't make the decisions. I'm just…," said the dragon.

"Transport," said Jemma, trying to look closer at the dragon while simultaneously trying to figure out her next steps.

"Right. And we're late. Time to head out. Things are bad, I'm told," said the dragon.

"But I can't just disappear," said Jemma.

"Must be some mistake. Didn't you get the summons?" asked the dragon.

"What summons?" Jemma was glancing around her office, assessing what she needed to take with her, what could stay.

"Apparently, that is a negative. Summons was sent, I was informed. You were supposed to be packed up and ready to go. Once I was out of the cabinet, out of the bowl, and into your line of vision, I was free and reporting for duty. Figures. Just one more indication of the dismal state of affairs," said the dragon, tiny brow furrowed as it looked quizzically at Jemma.

"No kidding. I—I don't understand. Something must be amiss." Jemma was trying to take in the information as she grabbed her things from the office and headed out. She sent a note to her boss, saying she was slipping out early to tend to a family emergency. Understatement of the century, she thought. She'd get in touch with Jake and Rhiona later.

Jemma got home, put the dragon on the counter, called her grandmother. Surely there was a reasonable explanation.

"Jemma! Thank heavens. Is Jing there?" asked her grandma.

"Jing?"

"Is there a dragon with you?"

"Grandma, this is crazy. Yes. There is a dragon here," Jemma said, turning toward the tiny dragon, who was walking on its two back legs along the counter, seemingly inspecting her kitchen, as far as Jemma could tell. "Is your name Jing?"

"Yes. We didn't have much time for introductions, did we?" said Jing.

"Yes. His name is Jing, yes," said Jemma.

"I'm not a he, I'm a she!" Jing said.

"Sorry. I, uh, sorry. Grandma, what on EARTH? Was there supposed to be a summons? And what does that mean? What is a summons? I never heard anything except just now at the museum. From a dragon, who just flew out of an ancient Chinese bowl! A dragon. Which I thought was not possible. Yet it—she—is now here. In my kitchen," said Jemma, extending her hand to Jing, who hopped on. Jemma walked the few feet to the living room and put a warm throw over the couch. Having never hosted a small, or large, for that matter, dragon, she thought she might just set Jing down on the sofa. Jing had other plans, and flicked her wings, flew up, and zipped around the apartment before landing, softly, on the couch. Jemma found herself following every move, entranced by the jewel-toned, iridescent creature. Also dashing for a hot pad to tuck under the dragon in case it was at all scorchy. Who knows, with dragons?

"Yes. Things have taken an unexpected turn here," said her grandmother. "As you know, we were planning for you to come and continue your training here, sometime this summer. But now, the Bay—Everland Bay Institute itself—has been attacked."

"What? How, when? I can't believe it!" Jemma said. She felt shaky inside.

"I know. It is horrifying. This happened just as the new director was being sworn in. The Institute awakened and must have sent out a summons to you and possibly to others; we don't know yet. We also don't know exactly why the Bay wanted you specifically. We think it was looking for your mother and found you. I wasn't informed; none of us human/fae/elf folk were told. The summons went out but somehow went without notice to us. I just heard about the whole situation and was about to call.

"What is most important for you to know right now is that our plans have changed. The Bay is in imminent danger; the attack is continuing and not yet under control. From what we can piece together, the Bay itself is planning for you to be part of a team of helpers. I'm not sure why you'd be in it since your training is incomplete. I don't have all the details yet. I am just learning about this in real time. I would have let you know the moment I did. Until today's ceremony, there was absolutely nothing terribly out of the ordinary going on, as far as any of us knew," said her grandmother. "We are being told that you will be protected, if you do agree to this summons."

"I'm just, I don't know what to say. Other than yes, of course I want to help. Where are the security forces, though? This all seems so strange," said Jemma.

"It *is* all strange. Very strange. What seems certain is that you are needed up at the Institute now. I am not sure whether I'll be there or at home, but either way I will see you soon."

Jemma took a deep breath. There was no question about leaving; she felt a pull that was nearly inexplicable, as if a dear family member was calling to her. "I'm in, Grandma. I'll be there. I do have some training, as you know, and I've been practicing with my friends here." Jemma struggled to take in all that she was hearing. How could her grandmother not know some important information? She always knew everything. Jemma was stunned, but tried to cover her fears with calm, if for no other reason than to keep functioning. Also, that's just what she did, she thought.

"It is a start. You know I've always said you're on your way to being as good a mage as your mother. Now. Pack your things and wear warm clothes. Jing will be flying you in and even though that will mean your saddle will be warm, it gets chilly up there. Don't leave anything important in your apartment. Bring your knitting," said her grandmother.

"How do you know about what to wear, but not know all of the important details? And yes of course, I'll bring my knitting. I have the usual project on the needles," said Jemma, fingering the knitting bag that she always had on her wrist, suddenly especially grateful that it was the shape-shifting variety. "I can't bring the piano!"

"Not right now. No time to downsize it. There is a lot that I will fill you in on. I wish I knew more, and I'll be trying to find out everything possible. Just get going and I will be in touch," said her grandmother.

"I was supposed to be practicing here tonight, and I have—" said Jemma.

"Who is your practice partner?" asked her grandmother.

"Partners. Rhiona and Jake. You remember them, yes?" said Jemma.

"Yes. I think Rhiona is a cousin to Keltie, here in the Village. And Jake has a brother up here, named Fletcher, if I'm remembering correctly. I will contact him, and he will let them know. Now be off, my dearest sprite!" said her grandmother.

Jemma rung off as she continued to rush around the apartment, gathering what she could, whatever would fit into her smallest suitcase. Jing was perched on the counter. "How will we get there?" asked Jemma. "I don't understand."

Jing looked up at Jemma, head tilted. "I told you I was your transport, remember? Didn't your grandmother mention it? I'll be flying you."

"But how…but you are so tiny. No offense."

"I beg your pardon!" said Jing, instantly becoming much larger. Her head brushed the ceiling.

Jemma jumped back. "Whoa! How? How did you do that?" Jemma was stunned. Jing was now huge, taking up a lot of the now very small-looking apartment, as her tail snaked through the living room and disappeared through the miniscule hallway, around the corner, and into Jemma's tiny bedroom.

"Apologies. I keep forgetting that you are not familiar with the way we work. I am a scaling dragon. Most of us have learned this skill. I can scale up or down as needed. I was in a state of suspension in the bowl. Freed by your presence, I am also free to assume the size that is most useful," said Jing, while simultaneously becoming smaller and smaller, and flying up to the counter, restored to her manageable size. About that of a raven. She snapped her wings smartly and tucked them neatly at her sides as she spoke. "But we are talking too much. We need to be off. Finish getting your things. Get whatever you wish. We will need to go somewhere that will give us room to have you climb up on me at a workable size. I'll scale up from there. It's not difficult. Bring a very warm cape, though. Also gloves and boots."

Jemma took it all in, shook her head, trying to clear her thoughts. "Right, then. I don't have a cape. I'll have to make do with my winter coat." Jemma finished gathering things, laying one hand on the keyboard of her piano, glancing at her favorite paintings for a moment. For a fleeting second, her shoulders and head drooped. *How can I leave all this behind?*

"My piano. And the paintings. I, will I see them again?"

"I don't have that information. And pianos are hard to move, you know, with such short notice," said Jing.

"I know. I know there is no choice," said Jemma, squaring her shoulders as she moved on to thinking about the best place for liftoff.

"The roof!" she said.

"Downscaling!" said Jing, at the same time.

"What?" they said in unison.

"I can do this," said Jing. "Place your satchel on top of the piano and bring one painting that you love the most in front of the piano, leaning back against it. Maybe between the bench and the instrument. Good. Okay, no questions, please, while I concentrate," said Jing, placing the tip of her tail precisely on Middle C.

Jemma watched in wonder as the entire jumble of her belongings—piano, satchel, painting, piano bench—got smaller and smaller, until everything was about the size of the original satchel. "How…"

"Later, I will answer questions," said Jing. "You said something about the rooftop?"

"Right, follow me," said Jemma. They went up to the rooftop. No one was there. Jemma let out a sigh of relief. "This should work."

Jing looked around, nodded. She grew to the size of a small pony, and out from under one wing, she let a small satchel drop. "Okay. Quick lesson. This is a MaryPop satchel. MaryPop is a satchel brand named for Mary Poppins. Legendary mage. You will find a small saddle inside. The saddle will size up correctly when you place it on my back. Ribbon reins will be attached at the front; I really hate reins, but you'll need something to hold on to. So, slip them around my neck, put the saddle on, and you'll see the straps below for your luggage. But try to hold more to the saddle horn than the reins. Don't choke me! Secure everything then get on," said Jing.

Jemma scrambled to accomplish all these very new-to-her tasks. Ribbon reins? *Sheesh,* she thought. *I don't even ride horses, let alone dragons.* With reins made out of hat ribbons, apparently. But she got everything done and climbed up. Just as she was getting settled, reins securely wrapped around her hands and very loosely around Jing's neck, the door to the rooftop scraped open slightly. "Go! Someone's coming!"

Chapter Four

Jing lifted off, growing larger and larger, into the size, roughly, of a rather large elephant. All the tack—saddle, reins—sized up to accommodate Jing's now-huge size. Jemma lurched back, grabbed the saddle horn, pulled too tightly on the reins.

"Watch the reins!" yelped Jing.

Jemma eased up on the reins, closed her eyes, and clung tight, breathing heavily. Riding on a dragon sounded great in theory, or in stories, but in real life it was very difficult. And a little scary. She felt herself going up, up, in an ever-widening spiral. But then she opened her eyes and cried out in delight as she saw the landscape unfurl below, felt the skies surround her, felt the solid warmth of Jing below the saddle. Washington was beneath them at close range, the embassies with their manicured gardens lush and green, dotted with what must be flowers, Jemma thought. Jing banked, flew along the Potomac River a short while, and Jemma could see the crews rowing, straining to pull their small boats quickly over the water. One small rower glanced up and stopped rowing. Then started waving his hands as he saw the dragon. Jemma could see the others trying to hold on to him and she worried now that they had been sighted. The rower dove into the water.

But Jemma couldn't focus on that for long; it was just too glorious up on Jing's back. The sun illuminated every detail. The river was incandescent with golds, blues, greens. Jemma felt the wind in her hair as they flew along, heading now toward the monuments; Jing did a banking loop around and Jemma looked down at some of her favorites. Jefferson Memorial, Lincoln Memorial. The tidal basin was exploding with the pink froth of cherry blossoms and Jemma was astonished again, as she was every year, by their impossible, fragile beauty.

"Uh, Jing?"

"Yes?"

"Aren't we in some kind of a rush?"

"Don't worry—we'll get there before you know it. I've been trapped inside that Chinese bowl for so many hundreds of years, though. I need to stretch my wings a little!" said Jing, in an unmistakably gleeful voice.

Down the long greensward, the National Mall, they went, then Jing banked again, and they headed west. Eventually they would head in a northerly direction as the approached the Great Waters region, where Everland Bay was nestled. Clouds slipped by as they went up higher. Jemma felt her hat blow off. She gripped the saddle horn tightly and rewrapped the reins to make certain they were tight, this time without strangling poor Jing. She felt her coat rippling in the wind and felt the slice of cold air rushing in.

Jemma felt alive as she had never felt before, tingling with delight and surprise, yet feeling a little precarious, perched on a dragon. A dragon! *This* dragon! How can this really be? Never mind, she thought. No time to figure that all out right now, as she looked all around, trying to take in every vista, every moment. Also trying to hold on. *This dragon-riding business is not so easy,* she thought again. They were now well away, following the contours of the land. Cityscape gave way quickly to woodlands and the unfurling quilt of farmland stretched beneath them, flashing peridot greens and fuzzy springtime yellows and pinks as they flew along. Cloud patches came and went, pretty as pictures but really rather chilly. And damp.

"I should have mentioned that you'd need a rain jacket," said Jing.

"No kidding. Those clouds were wet and cold!" said Jemma. "And I lost a glove!" Jemma felt icy cold wind blowing all around her. She shivered as the wind blew right through her. Knuckles white with exertion, she gripped the saddle horn tightly. She was grateful for the reins, even though they were sodden now. They still helped steady her. Her remaining glove was still on but proved no match for the cold. She could feel her hands stiffen with the icy winds. Then she felt her hands slip and begin to lose their grip. "My hands are freezing; I'm afraid I'll fall!"

"You can let go of the saddle horn. Carefully. I'll keep you steady and the reins will keep you attached as well. Place your hands on my neck or back. Wherever you can reach. I meant to say something about this. Forgot. Don't be afraid of my scales. Slip your hands under the edges of my scales somewhere, and…"

Jemma turned her complete attention to the task, letting the saddle horn go, one hand slowly, then the other. She wobbled a little, panicked, and felt her stomach do flips as she struggled to maintain her balance. The wind tore past her ears, making a torrent of sound, chilling her completely. In spite of it all, she righted herself. She then slipped each hand, still loosely entwined in a rein apiece, under the edges of Jing's scales, expecting everything to feel hard and stiff. She was hoping for a break from the wind and wet. Warmth flooded through her, and she closed her eyes briefly in relief. "What is…oh, so soft…is it feathers? It's like feathers!" The downy undersides of the scales startled her with delight; all of Jing looked so lacquered and hard on the outside, yet where her hands rested, there was nothing but softness and warmth.

"Well, of course. That's exactly right. Underdown, specifically," said Jing.

Jemma warmed up all over and after a little while, began to wonder when they'd get there, trying to remember how long it took on earlier, non-dragonflight trips, wondering which was quicker. "When will we be there?" Jemma asked, looking all around, trying, and failing, to see anything familiar.

"Dragonflight is quicker than you might think. We are getting close," said Jing.

As they got closer and closer to Everland Bay, the skies darkened. Jemma could feel a heaviness all around her and smelled smoke.

"We are heading in," said Jing. "But something's wrong."

"I see fire!" said Jemma.

Annalyn

Annalyn gathered herself together, put on the kettle, and got the tea things ready as she waited for Giselle to arrive. They never expected this turn of events, she thought, as she tidied the roomy kitchen and readied a plate of cherry scones, realizing how silly it seemed to focus on something so frivolous but also knowing as she did this that the ritual was a calming one for her, especially in the midst of chaos. She stopped arranging things for a moment and breathed deeply, trying to calm her skittering thoughts.

What now? she thought. Everything at Everland Bay Institute seemed to suddenly be coming apart. She only just missed being harmed, or worse, at what was supposed to be a charming little historic ceremony—the transfer of the directorship. But the crashing, raging mob overran the Institute, bludgeoning security forces, defacing the buildings.

And all this just as she was hoping to start a wonderful, intense time with Jemma's training and involvement in Everland Bay, both the Village and the Institute. This was going to be the time, very soon, when she and other experts could prepare and train Jemma much more along the lines of how they had always done things. Jemma and her training were a bit unusual and spotty up until now, but this upcoming deep training and tutoring would surely take care of the years she had missed by being away from the magical realms. The attack on the Institute meant that none of that could happen, at least for now. Annalyn felt a well of sorrow open up inside, one that she knew she had to put aside for now. It would live with her grief for her daughter, and other losses that were too deep to ever go away.

"Annalyn!"

Annalyn started and turned from her reverie at the sound of her friend's voice. Looking outside at the pathway in front, she was puzzled to not see Giselle. Then she smiled, shook her head a little, and walked down the hall. "I should have known you'd come this way. Sorry about any cobwebs, I haven't been tidying up in there much lately!" Annalyn opened the hallway portal stairs, and beheld Giselle, a frown folding her brow and eyes filled with worry.

"Oh, Annalyn," said Giselle, as she reached to give Annalyn a hug. "We are, and Everland Bay is, in great danger, as I know you know. I have called on Fletcher, you remember him, yes? He is my young tech mage. He will be joining us very shortly, and we may have another tech mage join us, along with the security detail.

"But it is good to be here," Giselle continued. "And it was wonderful to come through your portal again. Such a lovely one. Very well constructed. Makes the passage so much more bearable." She absently brushed off a bit of dust from her traveling clothes, which floated a bit around her before they settled down. The almost-invisible embroidery, stitched by the nimble fingers of the fae, shimmered an instant before subsiding to the background slate-blue color. The fabric was beautiful and rare, of elfin manufacture. It shed rain and snow, was warm in the cold and cool in the heat. No human understood this fabric, but it existed nonetheless, and Giselle always had her traveling garments tailored from it, which were then properly embroidered. Specially crafted spells stitched into the embroidery further enhanced its traveling fitness. Portal travel could be dicey, but with good traveling garments and the kind of sturdy, well-engineered portal that Annalyn had, the passage was not as difficult.

Annalyn brought her friend into the warm and sunny kitchen. "Thanks. These old-fashioned portals are the best. Okay, let's get to it. We have a lot to deal with. Jemma is flying on Jing to the Bay as we speak."

"Yes, I heard, most extraordinary, as you know, to even think of bringing in someone at her level of training," said Giselle.

"I'm worried, and was surprised, too. I believe the hope is that she and maybe eventually her friends can help with things there, despite her unconventional training. As you know, she is an unusual mix; dragon, fae, elf, and human. The Bay may be sensing unusual abilities in her; the Bay itself sent a Summons, then let me know belatedly, just moments ago. I barely had a chance to connect with Jemma, who was interrupted by Jing, a dragon, in the middle of her regular workday," said Annalyn.

"How did that happen? I didn't send for her, you know," said Giselle.

"I thought you would have told me, so I knew it couldn't have come from you. She said that Jing flew out of a small porcelain bowl that was in the Swain Museum's collection. She happened to be working on an exhibition that included it. Well, too many details to go into right now. But it flew out of the bowl and told her that it was transportation to the Bay, that she had been summoned. I've never heard of such a summons in real life; I think I've read about it in Everland Bay history books, but that's about it," said Annalyn. "And it terrifies me. What is the latest from your end? By the way, I escaped the revolt earlier by way of the back gardens. I was being pushed and pummeled, then security ushered me away."

"I saw you as you were just rounding the corner; they had collected me already and have kept me safe ever since. They let me return here and are stationed at the edge of your property. It's bad. Worse than we could ever imagine. Horrific."

"What happened? I am still confused," said Annalyn. "Who would want to harm you, or any of us?"

"There was a protest that turned violent right in the middle of my installation," said Giselle.

"I heard and saw the mob that started to attack us—I couldn't understand what was going on. What were they protesting? I am so glad you made it safely here," said Annalyn.

"Yes. I am now grateful that our officers saw you and got you out of there."

"What happened? You are the Director, yes?" said Annalyn.

"Well, that is part of what is so peculiar about this. I am *nearly* the Director.

"This ceremony, which was violently interrupted, as you know, is just the routine, final ceremony that acknowledges the new Director. All the official legal work has already been completed. We were just finalizing the routine recording of the transfer of power," said Giselle.

Annalyn stood up, began to pace the room. "Normally it's just a formality," she said.

"Yes," said Giselle. "But it is a necessary one. As you know, I had been vetted and appointed with the approval of the full Council. I have been on this path for years and it was all settled months ago. The usual ritual was taking place, with all the lovely touches in place and a reception to follow. You were there at that point."

Giselle stood up, walked over to one of the windows, and continued. "Normally, the names of the council are read, like a roll call; they all agree again publicly. It's all just completely ordinary public acknowledgment and celebration. Boring, even, though it is necessary. The public proclamation officially and completely transfers the power over to the new director. I was thinking I'd chat with you and other colleagues and friends at the reception, and get back to work, settle into my new role."

Annalyn walked back over to the couch and sat down. The shadow of a wry smile flickered across her face. "Most people are there because either they are on the council or are journalists, so have to be there, or they know the food it always pretty good at these things and are interested in the treats."

"Exactly so. Normally, the new director," Giselle continued, "accepts the ceremonial crystal wand with a few words of thanks at this point in the ceremony. The various leaders here have been doing this for hundreds of years. The transfer of official duties was already underway, in fact; my staff was getting offices lined up, tasks assigned, all that. Again, as usual!" She continued looking out the floor-to-ceiling windows that overlooked the rolling meadows, which disappeared in every direction into forests. The lake was visible as a thin line far on the horizon.

"But what happened? Was it robbery? The wand? Were they after the wand?"

"I don't think so, but again, we've been doing this for ever and ever. The wand was even given to me last week, so that I could use it to do some transfer and power work, but then it goes back into the vault, then comes out occasionally, under heavy security, as it did for the ceremony."

"And now—it's safe again? Was it stolen?" Said Annalyn. She reached over to Giselle's mug, noticed it was cold and headed over to the kitchen to start the kettle again.

"It's safe," said Giselle, walking in Annalyn's wake. "So, as I'm talking this through with you, clearly that wasn't what the mob was after. In fact, the wand was there in the Hall of Directors, ready to be used in the ceremony, and one of the younger security officers tucked it away for safekeeping once things turned violent. She was in my security detail afterward, and she handed it off to me, knowing that I could keep it safe.

"But," she continued, "the Institute is still under siege. The rioters don't know that they just interrupted the ceremonial transfer and that once we finalize the ceremony, which we will do, I'll be the official Director, and that their violence was—and is—all for nothing. They thought somehow that they could disrupt the ceremony and install someone they preferred. Unprecedented and impossible. Also frightening."

"I don't know what to say," said Annalyn. Or even think. This is insanity. We need you to be completely official. And we must get Jemma out of danger! I feel such a sense of despair, but I can't afford to think of that right now," said Annalyn. She refreshed the tea, handed the full mug back to Giselle.

"Thanks. I know," said Giselle, reaching for the tea. "And I need to get things back under control, finish the ceremony, put things back to rights, and figure out the next steps. In fact, the grounds are not yet completely secured, though I'm told security is doing a sweep and we should be able to start directing the cleanup and rebuilding as needed. Which reminds me—I need to ask you for hospitality, if possible, so that I can set up offices here for a short while, as our security forces continue to secure the Bay. I am truly sorry to have to ask, but…"

"Of course; consider this your home and place for as long as you need it. We will figure out details later. I'm afraid we are on the way to a rough time, my dear almost-Director," said Annalyn. She felt a terrible sense of foreboding and a pit in her stomach.

"We are there already," said Giselle.

Annalyn heard a small ping from across the room. "That's the scrying stone. It must be Jing," said Annalyn. "I'll bet they are approaching the Bay."

"Let's take a look. Where is the stone?"

"All set up, over there," said Annalyn as turned toward the great room.

The two went over to the scrying stone, a large, perfectly flat, perfectly polished obsidian stone surface submerged under a thin film of water.

"Annalyn, you are better at this than I. What are you seeing?" asked Giselle.

Annalyn took a deep breath, closed her eyes, and gathered herself for a moment. She slowly opened her eyes, gazing at the surface. An image of Jing, in silhouette, with a small rider on her back, came into focus.

Annalyn adjusted the scrying stone a little. "There they are. What is Jing saying? Can you hear her? I don't get audio in the scry, just visual," said Annalyn, keeping a soft gaze on the watery surface of the stone.

"Jing says they are seeing smoke, could be magefire or mageflares. Hard to tell. Not good, whatever it is. Windows are broken, and a crowd has overrun security. Oh, God, Annalyn, they're inside," said Giselle.

"We must tell her to turn around and come here. Jemma won't be safe there. Neither will Jing," said Annalyn.

Jemma

Jemma started coughing as they flew into the gritty, greasy smoke. And within the down-lined scales she felt a buzzy sensation, one she could not place. "What is happening? I can feel something buzzing," shouted Jemma. They were going faster, and the wind tore the words from her mouth.

"Perimeter. Trying to find a way in," said Jing.

Jemma tried to make sense of what she was seeing. It was hard to see anything at all under the smoke. Darkness enveloped the landscape. She thought briefly about her earlier visits; they mostly spent time in the Village, walking down the charming streets, stopping in here and there, at her grandmother's and mother's favorite shops; the bookstore, Folio, the second-hand store, Time and Time Again. Sometimes they stopped in to visit; the owners were all friends. The visits were a child's delight that grew to a comforting mainstay in her life and continued to lay the foundation of her grandmother's home and Everland Bay Village as safe and stable places, no matter what craziness or unhappiness was happening at home. She only visited the Institute itself once or twice, and her memory was of glorious stone buildings, a castle on a hill fit for a fairytale, and beautiful, manicured grounds, just like the miniature version she manifested during her drill with Rhiona and Jake the other day. But an entirely different world was on view below as they flew over. Now all was grim, sooty, gray. Billowing smoke created a nearly impenetrable veil. She glimpsed a few scattered figures running toward the once-majestic castle.

"We can't go in there. We are going to have to turn around, get out of here," shouted Jemma.

"But where? I have no orders for this," said Jing.

"Borderlands. My grandmother's place. The big house," said Jemma.

"I know that place. And yes. Okay. I'm just hearing from Dr. Azule. She's there, with your grandmother. Redirecting, redirecting.

Borderlands, onward!" said Jing. "Hold on tight. Going back through the perimeter," said Jing.

Moments later, Jing landed in the meadow outside her grandmother's kitchen. Jing began scaling down in size, pausing to let Jemma dismount. Jemma ran to her grandmother, who had come out onto the stone courtyard. She ran into the comforting circle of her grandmother's arms for a long embrace. "Oh, Grandma. It was terrifying. And amazing."

"Oh, my dear. Oh, thank all the heavens. We are so, so relieved that you are here and safe. You will both stay here," said Jemma's grandmother, giving directions to everyone quickly.

Her grandmother was a whirlwind, directing, gathering Jemma's things. "The piano—good thinking! Leave it scaled down for now." Then, giving Jemma another quick hug, she turned back to Jing. "Jing, there's enough room for you to be in or out; just remember to scale down a little smaller than you would at the Bay. This place is tight quarters for an energetic dragon. You are welcome here for as long as needed. Now, some introductions, though brief ones. Giselle, this is my lovely granddaughter, Jemma. Jemma, this is Dr. Giselle Azule, my friend and the new almost-Director of Everland Bay Institute."

Jemma was on her way to the kitchen sink to wash her hands while she was talking. "Oh! I've heard so much about you! I have wanted to meet you. But I was thinking that would happen someday on a terrace or classroom at Everland Bay Institute, if I was lucky enough to get a fellowship," Jemma said.

"And I have heard about you since you were a very young thing. Well. Despite the disarray, welcome to what is now the annex for Everland Bay Institute. We don't know what is left of it or what will be next," said Giselle, reaching for the small, framed photo of Annalyn and Elise on the coffee table. "And I cannot help but say how much you favor your mother. You look so like her."

Jemma smiled, leaned over, and picked up the photo. "I've heard that. You know my mother said to look for you if I were ever to come here, and so did my grandmother," said Jemma, drying her hands, looking at her grandmother and back to Dr. Azule.

"Your mother was one of my best junior magefellows. So long ago," said Director Azule.

"And now," Jemma's grandmother interrupted, "we have a lot to do. We need to get to work on the next steps. Dr. Azule can direct things down here. Jemma let's get you settled quickly upstairs. You haven't been in your room for a while. I think it's been a couple of years since you've been here overnight."

"I know, and now, of course," said Jemma, "I wish I came here much sooner and more often. I always thought there would be so much time to train, then apply, then come here, then…" Her voice trailed off, trembling just a little as she followed her grandmother up the familiar staircase. She took a deep breath to steady herself. *I can do this*, she thought.

"Things are different than we had all expected. It is a scary time, I know. There is so much to catch up on. We've been in touch with short visits and by phone, but it's just not the same as being together over a long run of days and nights, is it? This will change that. See? Here's your room, as usual. Come down as soon as you can. We will get through this time, my dearest girl," said her grandmother, giving her another hug, looking squarely into her eyes, then heading back downstairs.

Jemma could feel her shoulders relaxing as she took in her grandmother's comforting words. She wasn't quite sure how they would get through all of this but felt deeply relieved simply to be right here. To see her grandmother, be in this beloved and familiar place, connected again in person. The burden of figuring everything out would no longer be hers alone, and she knew she was in the hands and home of the wisest and most loving soul in her world.

This place was a sanctuary for her, and she knew it had been that for her mother, who had grown up there. Jemma took a shaky breath as she thought of her mother, wishing yet again that she was still alive. That ache, she knew, would never go away. But she also felt a sense of calm inside, despite the utter craziness of the day. While she had been working hard at building her career and getting along in Verandalands and the museum, she was, in some ways, living in a waiting room, still a child. Not quite a grown-up. Waiting for the next chapter in her life, waiting to get to Everland Bay Institute, to train there, to launch her real life in a more complete way.

She understood now that *this* was the next chapter. This messy, scary, unplanned situation. Right now. She was exhausted from the flight on Jing, exhausted from the frightening reality of the events and violence taking place, even now, at the Institute. But she resolved to be part of the solution. She didn't yet know what her role would be, but she was determined to step into it and give it her best. This was the time she waited for. She would do this next thing, whatever it was, for her mother, for her grandmother, and for herself. She took the Storybook out of her satchel, set it down on the dresser, gave it a loving pat, and turned to go downstairs and join the others.

There were a few unfamiliar-to-Jemma people sitting in the kitchen. A lanky fellow was focused on the screen in front of him, barely looking up. Maybe a tech person, Jemma thought. Two young, athletic-looking women seemed sort of military in their bearing. Formal, watchful. Maybe security? All were gathered at the sturdy, well-worn kitchen table scavenged by a long-ago farmhand from one of the old outbuildings on the property. The inviting clutter of mugs and cherry scones belied the serious tone of the gathering.

"First, we have to finalize the ceremony," said her grandmother.

"Yes. Even though my position is already official, the ceremony is a requirement, as it seals the appointment legally."

"How far along was it before the chamber was breached?"

"Nearly done; just need the final bestowal with the ceremonial crystal wand," said Dr. Azule.

Jemma spoke up. "Can we do the ceremony here?"

Silence ensued. Jemma worried at first that she far outstepped her place. Who was she to make a suggestion like that? She glanced down, busied herself with pouring a cup of tea, hands shaking a little.

"Is this your granddaughter?" asked the tall, serious looking fellow who had been focused on the large screen.

"Yes, Fletcher. Everyone, this is Jemma, my granddaughter. She just arrived from DC, in the Verandalands. Jemma, this is…everyone. Fletcher is our tech wizard. He keeps us up and running and connected to everyone. Shayna and Emma are security," said Jemma's grandma, nodding briefly at Fletcher, and the two members of Dr. Azule's security detail.

"My brother has spoken highly of you. Welcome," said Fletcher, with a nod.

"Thanks. Your brother? You must mean Jake. He's always talking about how much he misses you," said Jemma with a smile. She looked at him closely, seeing the resemblance to Jake, but noticing the deeper grin, the curls in his hair.

Dr. Azule chimed in, answering the earlier question. "It sounds a little outlandish, but I think there might be some merit in the idea of doing the ceremony here. We certainly can't go up to the Institute now; it is too risky. Can you run it through Legal?" She nodded toward Fletcher.

"I'm on it," said Fletcher, focused completely on the task before him. "We can do it, but the wand has to be the official one. No substitutes. Must be the real thing. Which was last seen in the ceremony room at the Institute, I think."

A general outcry rang around the room. Jemma felt her spirits sink as she realized that their hopes for a swift resolution and final ceremony could not happen.

"Thanks to Shayna's quick thinking," said Dr. Azule, "I'm happy to report that we have the wand. She took it and brought it here as we were escaping the violence at the Institute."

Jemma looked with admiration at the security detail.

Her grandmother said, "We are in your debt."

Jemma could see the two sit up a little straighter, nod, and smile just a bit. "Well," said Shayna. "We're security. Emma and I both thought of the same thing. She was right there. We were both assigned to the ceremony. When everything blew up, we…" Shayna paused, looked at each other and with a nod, said in unison "Secured it."

"Excellent." said Fletcher. "We should be okay now for the ceremony."

"Jemma, help me set up a sacred space," said her grandmother.

The two paced out the circle, a simple ritual that Jemma learned when she was a tiny thing. Now she stepped with confidence into the familiar pattern and when they were done, the shimmering air around them all confirmed the active presence of the circle.

"I need clearance for the ceremony," said Fletcher. "Hang on. Okay. Got it. No. No?" Fletcher's face, full of hope initially, fell. He tapped the table with frustration. "No can do, says Legal. Need another mage. Director cannot serve as her own ceremonial mage. Ms. Annalyn is qualified, but we need another. Needs to be female, otherwise I'd qualify. Don't ask. I don't make the rules."

"But who?"

"I can talk someone through it," said Dr. Azule.

"I have limited strength on my own, but can join with another," said Jemma's grandmother. "I would never normally suggest this as a first task, but Jemma, I think we're going to need you."

"I'm here." Jemma squared her shoulders and grasped her grandmother's hand. She felt a jolt of energy, stepped back a moment, then felt a sense of strength and determination as she stood ready. They followed Giselle Azule's instructions, reciting the ancient words, ending with, "and so it must be."

Silence infused the room. And continued. After an uncomfortably long time, people began to stir. "No good," Fletcher started to say.

But all at once, a rippling occurred throughout the air around them. And as if it had always been thus, the ceremonial crystal wand shimmered brilliantly and sent light beams through the clasped hands of Jemma and her grandmother. Jemma felt the amplified energy as the light pulsed in her hand holding the wand. Her eyes grew wide as she grinned. She felt shivery inside at the wonder of the moment.

The wand was glimmering. Magnificent. A rainbow of light beams, silver, indigo, fuchsia, peridot, golden yellow, poured out of the wand and illuminated the room.

Jemma was dazzled. Awestruck. She had experienced minor light emanation, but it was mostly routine; small shimmers here and there as she shifted her knitting around, minor light trails during practice drills. Or sometimes she'd create a little magelight, like back when she first met Jake in the museum. Never for such a high purpose as this. Never from a sacred ritual instrument. This was energy work of a higher order altogether. And it was breathtaking. She sensed the electrical power coursing through her and felt her hair lift and blow up and around, a halo of swirling curls. The others experienced such lofty ceremony at other times, she suspected, but she could see by the expressions on their faces that they, too, were awed by the majesty of this magic.

"And now the rest of the ceremony," said Jemma's grandmother.

"And now the rest," said Dr. Azule. "The words are yours to speak out today, as our most senior mage. I took a copy of the oath and proclamation as I left the chamber. You can do the honors now."

"Wait," said Fletcher. Someone groaned. "Legal is questioning our mage choice. They're saying we must have someone else with lineage. Sorry."

"Oh, mercy. And we are so close. To both failure and success," said the Director.

Jing interrupted. "Bad news in the Institute and in the skies. The rogue mage surge is continuing, and they are bringing in mercenary flying tribes. Not dragons, but chimera and possibly gryphons. Their strength is legendary. If they get in, they could hold it for good. Dr Azule, are you hearing from Council? Or Legal?"

Dr. Azule and Fletcher started talking at the same time. Fletcher deferred.

"We can definitely do the ceremony here, we just need—" said Dr. Azule.

"One more lineage mage. With, like, perfect lineage," said Fletcher.

The tension was high in the room and Jemma turned to her grandma. "Can I count as the second lineage mage as well?"

"Well. You are certainly qualified." Jemma's grandma turned toward Fletcher and Dr. Azule. "She has lineage. And they just cleared her moments ago for the opening part of the ceremony. Why not this as well? They are being overly bureaucratic here."

"Indeed. This should solve things." said Dr. Azule. "Fletcher. Jemma has impeccable lineage."

"Hang on, Legal is responding. And…confirmed. We are a go," said Fletcher, grinning, raising his hand in the air in a triumphant thumb's up.

"Brilliant! Jemma, keep hold of my hand; you are now empowered for this ceremony."

Jemma tightened her grip on her grandmother's hand, feeling buoyant at being able to help. She held her breath as her grandmother stated the formal proclamation, which ended "…and so it must be, and so it now is, with all rights and powers granted and proclaimed." The wand sparkled as if it was alive.

"And we are now in the presence of the newest Director of Everland Bay Institute," said her grandmother. "Allow me to be the first to say congratulations, Director Azule."

Giselle Azule smiled briefly and gave a quick nod. "Jing, please let security know the ceremony is complete and activate all the rest of the backup. Fletcher, please translate and proclaim this through all platforms and communication relays. Now. We have some work to do." Jemma sensed with admiration how Dr. Azule had stepped fully into the authority of her new position.

Jemma helped her grandma and Dr. Azule arrange the large back great room as a temporary control center. Everyone bustled around, Fletcher getting tech set up properly, all the while in touch via headset as well as internal magespeak communications. "I'm checking those reports about flying mercenaries and rogue mages," Fletcher said.

"Right, good," said Dr. Azule. "Jing, please join the security flight team now; keep us informed as you are able. Please pull in others in the dragonclans; we need all the old families to help. Annalyn, activate all the elven peoples, all the fae who are with us to reclaim the grounds and the Institute. I'll be over here in command and control." She looked around the room, searching the faces around her, and nodded. "With a team like this one, there's no chance that we will fail." Everyone got to work. Fletcher huddled with Dr. Azule, Grandma Annalyn started contacting her network. Jing headed outdoors, scaling up and flying away to connect with the others in the skies.

Jemma took it all in, momentarily recounting the swirl of emotions, fear followed by pride and awe as the ceremony unfolded. Now she stood in the kitchen as the others went about their tasks, not sure exactly where she should be or what she should do, but knowing it felt exactly right to be here. She turned to her grandmother and caught her eye, raising her eyebrows in a question.

Grandma Annalyn smiled warmly at her and reached over to give Jemma a little hug. She paused in giving orders over her device. "All right, my sprite. We've just accelerated your training schedule. We begin now in earnest. Though, really, we've already started, haven't we? For now, I'll have you shadow me as we go through all we are doing. I don't have a specific assignment list for you, as we are all in the middle of it all. Just stay alert and stay with me and we will do this work together. I will explain as best as I can, will give you tasks along the way, and we will debrief in stages when we take breaks. Here begins your next chapter."

Jemma felt her shoulders come down, taking in her grandmother's comforting words. *Okay, she thought. I'm going to be okay.*

Chapter Five
Agni

Back in his study, Agni was distraught. He could not stay still. He paced the room back and forth, trying to make sense of things. His willful, fiery, wonderful, frustrating daughter stormed out of the restaurant their last time together and hadn't been in touch in weeks. His calls went unanswered. I failed her, he thought. I failed the last person on Earth who means anything to me. Agni looked out the window, as if trying to see her in the darkening skies. Turning away from the window, Agni felt a deepening sense of despair. And shame. How could I have lost her this way? He knew that he was too harsh with her mother, was too strident, insistent, fierce. Fiery. He thought he was saving them and making them safe, but now, he was beginning to sense that, in gaining all the wealth and power, he was losing all that mattered.

He shook himself. "Too dramatic," he said out loud, standing up and pacing the room. "No need to be maudlin. She'll call soon." But his words felt hollow and small as he spoke them into the dark solitude. He was not convinced. And he was beginning to know that things had to change, if there was going to be any chance at all that he would have a life with Jemma in it. He realized, as these thoughts were swirling uncomfortably through his mind, that this was more important than anything else. And that it might just be too late.

At work, another kind of storm was gathering, as his disgruntled competitors had gotten wind of a possible identity problem. He knew they were whispering about his dragonmark. He carefully camouflaged it each morning, as always. He was due to speak to his boss tomorrow and believed the reason might be linked to the whisper campaign, though his boss did not say. He would stamp this out, he thought fiercely. He fought for his position and brought in so much wealth for the bank. He helped build this bank into one of the most important of the banks in Verandalands. They owed him. And he would fight this.

Or would he? And could he? He stopped pacing, sat down heavily. His shoulders dropped and he put his head into his hands. His fingers instinctively sought out the mark. He could feel it, ever-present. Slightly warm, slightly pulsing.

Why did he have to have such a mark? So many like him didn't. He knew that. Throughout his life, he shared glances and sometimes friendships with others who he knew were part dragon. Those friendships mostly dissolved after college, but he knew there were others. Mostly, they were in the Northlands and Great Waters areas, regions that were magic-friendly. Dragon-friendly. Indeed, magic and magical creatures were simply the norm. Welcomed and not unusual. Dragonmixed folk were rare, partly because the mix was inherently unstable; humans had lower ethics than dragons as a whole, and the internal conflicts could add up to hot-headed choices and poor results, as he ruefully reminded himself, knowing he fit that profile. But even in Verandalands, there were some like him. They didn't stay long, usually, but those who did completely hid their true identities. Those in the Verandalands tended to have very small marks, ones that had no glossiness or sparkle to give them away. His was larger, sparkling with iridescence, pulsing with his every emotion. He had worked hard to hide it ever since he began thinking of moving his family to the area, to take this very lucrative position at the bank. The bank had been the only place he had succeeded so well. But things were not looking so solid anymore.

And now he wondered. Was it still really what he wanted? Surely it was. And yet…

His thoughts were interrupted by his phone's chime. Relief cascaded through every part of him. Jemma. "Jemma! Are you okay? Where are you? I've been trying to call."

"Dad. I'm fine. Things are kind of crazy right now and I'm at Grandma's."

"What? How? Aren't you supposed to be at work?"

"This is more important."

Agni swallowed. He took a deep breath, forcing himself to stay calm. What happened? How could she just leave and not tell him? How could she just walk out of work? What was going on? But this was one time, he realized, that he could listen to what his daughter was saying to him, even if it seemed ridiculous. No, he said to himself. Maybe not ridiculous. Must listen here. Another deep breath. No fire. "Tell me," he said.

"Okay, Dad, don't get mad. I got word from, uh, folks from Everland Bay that I was supposed to go there. I was planning to go to Grandma's to train and prepare for the formal application this summer. I was going to tell you that last time we were together, but, well, that didn't work out. But something happened up there, and they suddenly decided to bring me in much earlier. Then there was a, a problem at the Institute, and I had to go to Grandma's instead. I'm safe, and so is she, and I will be here for, well, I don't know how long. But I wanted to make sure you knew right away," Jemma said.

Agni could hear that she was hesitant, and tired, and something else. He couldn't pin it down, but he knew he wanted her to know he was there for her. Somehow. "Honey, I, I don't know what to say. But I'm so glad to hear your voice and so glad you are safe. Is there anything I can do here? Are you going to be there long?"

"I don't know much yet except I'll probably be here for a while. But I don't know. Can I call you when I know more?" said Jemma.

"Of course. Please let me know what is happening. Call even if there's nothing big to report. I just want to know you're okay."

"Will do. Dad?"

"Yes?" said Agni.

"I love you," said Jemma.

"Oh, honey. I love you, too," said Agni. He could feel a catch in his throat, and he felt uncomfortably warm. His mark was pulsing, and a tear threatened to slip down along it, marring his careful camouflage yet again. The call ended.

Impatiently, he brushed the tear away and stared down at his phone, then out the windows, into the darkening tree line outside. He could sense his world was changing. He did not have answers right now, and it was a very unsettling feeling. What could he do? How could he make things better? In the quiet dark, he found he had the most surprising thought. What if he joined her? What if he went to Everland Bay someday? No. Who was he kidding? That would be crazy. He couldn't leave everything here. Or could he? The unexpected idea felt rather like something Elise would have liked. A lot. Crazy as it was, it felt, just possibly, like a good idea. And for the first time in a very long while, he felt a sense of hope.

Jemma

At her grandmother's, Jemma was ready to work harder than she ever had, and knew she needed to be nimble in the midst of chaos. After the flurry of activity right after her arrival, and the ceremony, a couple of days passed, and things remained uncertain. The Institute was still under what was a murky occupation; the rogue mages had not been routed. She knew an important meeting was happening the next day with the Village leaders as well as Dr. Azule, her grandma, and some others from the Institute. They would be deciding what to do next, Jemma knew. While she was gathering her thoughts, she was putting things to rights after the others left. Her grandmother came into the kitchen.

"Grandma, we saw such devastation at the Institute—the grounds were torn up, there was smoke billowing up beneath us as we flew. It was hard to see, but the glimpses we saw were terrifying. What is happening there now?" Jemma turned to her grandmother, who was intent on the small scrying stone she kept on the kitchen counter.

"Things are in disarray, and we are in a bind. Those of us who are determined to get things back in order—Director Azule, key faculty, and council members—are trying hard to do that. Apparently, however, there was a very small faction of lawless, extremist faculty. The most prominent was an old classmate of mine, Dr. Max. They were supporting the rogue mages and their leaders and opened the grounds to them. We were all shocked, horrified. They dispute Director Giselle's position simply because they disagree with her approach and are trying to wrest control of the Institute from the Council and loyal faculty. The Village leadership is also part of things; they have been angry for a long time about not being consulted regularly for overall direction of the area and are furious about the violence and fall of the Institute and what the fallout will be for them. Years of resentment are boiling up."

Jemma took all of this in as she walked over to look at the scrying stone, trying to see. This was a skill she had yet to learn, and she only glimpsed shimmering on the surface. "I wish I could see things clearly in here. I wish I knew what was happening," she said.

"As do we all," said her grandma. "But right now, we can correct a tiny portion of that; let's teach you more about scrying."

Jemma nodded, relieved to have something useful to do. To learn. "That would be great."

"Here. When two read, we center together first, to align our energy," said Grandma Annalyn.

Jemma felt a calming inside as she closed her eyes, breathing quietly with her grandmother.

"And now," her grandma said, "lean over toward the scrying stone, and keep your eyes in a soft focus. Shoulders down, stillness inside. Just glance lightly at the surface, let it unfurl."

Jemma looked and looked. And couldn't see anything but liquid jet, like a pool of ink. She felt a slight giving up, resigned herself to needing more training, when "I see something!"

"Hold it very gently, that's it. Now, let it unroll, like a little movie,'" said her grandma.

"Yes—the people there. Mages? Campsites, it looks like. The grounds are churned and torn," Jemma said, rubbing her temples. "It looks frightening there." Jemma glanced up at her grandma.

"Good work, my sprite. That is probably enough for a start; we don't want to strain your abilities by overtaxing them too soon."

Jemma turned away from the small scrying stone and went into the living room, pacing the length of it as she tried to think things through. It felt so good to learn something new, something that she could build on and get better at. But now she felt a little queasy. It hurt to see so much, even just that one small glimpse.

And now what? As the chaos of the crisis up at the Institute continued, she could learn the practical details of helping her grandmother run Borderlands. She knew she could assist with the portal, flex her magic skills with constant use, whether drilling in quick-glamour or practicing moving landscape out back with her visualization and manifestation skills. And now, some scrying. Which felt great. But she wanted things to be happening sooner. She felt an overwhelming sense of urgency. After the huge rush of flying there, it was as if she had run into a wall. She knew her grandmother and Director Azule probably knew what was best, but she was worried that things were mired in a sticky muddle of inaction. She heard the stair portal creaking to life. "I'll go get that," she said, running to open the door at the top of the stairs. "Hello, Director Azule."

"Jemma, dear, hello," said Director Azule crossing the room and settling near the large scrying stone. She paused, breathed in deeply, and Jemma could feel their energies aligning. Dr. Azule peered in, next to Jemma's grandmother.

"You can see—see here? Those are rogue mages. They are camped all over. Our security collapsed. That faction—Annalyn, I'm still stunned. I just had no idea this was more than a fringe threat. None of us did. Our threat assessors dismissed the group entirely. Minimized it all, saying it was chatter. And I heartily wish for my landscape map. It is in my office, and I'd really like to get it out of there. I need it. Right now, there is a solid spellwork shield around my place at the Institute, but I don't know how long it will hold. If they breach it and get the map, they could further deepen their hold on the Institute. I've cancelled all activities, ordered resident faculty and fellows to move off the grounds temporarily. I've also invited Fletcher to join us; he should be here any moment."

As if on cue, the portal door thumped. Jemma headed back over and opened the door. She nodded to Fletcher as he strode in and headed over to the room.

"Hey, everyone," he said, nodding.

"How can the map help?" asked Jemma, looking at Dr. Azule.

Fletcher looked over to Dr. Azule, who gave him a quick nod. "It's one of those unusual landscape maps that came with the original deed to the land," he said. "A 3-D scaled-down model of the whole Institute and grounds, and it shows precisely what is happening. It is a living replica that displays all that is happening in real time."

"I've never heard of one of those," said Jemma.

"They're pretty rare, but some of the oldest, largest properties with significant buildings have them," said Fletcher.

"I have not fully explored its capabilities," chimed in Dr. Azule. "Those of us below the directorial level had always been told that you cannot breach the map or change what is happening within, but you can see everything. When or if one becomes the director, more possibilities and rights are granted. I haven't yet had time to explore that, but I don't know what the rogue mages may know or be able to do. I don't know if the map could be vulnerable and create risk on its own."

"We should somehow find a way to get it. And don't we have to get the rogue mages and their leaders to move out of there?" asked Jemma. "There's got to be a way. How could they be so entrenched, so quickly?"

Fletcher jumped in. "We are secure here, so I can speak to this. They are acting as if Everland Bay is theirs to control, and that they are not recognizing any Everland Bay authorities. They have just attacked and are claiming the ground. We are hearing that they are having properties like Everland Bay falsely condemned and manufacturing documents claiming their right to the land."

"This is insane!" said Jemma. "I know it's only been a couple of days since I got here, but things seem so stuck."

"It is insane. You are right. The meeting at the Village tomorrow should go a long way toward getting things back on track," said Grandma Annalyn. "There is some foot-dragging, though, on the part of some of the leadership. We were all hoping for consensus but there are a couple who think we can still negotiate and win over the rogue mages. I disagree with those, but I am only one voice."

"Fletcher, what are you hearing?" asked Dr. Azule.

"We are hearing that they are digging in and are talking about gathering in more like themselves, attracting even younger, more impressionable mages, and cornering the market on evil magic and budding evil mages. They don't care that the grounds are torn up and debris-strewn; they think it looks more menacing and apocalyptic, so they are not bothering with repair or cleanup. They *want* it to be ravaged and chaotic; they want there to be no real seminars or learning or normal civilities but a militia style evil magic boot camp, on an ongoing basis. They find chaos exhilarating and right now that's all we know about their agenda," said Fletcher.

"They seem to have no agenda other than disruption and encouraging evil," said Jemma, standing up and pacing the room.

"All of this is true. And yet we have others to consider. But let's see how the meeting goes. If we need to, we could convene a small team that could be more nimble; Fletcher, Giselle, you, and me. But Fletcher, how do know all of this?" said her grandmother.

Fletcher looked down at his keyboard. Took a deep breath. Jemma could see him hesitating. "They tried to recruit me. It was a while back."

The room fell silent.

"I could never be part of them."

"You know, I remember. Jake said something about that when we were practicing together. And that reminds me—we should bring him into this group," said Jemma.

"Are you sure?" said Grandma Annalyn.

"Positive," said Jemma. "And a local young mage named Keltie. Who is already here, down in the Village. I think we'll make a good team. We've been training with her cousin, Rhiona, who lives near where Jake and I do, in D.C. And we have remote trained with Keltie, back at my place."

"That is a relief to hear," said Jemma's grandmother. "I didn't know how much you were doing. I am glad you've been working so hard, though. We had no idea that all of this was coming. I would have included Keltie on this end if I had known."

Jemma felt a pang of regret. It would have been good to have Keltie involved openly earlier. She felt a little guilty, wishing she told her grandmother earlier. Somehow the right time hadn't opened up. But also, they were a little unsure of the older mages' reactions—they were all worried that their training and planning together might be discouraged or minimized as being unimportant, less skillful. Jemma watched her grandmother turn to leave. She followed and put her hand on her grandmother's shoulder. "I love you so much, Grandma, and I've always loved this place. I want all of Everland Bay to be wonderful again, like it was when my mother was here."

Her grandmother turned to give Jemma a quick hug. "I don't think it will ever be the same, dear girl. But I know you are coming into your strength, and I welcome it. Know that we, Giselle and I, and others, are also very strong and we, too, see what is happening. With you, we can make it even better. With all of you. We just don't know what that looks like right now. Why don't you go ahead and contact Keltie?"

Jemma watched her grandmother leave and though she sensed a lingering sadness, she felt reassured and stronger inside. It was such a good feeling to know that her grandmother loved her and was a brilliant mage in her own right, but also gave Jemma credit for her own growing strength. She was not dismissed, the way her father dismissed her. Or just dismissed because she was young. A sense of resolve was taking root inside, along with her worry that the older mages were not moving as quickly as they needed to.

And at the same time, she felt a little thrill of discovery and hope, and a sense of lightness. Her little team, working on this for real. They could do just about anything together, she felt, including, somehow, taking back the Institute. Jemma realized that she had been wiping down every corner of the kitchen, mindlessly, for a while. She walked out into the garden to regroup and get ready for the days ahead. On her way, she sent a contacting thought to Keltie. Now. Maybe just a few moments on the garden bench, she thought, taking a deep breath as she sat down, and taking a moment to see the roses in bloom, the lilies reaching toward the sky, the deep green forest of fern-skirted trees in the glade beyond the sunny beds.

A crunching sound startled her, and she turned to find the source. So much for a bit of quiet, she thought, feeling intruded upon. Her alarm and annoyance melted as she turned to see a familiar, lanky figure heading toward her. Jake. How? "Jake!" A bloom of delight opened up inside as she saw his smile.

"I made it! They let me come sooner than expected!"

"You're here! I didn't know when you'd get here." Jemma's and Jake's words passed by each other as they spoke in unison while hugging. They laughed. "How did you make it in? I was on, well, you won't believe this, but I came by dragon. We went through the perimeter around the Institute but had to change plans and come to Borderlands," said Jemma.

"Yeah, after you disappeared, I was talking pretty much constantly with Fletcher. He sent a request up the chain to have me come through, even though my internship at the museum wasn't up yet. But I just came into the Village, checked in with my brother, then came up to your grandmother's from there, so no need to deal with Institute perimeter wall or anything like that. Just completely ordinary. And no need for a dragon flight, though I admit to being jealous!" said Jake. "I want to know everything about that."

"I definitely have a good story for you, once there's time. It was pretty wild. Also kind of amazing. For now, though, we have got to get moving on things here. I'm sure Fletcher is keeping you up on things, but there is a sense of waiting around and inertia that just seems to be bogging things down. With the three of us, I think we can get things moving," said Jemma.

"Three?" Jake said, looking around dramatically for a third.

Jemma laughed. "We're going to include Keltie. In fact, I just pinged her. She'll be coming up from the Village. As you've just demonstrated, it's not all that far, but she wants to use the kitchen portal."

The two ran back through the garden and went through the back door into the kitchen.

"Those older portals are pure genius. I want to try it sometime, too. And, wow. This place is great," said Jake.

"I love it here. Despite all the chaos, it is so good to be here. Feels like home to me," said Jemma.

"I get that. It was amazing to see my brother again. And just be here. Definitely home. So good to be home and so good to be somewhere magical again. I haven't been back in a while," said Jake.

"No kidding. Just feels so much cleaner here. So safe. We are free to just be ourselves. And yes—so good to see family. Your brother is in and out of here a fair amount; you'll see him here a lot," said Jemma, smiling. As they turned toward the gathering in the kitchen, she called out, "Everyone, this is Jake. And I think many of you know Keltie," Jemma said, opening the portal door next to the pantry. A tangle of red curls stood out at all angles from a smiling, befreckled visage as the door opened. Jemma, Jake, and Keltie all beamed at each other.

"Nice to see you in real life!" said Keltie, grinning. "Practicing via remote scrying screen is cool, but nothing like being together in person."

"True, that," said Jake. "No idea you were so tall."

"We're all here now." Jemma felt a sense of delight all the way through, despite the somber situation they were in.

The three hugged, and sparks flew all around the room.

Jemma started to laugh, and she could see her grandmother and Dr. Azule looking astonished.

"Clearly," said grandma Annalyn, "you three are meant to work together."

We can do this, she thought. Not sure of the details, but somehow, everything will come together. Jemma knew she was becoming strong on her own, but it was so much better to be working as a team. Their skills complemented each other's and somehow just being together, working on things, made it all a little easier. And they were just beginning to learn that it amped up their magic.

In one of their last practice sessions before she came, Rhiona had brought Keltie in via scrying screen so that they could get a bit of a start on working together. Individually, they were becoming good mages; together, they had the potential to be phenomenal. Jemma grinned and glanced around the room and saw answering smiles and nods.

She heard a ping from the scrying screen, murmuring as her grandmother and Dr. Azule assessed the information. Jemma was immediately reminded that things were coming apart up at Institute.

Jemma looked around the familiar kitchen, filled with favorite things, from the small teacup she had used as a little girl to the beautiful artwork—framed oil paintings by her mother of pears and peaches and simple watercolor sketches of flowers and landscapes—that graced the roomy kitchen and breakfast room and set the gracious and usually calming tone. Today none of these were comforting as Jemma began to take in the enormity of truly being in the midst of this mage war, this horrific time. How could this terrible mess be solved? What could she possibly do?

She had longed to move here for so long. She was beginning to realize that some of what she had been hoping for were happier days. Days filled with reading and picnics and walks along the creek. Visits to the shops in the Village with a stop for frozen custard every now and again. Watching the meadow fill with spring flowers and settle into summer blooms. Someone else taking charge of things. A time when her mother was alive and strong. That was how it had been when she was a little girl, visiting here with her mother throughout the soft, sweet summer days. That was what she had been hoping for upon her planned return to Everland Bay. So completely different from the chaos and destruction that greeted her instead. Would those beautiful summertime days ever return?

Her grandmother sat down across from her at the battered table and folded her hands over Jemma's. "This is exactly as you sense. We are in an in-between time right now. Times like this are very, very difficult. And none of us knows exactly what to do. And now that you are an adult, you will be part of the solution, helping along with all of us to solve this messy, painful situation. But you are not alone in this. And it is not yours alone to solve. Remember that Dr. Azule and I and some very good souls in the Village and the Institute have many years together, solving difficult problems."

"But things fell apart anyway," Jemma said. She still felt the sting of despair and the heaviness of worry.

"Yes. They did. And it is a disaster. For now. And I don't know exactly how we will move forward. But we always have, and we will now. Coming together to solve it will be a big part of that. And you, I have a feeling, will be a big part of this."

"And Keltie. And Jake," said Jemma, glancing across the room to see her two friends in an animated discussion with Fletcher. She brushed a tear away and looked into her grandmother's eyes.

"Indeed. We are none of us lone saviors. Giselle and I have been a team for a long time, and we are going to partner with the Village more closely than ever before. We have been wrong in keeping the Village wisdom apart from the more academic group at the Institute. We need them. Probably even more than they need us," said her grandmother, with a wry smile.

Jemma closed her eyes and allowed herself a moment of comfort as she felt her grandmother's hands, still folded over hers. She turned and looked up at her grandmother, and behind her, Dr. Azule, who was just leaving the room. Dr. Azule turned and looked at Jemma. "Welcome to our mess, my dear. We will get through this together."

Jemma felt a glimmer of strength and hope. She squared her shoulders and allowed her lips to quirk up into a small smile. "It's hard, being all grown up."

The three laughed and nodded, rueful but resolute.

Chapter Six
Annalyn

Annalyn was deep in thought as she walked down to the Village the next morning. Barely registering the drifts of summer meadow flowers and grasses, she thought through the next steps. To finally evict the rogue mages as well as create a new system, every person and creature would be needed. Each shop, café, and business in the Village was necessary, as well as all the academics who had not been corrupted. Old fault lines were exposed with the assault on the Institute, with some in the Village suggesting that the Institute was not such a wonderful place after all and questioning the need to rebuild. Others felt this was a time for the Village to shine, and still others just wanted to get things back to the way they used to be. Those were generally the ones who prospered for generations and had nothing to fear in returning to old ways that mostly served them and their families.

But how to do things differently? Annalyn thought. She reached over, pulled on a long blade of grass, and absently twisted it in her hands as she strode along. This question, of course, was the hardest. And complex. One difficulty was the lack of career-track work in the Village, thus the ongoing pattern of academic mages coming in as young practitioners and leaving to go elsewhere, and a bias against ordinary, practical magic and practical work, including skilled magical trades, retail, hospitality, local banking, and local businesses of every imaginable kind.

Annalyn bent down, examined a leaf, glanced around for the flutewood it came from. A small grove just over the next hill. The flutewoods connect every part of the area, she realized.

Shaking her head a little to help clear her mind and focus on the problem at hand, she continued thinking and walking. Despite the limited types of work available, the Village business owners, both mage and non-mage, needed new workers and young people to continue the work after their own retirement.

Annalyn and Giselle were going to present an Institute-to-work model, which would create a supply chain of talent that would weave through the Village and, in some cases, retain valuable working mages. Annalyn glanced at the sheaf of paper in her hand, which detailed the plan.

How to present all of this while the Institute was still in such turmoil? The plan was that those young mages who went through the new pathway and then went on to other places would have a deep understanding of small-town magecraft and would be better able to do their own work in the widening world and could remain connected to Everland Bay by encouraging folk to move there or take part in organized events. Internship/apprenticeships would be created for every Village concern, from the thrift store to the grocery store to the tavern to the bookstore, library, museum, attorney's office, and all the other trades and businesses. Institute-bound young mages would begin their Everland Bay journey in the Village, choosing a place to learn a trade. This would create a home base that would be a warm and nurturing spot throughout their time at Everland Bay as a whole.

Annalyn stopped and leafed through the rest of the pages, glancing quickly, reminding herself of her key points: The young mages' first year would be spent mostly in the Village, learning from their supervisor, living and working in the Village and training in basic magic skills. Skill assessment could be done in the Village, which would delegate some of the formerly Institute-only tasks to the Village. Trainee mages could attend Institute lectures that fit their needs and interests, and they would be paired with a mentor from the Institute, who would be in the Village from time to time. Each business in the Village would be paired to an Institute division, ensuring a steady supply of employee talent. This would ensure work-and-life training for the young mages, who would continue to work in the Village throughout their years at the Institute. Many, perhaps most, would leave afterward to go on to work outside of the Village, but those who stayed would have guaranteed jobs, and the Village would stay strong, vibrant, and more deeply tied to the Institute in a sustainable and mutually beneficial way.

Those mages who were primarily academics, and who joined the Institute later in life to round out their magical work, would be required to give workshops and talks at various Village sites. The two places would open their borders so that there was no magical or other barrier between them, as there had been for centuries. Instead, a new perimeter would be created that would encompass both the Village and the Institute. Barriers would be removed and reshaped, with inviting and beautiful pathways linking the two areas. The old perimeter, which was constructed without the agreement of the Village centuries before, would be dissolved.

Annalyn finished leafing through the presentation and continued on her way. The trouble, of course, was that she and Giselle needed energetic, visionary young mages to start this work with them. They needed to be a special group, who would be interested in creating this new way of being in and running Everland Bay, and not so enthralled with the old Institute that they would be resistant or half-hearted. Same with other more seasoned mages and Villagers.

Her brow was furrowed as she found herself at the café. She looked up and smiled at Giselle, who was there already, beginning the work of the meeting. She glanced around the room and saw all those who gathered, including the younger ones. At a table noticeable for the laughter ringing out in its vicinity sat her sweet granddaughter and her posse, Keltie and Jake. Fletcher was no doubt on his way to join them, she thought, along with another small group of younger mages who were just a few years older; journeymages. Inwardly, she smiled. Maybe I don't have to look too far for my dream team, she thought.

She took a seat as Giselle nodded, listening as Giselle laid out the plans.

"First," said Giselle, "we must secure the Institute. We never thought we needed a large security force at the Institute, so we never had one. I regret our lack of foresight but have taken steps to put things to rights. Our head of security, Merywinkle, has joined forces with the elite crew from our neighboring province in the wider Great Waters Region to come in, and they arrive today to assist our team in clearing the rogue mages out, securing the grounds, and restoring the current perimeter. The work is underway even now and will accelerate as soon as they arrive. We have added a great number of willing folk of all sorts to our cleaning crew, who will go in after them to handle cleanup and repair. Within a few days, we hope, Everland Bay Institute should be safe and ready for restoration. We're hoping to get things back up and running as soon as possible."

Cheers erupted as all took in the good news. Annalyn glanced around the room, smiling. A movement in the back caught her eye. A large man leaned over, passing a note to another sitting next to him. Their faces were grim, unsmiling. Abruptly, one stormed out, spewing vicious expletives. The other rushed toward the podium, shouting as he went, "She did not earn this office! She is not legitimate! No woman can do this work and surely not a woman with mixed blood!" The town police officer tackled him. The sheriff handcuffed him and led him away, shaking her head.

The room was filled with answering shouts of shock and anger at this outrage. Giselle made a shushing sound, smiling and shaking her head. "We have been hearing from this fellow for some time, according to our sheriff; we hadn't expected him at the meeting but thought he would pose no harm. It is clear that he has some mental health difficulties. Let us move on."

Some nodded, others expressed some murmuring concern. It was widely understood for generations that the most effective leaders at

Everland Bay were more often women than men. The very thought of illegitimacy based on gender or ethnic heritage was so outdated as to be puzzling to most present. Some of the older ones heard that in very ancient times, mostly men ruled, but the younger ones rolled their eyes at such stories, and generally believed that they were simply folk tales, meant to teach young children to pay attention to all their elders, even the men, who tended toward gentleness.

Giselle concluded, "We will look into this fellow's associations again, to make sure he is not connected to fanatic or terrorist groups, or to the insurrection."

The momentum for the meeting shifted with the disruption. Humans, many of whom were mages, as well as magical creatures of many kinds—mostly gryphons and fae/elf/human folk of various lineages—were shifting in their seats, murmuring, shuffling papers. Chairs scraped noisily a bit here and there as the occasional wing or tail needed accommodation. Gryphons were quite fond of their felted and embroidered hats, which they customarily wore indoors and out, causing difficulty from time to time, as the taller ones obscured the sightlines for those behind them. Mutterings of "Down in front—hats, please!" rumbled here and there.

Annalyn wanted to take advantage of the gathering to move things back to a positive direction, so she quietly made her way nearer the front, and caught Giselle's eye. Giselle addressed the crowd. "I now have the honor to invite a good friend of the Village, Annalyn of the Borderlands, to join me up here. Annalyn has kindly agreed to take the reins on a new initiative, to talk with us about a way forward."

Annalyn smiled warmly at the group as she walked to the front of the room. "We have thought long and hard about how to do things a little better around here, and thanks to you in this room, we now have a viable plan. From the tiniest café to the largest law firm," laughter erupted, as all knew that the largest law firm consisted of two lawyers and their cat, "we think this plan will give our incoming mages good work, give our businesses a reliable ongoing source of labor, and give our older academic mages a way to get involved in the village and share their wisdom."

Annalyn presented the plan briefly, paging through her papers as she noted the overall ideas. A long pause followed.

A hand went up. "This plan sounds like it might be okay for us, but how will we get our kids interested? Looks like they will have the back end of this plan. Not sure we want some privileged baby-mages down here taking good positions and taking up space with us, when our own kids don't have work to do."

"But our kids are leaving, too," said Ms. Jan, owner of Folio. "You know that. We can't get them to stay and work in our places. They go off, as far away as they can get. How does this solve that?" Murmuring commenced around the room.

Annalyn nodded to Giselle, who moved toward the podium. Annalyn spoke to all. "Our Director will be answering some of these questions now, and I will be available after this meeting." She walked back to her seat with mixed feelings. It was good to finally present this new direction, but with the ongoing unrest up at the Institute, making big changes at the Village seemed futile. Annalyn closed her eyes as she sat down, willing herself to an inward calm.

Jemma

Jemma noticed another man in back, who had stood up and seemed to be leaving. He turned and glared at her with a look of pure hatred and slipped out the door. Jemma was jolted and met his eyes with a steady stare and a frown. She glanced over at Fletcher, who was sitting with her group, wondering whether he noticed anything out of sorts. She caught his eye and leaned over. "Who was that guy?" she asked, noticing that he was slipping out the door.

"I'm not sure," said Fletcher, looking around the room.

The man's disappearance was lost in the shuffle as Dr. Azule finished answering questions. "That concludes our meeting today, everyone. I will be in touch if our team needs assistance from any of you," she said. The room erupted in chatter. Chairs scraped, people scattered and streamed out the doors.

Jemma was on high alert and turned toward Keltie, Fletcher, and Jake. She knew there wasn't much time for the three of them to talk.

At a nod from Jemma, they all headed out together while the room was emptying. "Something tells me we're about to put our training to a test. Meantime, though, you all know I've lined up an interview at Folio; I know it might sound a little crazy, but even with everything going on, I need to figure out where I'm going to work for the long term. I know the timing is not great, but I really want to be here for real, not just a visitor at my grandmother's, you know? And obviously, there's no way into the Institute as it used to be. Could be a long time before things are back to normal."

"I get it; I've already started talking with the guys over at Heartwood, you know, the magical gear and wilderness outfitting place? I can't just hang out with Fletcher or at my mom and dad's place, holding my breath while we see what happens up at the Institute," said Jake.

Fletcher chimed in. "They love having you, you know. But you have a point. It feels better to get going on whatever your work will be, even while things are a mess up at the Institute. Speaking of, I've gotta go back to work. See you when I can. Keep your spirits up, everyone."

"Okay, bye Fletcher," said everyone, including Keltie, who continued. "I'm in the same boat as you two, pretty much. No possibility of Institute entrance now. But since I am local, I've been out of my folks' place and working for a while now. I'm up at the botanical gardens and research institute, learning botanical and myco magic, different kinds of living magic," said Keltie.

"What's myco magic?" asked Jemma.

"Mycoremediaton. Fungi to the rescue, basically. Kind of amazing, what it can do," said Keltie.

"Cool," said Jake.

The three walked away together, chatting as they went. "You know, I do think Dr. Azule's plan is a good one for the long run," said Jemma. "But not until the Institute is really back in good hands. So that everyone could be involved. The fatal flaw, I think, is that they need to let the local young people choose where they want to work. Give them as much flexibility and as many options as the Institute kids. That way they're on more equal footing. But that's a ways off. Right now, we need to make sure the Institute doesn't collapse for good! Let's figure out a plan for what's next."

"I can talk with the senior level botanical and earth works mages. They literally have an ear to the ground and will know a lot about what is happening on the land up there," said Keltie.

"And I will ask my grandmother about what they are planning at Institute-leadership level. Or at least, I can find out whatever they are willing to let me know," said Jemma. "I just don't think they are moving quickly enough."

"I'll check in in with Heartwood and will keep my ears open," said Jake.

The three of them walked and talked, hands gesturing in their intensity as they headed toward the crossroad where they all needed to go in different directions. "I'll let you know how it goes with my interview," said Jemma. "I'm really hoping it works out—I definitely need a job, and I've been thinking that maybe Folio can somehow also help with the insurrection. Anyway, I can't just be a no-show. Let's meet back here—when? Maybe after the interview tomorrow morning? Will you two know more by then?"

"Definitely," said Keltie.

"Same," said Jake.

"Okay. Here tomorrow. See you then," said Jemma.

Chapter Seven

The next day, Jemma was nervous. As she was getting ready, she felt herself torn between going ahead with the interview and doing something, anything, to somehow help with the attack at the Institute. But her wiser self knew that this was not, right at the moment, in her hands. She gave herself a little shake as she glanced in the mirror and made sure her usually messy curls were behaving, made sure she was presentable. Even nice-looking, if possible.

She made a face in the mirror, then tried to smile. Squared her shoulders and turned her thoughts to the interview ahead, sorting through her experience and trying to anticipate questions. It didn't really matter that she already clocked in some years of work in a good museum before she got to Everland Bay Village. Folio was her potential first employer in the Village, and who knows, maybe for the rest of her life, and it all felt nerve-wracking. Even though she knew she could stay with her grandmother and not get a job, it just didn't feel right, or normal, to her. She wanted to contribute to the household finances, and she wanted to be a real Villager. She wanted to be part of things, no longer just a visiting relative, the grown-up child or grandchild of someone else. And to do that, she needed to get a job.

As she walked downhill to the Village, she remembered her visit to Folio with her grandmother just a few summers ago. And now, with everything so tumultuous and uncertain at the moment, it felt soothing to think back to those calmer, happier days.

The pathway from her grandmother's went downhill and ended at a small park. The town spread out from there. The lake was farther down the bluff, and a wooden staircase meandered all the way down to the strip of pebbly beach.

Back then, she and her grandmother followed the path into town. The main street was crowded with shops and offices. The town had been there for hundreds of years; stone buildings were jammed against wood-and-wattle shops. A café was just opening, and the owner was putting out umbrellas, clearly hoping that the day would stay sunny enough for outdoor lunching. She looked up, smiled, and waved. Jemma remembered how welcoming it felt that day.

The bookstore, Folio, sold both new and used books.

"This is a special shop," her grandmother said. "They have books from the earliest days of printing, and before, as well as new things. And there are also some very unusual books, which you'll see here and probably nowhere else."

"I heard some kids in town talk about vampire books. Is that what you mean? What are those? Are they for real?" asked Jemma.

"Oh, please don't use that word. That is considered an insult to the books here. No. There are special books with, well, unusual attachments to their owners. We might see some one day, but they are shy," said her grandmother.

They went inside, looked around. The newer titles were at the front: *Magic and Me, Under Her Spell, Visualization Mastery in Seven Days, How to Manifest, No-Fail Fire Magic, Volume 2.* "Do people who live here buy these? I thought this was a normal town," Jemma said.

"Well, it is normal for here. This is a mixed-magic town. So many people have gone to the Institute and left for one reason or another but wanted to stay close. They intermarried with the locals, and all kinds of magic have emerged over the years," said her grandmother, pausing to look at the sale table, picking up a small book, turning it over and setting it down again. "Some just like the town and live here with the benefits of borrowed magic."

As they walked deeper into the store, which seemed larger on the inside than on the outside, the new and crisp gave way to the old and musty. Her grandmother was struggling with her bag. "Stop it," she whispered, looking down into her bag, where a tiny leather-covered book was crawling out. "She gets restless in this place—this is where she came from," said her grandmother, not moving her eyes off the green book cover that was still struggling to crawl up and out of her bag. A corner of tooled leather slipped up out of her bag again, looking for all the world like a tiny hand, and folded itself over the edge, clearly trying to climb.

"What is that?" asked Jemma.

"She—she's a she. She's a mini portal book. Very old. Definitely helpful. Spells and charms and portal all in one, plus practice sheets. Anyway, she, and books like her, are one of the pathways into Everland Bay. The portal book shapes itself as the selected one is growing up. When it is their time, it goes to that person, usually as a gift. For me, I came through a different way, since I am mixed fae and human, but this is a mini portal book that just wanted to be with me. So, it is a little magic meditation book for me. She goes everywhere with me, and if I don't have a home portal nearby, I can use her. And she loves coming back here to visit."

"Why is it—she—so upset? Or at least, it—she—seems upset, or something," said Jemma, not taking her eyes off her grandmother's purse.

"She can feel her family. They're in the old part of the store. See those over there?" A shelf was full of tooled leather books that were swaying gently. "They're waving at her."

"They sound amazing. I would love to have one of those," said Jemma.

Her grandmother smiled. "Well, you can't just buy one."

"Why not?" asked Jemma, looking longingly at an azure-covered, hand-tooled journal, whose closing hasp was a beautifully wrought bronze dragonfly.

"They are self-secured."

"Meaning?"

"Meaning they cannot be opened unless they want to be opened," said her grandmother. "And they can't be bought unless they want to be bought. Also, they sometimes just go and live with a chosen person, which is what happened to me."

"Kind of a funny way to run a business," said Jemma, her nascent family business genes on full alert.

"No kidding," said the owner, Ms. Jan, as she walked by. She gave the books a little pat on their spines. They moved even more, as if they were cats that had just been scratched behind the ears.

Jemma blushed and felt a pang of awkwardness as she looked down at her feet. "Oh, I didn't mean to criticize. But how, how can you run a shop if you can't sell the books, if the books don't open unless they want to?" asked Jemma.

"Only the portal books are like that. I must keep them here because they need to live together and be taken care of. But they come and go as they please. Then, once they find their new person, that person knows where to come for supplies and other books. It is really a good way of bringing in repeat customers, especially those who do not have family portals. Annalyn, it is good to see you and your lovely granddaughter."

Jemma emerged from the pleasant memory and shook her head a little as she found herself in front of Folio now, in real time. A part of her wished that she was still that younger self, just enjoying a summery day in the Village with her grandmother. It seemed like a different world, a different land, a different time, as she looked at the door and braced herself for the interview.

"Jemma!" said Ms. Jan, as she opened the door wide.

"Ms. Jan," said Jemma, finding a smile emerging despite her worries about the terrible mess up at the Institute, and all the uncertainty there.

"Let's go into the reading room, where we'll be surrounded by friendly books. We will get down to business in just a moment. I need you to know that I may need to break away if anyone needs me to help out at the Institute. I know it is not ideal timing for an interview, but it seemed better to keep our appointment," said Ms. Jan, glancing at her elf-wrought timepiece. It sparkled a bit. "I hope you understand."

"Of course! I was thinking along the same lines; I didn't want to leave my grandmother's with all that is going on, but I couldn't think of cancelling," said Jemma.

"Yes, it is a dilemma. My previous assistant left about two weeks ago, and I really need the help, but nothing will matter if the Institute isn't saved. I tell you what; why don't we do our best to continue with our business together, knowing that we are going to need to be flexible with what we do here," said Ms. Jan.

Jemma felt her shoulders relax. "That sounds exactly right. I was really torn."

"As was I. Okay." Ms. Jan cocked her head to the side a bit, smiled, and continued. "Putting my regular interview hat on now: Tell me about why you'd want to work here."

Jemma described her love of books and reading. The interview went along expected pathways, and Jemma felt more confident and comfortable as the time went on. They left the reading room and walked over to the shelves, where Ms. Jan showed Jemma different areas and described the tasks of a bookstore employee. After a little while, Jemma could sense the portal books leaning in, and they rustled a little, pages and leather covers nudging each other a bit. Jemma looked up, wondering.

"Don't pay them any attention. You remember those portal books. They are very nosy, and they are especially interested in hearing why it is people like books and want to be around them."

"Hello, everyone," Jemma said to the shelves of portal books, with a wave. "I do think you are rather wonderful." She grinned as she saw them stir and preen a little. They were sitting on two shelves that were set aside just for them. Each volume was different. Some were covered with plain leather, some were fastened with elaborate tooled silver or brass. Some were covered in fabric shot through with golden, shimmery threads. The smallest flitted around, alighting in different places along the shelves. All of them were ancient. "I honestly would love to be the caretaker of one of those amazing books one day," Jemma said, tearing her glance away from the books and smiling at Ms. Jan.

"I know the feeling. I do love them. They are a bit of work, but they are truly wonderful to be around. More on that later. But you know that being in a bookstore as an employee is very different from being a customer. There is a lot of heavy work. Lifting, sorting, waiting on customers, some of whom are very difficult. Mean, even. But then bouncing right back and juggling a dozen things at once. It can be very repetitive, too, really.

"And the reading you do, you must tuck in, and only at the end of your task list. Also, sometimes you'll need to stay late if we get in shipments, or if the books get restless. The portal books' care will be part of the work, too, eventually. They usually need time to get used to a new person. And there is the matter of these difficult and new times. It used to be that the Institute academics, whether professor, senior fellow, or the younger fellows, would come down here to buy books, have a meal or frozen custard treat somewhere, then scurry back up the path to the Institute. Now that the Institute is, well, going through whatever it is going through, we will be adjusting to things," said Ms. Jan.

"What will be different, do you think?" said Jemma.

"That's the hard question. I don't know yet. We can think of you as an example. Normally, you would have been going to the Institute, correct?" asked Ms. Jan.

"I'm probably a bad example. I would have loved to have gone right in, in the usual way, but my training was spotty, since I was living with my mom and dad, then just my dad, in Verandalands. I had some training over the years here, and had a small practice group there, but never had the ordinary magic training most incoming fellows would have. So, I'd be in remedial training, mostly likely. Then after remedial training I would be, I don't know, maybe tested. But with all that happened, I was summoned to come, then when I got here, the Institute was in flames."

"How did you get here?" said Ms. Jan.

"I came on a dragon. On Jing," Jemma said, shaking her head a bit.

"A dragon! Oh, my. This really is serious. Normally there's no need for dragon transport. It can be risky for an untrained rider," said Ms. Jan. "You probably figured that out when you were up there."

"There were some scary moments, that's for sure. When we saw that the Institute was burning, we changed plans and landed at my grandmother's. So, I have been there, doing whatever I can, and trying to figure out what's next," Jemma said. She fidgeted a bit with the papers and books on the table between them. "This,'" she continued, gesturing at the shelves of books, "working here, could be what I do for the long term."

"There is so much to think about. Everything is different now. We are all finding our way," said Ms. Jan, looking around the room.

Jemma noticed Ms. Jan's softened expression as she glanced around the crowded, overstuffed shelves. "You started this shop, didn't you?" she asked.

Ms. Jan came out of her momentary reverie. "My grandparents started it. My mother worked here all her life, and I grew up in the shop. I have always loved it, I think. Though I did have a time during my teens of deciding for a while that I hated it and didn't want anything to do with it," Ms. Jan said with a rueful smile.

"I wanted to be like the polished young mages, going up to the Institute as fellows and then breezing down here occasionally, with seemingly limitless funds for whatever they wanted to scoop up. But in truth, that wasn't me. I learned to care for these books and this place from the time I was a tiny thing. Some of the larger portal books used to keep an eye on me when my mother was too busy to watch me. Folio, and the books who live here, really have a life of their own. We just help them live it. And now we must figure out a way to do that, and protect them all, despite these strange times."

"I had no idea," said Jemma. "Did you know my mother?" She stopped short of asking what her mother was like. She almost wished she hadn't asked. What if her mother wasn't who she always thought she was? What if she was a snooty person in her younger years? And what about her grandmother? Jemma had never really thought about her parents and grandmother as people in their own lives, or as younger people.

"Ah. Yes. Of course I did. I knew your whole family. Your grandmother and my mother were dear friends, and your mother and I, well. She was a special friend. She wasn't like the wealthy mages I mentioned a moment ago. She was part fae, as you must know, and maybe elf? So, she wasn't as oblivious as the fully human ones were. She had her blind spots, but she was in love with this shop. And the books, well, they loved her very much," said Ms. Jan.

"I'm so relieved to hear that. I had hoped that would be so, but who knows what one's parents are like before you are born?" said Jemma. "I do remember how Folio was always spoken of with reverence, and she said you were a friend."

"Yes, and she and your grandmother and I were working in our quiet way to change things here, not just at Folio but throughout Everland Bay. We didn't think we'd have any violence along the way, though," said Ms. Jan. "That part is unexpected and frightening. I don't know what it will require of me or the shop. There is going to be a lot of uncertainty as I figure out the way forward with your grandmother and everyone else. But now, we must get back to the business at hand, your interview. And…" Ms. Jan trailed off and Jemma saw her turn her head quickly.

A book flew through the air with great force, plummeting into the room from a high shelf. Papers scattered and the portal books woke up and started chattering and rustling in alarm, covers waving, pages riffling. The smaller ones peeped, looked for cover under the now-outstretched leather covers of the larger ones. The great flying book, with its menacing, steely, charcoal-gray silk cover and its red-satin ribbon trailing behind, landed with a noisy flourish on the chair beside

Jemma. It fanned and snapped its pages and covers a bit as it settled onto its perch.

"Whoa!" Jemma said, flinching and edging away while also trying to get a good look at this creature. "What *is* this?"

"Felix! Knock it off," Ms. Jan said. She stood up quickly, raising her hand in a "stop" motion. The book, clearly chastened by the harsh tone, drooped a little, and hopped over to Ms. Jan, jumping on her shoulder and trying to hide, huddling under its covers as if they were proper wings.

"Is it a portal book?"

"Well, it is a cousin of the portal books. He's another sentient book, one we call a symbiotic volume. A class by itself," said Ms. Jan.

Jemma could hardly breathe. A vampire book! Her eyes were wide open as she watched the book's pages riffling slightly at Ms. Jan's neck. It looked as if it might actually bite her. "Ms. Jan? Are you sure you're okay?"

"Yes, he's all puffery. No real bite. Not with me, anyway. He is very inquisitive and wanted to get a good look at our prospective new person, though right now he's feeling a bit embarrassed by having lost his composure and then getting a scolding. He's trying to hide, silly old thing. There is a shelf of symbiotic books below the portal books. The locals call them vampire books, but that is really rather unjust. They tend to be a little brusque, but they do no harm to humans or human-mixes who are good and kind. They will, however, sometimes nibble at you a bit, and the stories in their pages stay for a *very* long time as a result.

"Rather like a song that won't stop playing in your mind. No need to worry. I will fill you in more on those books later. They are rather special, if unruly sometimes. They can be quite protective. Like small terriers. He was probably just overly curious about you and making sure to defend me. Well, now." Ms. Jan put her hand up and Felix climbed on, just as a parrot would. She walked him over to a shelf and set him there. "Stay there, please, Felix," she said, turning back toward Jemma. "Okay. Once again, back to our interview. I have one more question for you. Why aren't you applying for a place at the museum? That's what you were doing in Verandalands, before you came to us, correct? Working in a museum?"

"Ah. Yes. I was. And I loved it, in so many ways. And I did think about it, about applying to the one here. But as it turns out, they are closed right now. They have always had a very high-traffic portal to the Institute, according to my friend Jake. He also said that the security risk is too high to open in any capacity right now, and will be for, well, no one knows, I guess. And no way are they going to do anything with new staff for now. So, part of it is that it really isn't an option. But I was thinking about that and in a way, it is a good thing, because I wanted to try something else. I really, really love books and reading. Some of the most magical days when I was little happened right here, when I walked down here with my grandmother."

"I remember at least one of those visits; your grandmother had a knack for choosing the best of our new books," said Ms. Jan.

"She still has that knack! But yes, I was just remembering one of my visits as I was walking here this morning. And to be able to be part of a bookstore that is magical in the ordinary 'there-is-no-frigate-like-a-book' way, but is also really, truly, amazingly magical, complete with the kinds of books that probably don't exist in many places, just sounds kind of great." Jemma blushed a bit, as she found herself getting worked up.

She loved this place, and the idea of being in a less stressful environment than the museum also sounded inviting, though she hadn't mentioned that part of things. She didn't want it to seem like she thought of working at Folio as an easy job.

But it did seem less stressful to her than her old job, and still conjured up happy feelings inside, just by being so close to so many books. She also longed to be a part of the community. Being right on the small main street, in a beloved shop, seemed more likely to give her that chance. But she didn't know quite how to say it. A deeper thought for her also bubbled up. She wanted to be closer, somehow, to her mother, or at least her mother's memory, and she liked the idea that Ms. Jan had been a friend of her mother's.

Ms. Jan smiled and nodded. "That all makes sense. I love books the way you do, I believe. And Emily Dickinson, whom you quoted just now, is one of my favorite human poets. We have a whole section of poetry over there, and we have many editions of her work. Not everyone can quote her."

"Just about every reader can," Jemma said, grinning. "You know, back to the portal books; I wanted to ask about another thing."

"Yes?"

"I know that if I did get this job, I would be here to work very hard for you. For Folio," said Jemma. "I know that this might be a difficult time for me to get started, though, with everything that is going on. But one day, it would be very interesting to know more about all these very beautiful and intelligent books." She waved at the portal books, who were practically falling off the shelf to get closer. One clearly couldn't contain itself any longer, and flew over to Jemma, landing on her forearm like a very stocky little bird. Jemma's eyes went wide as she lifted her arm a bit and laughed in delight. "And who might this be?"

"This is one of our mini portals; she is related to the one your grandmother has. Their names are hard to pronounce for us, so they like us to call them by nature-themed names. See the dragonfly clasp? We call her Lula, short for Libellula—the Latin name for one of the dragonfly families, derived from *libellus*, 'little book', or for *libella*, a diminutive of *libra*, 'balance, instrument,' for the way their wings open and close, like a book or a balancing scale. Clever, yes?"

At that, the tiny book on Jemma's arm wriggled a little, as if in assent. Jemma gingerly reached out to it with her other hand. "Very clever. Hello, Lula. May I touch her?"

"Yes, I think she'd like that. Like stroking a bird. And there's a lot of magic associated with the dragonfly; you'll probably find out about that over time with our Lula."

Jemma gently stroked the tiny book, and Lula curled into her hand. "She is so beautiful," Jemma said, as she admired her aquamarine and moss-colored leathery cover, hand-tooled with fern fronds and flowers.

"This one is quite ancient and has not been actively used as a portal for a long time. But she is clearly ready to come out of retirement." said Ms. Jan, shaking her head and moving her shoulders into a what-can-you-do shrug. "I have a feeling they'd all like you here. But," she said, and Jemma saw the professional expression come back on to Ms. Jan's face. "I have to make my decision on my own. I will be in touch very soon."

"Of course. Thank you so much for taking time with me today." Jemma placed Lula carefully on the table between them, got up to leave, and shook Ms. Jan's hand. "You know, there is one more thing I should mention," said Jemma, a little hesitantly. She took a deep breath, readying herself.

"What is that?"

"Well, I really want to be part of things here. Not just a visitor. Not just my grandmother's granddaughter—a guest from far away. I want to belong to Everland Bay Village. No matter what happens up at the Institute. And Folio, well, it is right in the middle of things, isn't it? It is part of the heart of the Village. I want to be someone who is in the midst of all that," said Jemma.

Ms. Jan looked at Jemma intently. Jemma worried that she was being overenthusiastic. Too emotional, too needy. She was kicking herself inwardly, even though those were her true feelings. But Ms. Jan was just looking at her and Jemma felt awkward in the gathering silence.

"Oh, my dear," said Ms. Jan, with a sigh. "What a lovely thought. How can I *not* give you this job?"

"Really?"

"When can you start?"

Jemma clapped her hands, unable to reign in her excitement. "Thank you so much! I am so excited! I can start right away," she said, the words rushing out of her.

The portal books rustled with evident delight and Lula flew up to land on Jemma's shoulder, nestling in a bit. Jemma looked at her and smiled.

Ms. Jan laughed as she stood up. "It is clear we are all agreed on this. Okay then. Let's start you on Monday. And why don't we let Lula stay with you over the weekend? She can visit with her cousin at your grandmother's and your grandmother will know how to teach you to care for her. She will have fun going on a sleep-away adventure."

Jemma said her goodbyes and started her walk back to her grandmother's, feeling as if she were floating just a little ways above the pathway. She reached up to stroke the tiny portal book, who was still nestled in at her neck, and felt a sense of delight and happiness that she hadn't felt in a very long time. "Well, Lula, I guess we are going to be on this journey together. Let's go to my grandmother's and let you visit your cousin." She felt the small book teeter a bit and Jemma tucked her into a pocket, then moved along with her characteristically brisk stride. "Hang on!"

Jemma could hardly wait to talk with her grandmother. She felt a surge of hope and happiness building inside as she walked to Borderlands, which, she now realized, had become home. She barely registered the beautiful trees, flowers in bloom, or the charming winding path that provided the last leg of the journey. And though today she knew she was rushing it, she loved the walk to and from the Village. It gave her a chance to collect her thoughts, thoughts that were, right now, simply soaring.

Chapter Eight

"Grandma! I got the job!" Jemma called out, as she ran the last few yards and dashed through the back door into the kitchen to look for her grandmother.

"Oh, what wonderful news!" her grandmother said. "Come here and give me a kiss. I'd hug you right now but, as you can see, my hands are too full."

Jemma dashed over and kissed her grandmother and gave her a little hug. "A bigger hug later—but what are you doing?"

"Well, here, you can help me with this as we talk. I'm restoring some of the spellwork and also doing some updating," Grandma Annalyn said, as she handed Jemma a small paintbrush, and demonstrated as she spoke. "Here, see? I will show you the restoration work and then will be able to go on to the updates. Take the brush, like so, and look for the spells in the trim around all the doors and windows."

Jemma looked and looked again. And saw nothing. Her shoulders sagged. "I, uh, really don't see anything at all," she said. She could feel her face redden. Probably a more adept young mage would be able to see it all immediately, she thought.

"Do not be alarmed. Takes a little bit of practice. Also, your magelight might help. Go ahead and illuminate but turn the beam to catch things at an angle. Raking light, it's called. It will help the spells pop out. They will look like shiny areas of pattern on top of matte areas," said her grandmother, matter-of-factly, while continuing her own areas, dipping the brush into a clear varnish, and applying it. Carefully.

Jemma concentrated, as magelights were still sometimes a little tricky for her. "There!"

"Do you see the spells?"

"Well, not yet. I was just happy to get the light on!" Jemma concentrated, turning the light beam this way and that, and looking over at her grandmother.

"Relax, now. I'm trying to think back to when I was learning this from my mother. Soften your gaze, and think about something ordinary, like walking along the pathway home."

Jemma thought about her walk home, and, glancing at the trim around the window in front of her, could suddenly see the spells. "Oh! There they are! Wow. They are so intricate. Now what do I do?" asked Jemma.

"Oh, good. Now you have it. Just take the brush, dip it in the spell varnish, here. Don't overload the brush, it's all sort of drippy. I keep thinking I need to get the better brand from our hardware store, but I never get around to it. Next time. Anyway, now just trace over the spells you see. Some of them might glimmer a bit, some of them might be hard to read. Don't worry about any of that, as some are in earlier languages of magic. I will go over things afterward, and then will spot check, just to make sure things are going along well. In the meantime, I'll be able to get so much more done on the more complex upgrades. We will get through all of this in no time. Now, tell me all about your good news."

Jemma focused on the spell tracing as she talked. Her words tumbled out in a happy torrent. "Oh, Grandma, I really like Ms. Jan. She went over all of what the job would be, and I know I can do it. She also asked about why I wasn't looking for a job at the museum. So we talked through all that. But you won't believe this. A vampire book—well, actually, now that I work there, I shouldn't say that—a symbiotic book flew off the shelves and headed straight toward me! It landed next to me, looking very menacing. Then Ms. Jan put it on her shoulder, as if it were a, a parrot or something. It looked as if it was going to bite her!"

"Gracious. Maybe they are getting feistier these days. Did it bite?" her grandmother glanced over, eyebrows arched in with concern.

"No, though I was really worried at first. Ms. Jan said this one's name was Felix, and that he was just being protective. It was a bit scary, but Ms. Jan is fine, and all is well."

"I didn't know any of her vamp—er,—symbiotic books were so aggressive," said her grandmother, with a furrowed brow.

"Well, they are interesting, that's for sure. I will find out more about those eventually. I'm not worried, really. But…" Jemma looked down as little Lula emerged from her pocket, and crawled up her sleeve, perching again on Jemma's shoulder. She made a peeping noise, and the small portal book that mostly lived in her grandmother's pocket emerged and crawled up to her grandmother's shoulder.

"I wonder that they didn't fly into each other's pages the moment you came through the door! How nice this is! There is so much you must tell me. Can this one stay here? How is it that she can be gone from the shop? Here. Let's settle them over here on the open shelf by the reading chairs. They can get caught up. I am sure they have a lot to talk about," said her grandmother.

"It all went by in a blur, and we were talking about portal books, and this one flew over and seemed to want to be with me," said Jemma. She felt a sense of wonder and delight as she looked over at Lula.

"They will do that sometimes, but it is unusual for them to leave the store, unless they are in current work as portals, or actively seeking their new person."

"Well, since I'll be back on Monday, and Ms. Jan knew you had a related portal book, it just seemed like it would be fun for us all. Nice for Lula and her cousin to be able to visit, and fun for me to be able to learn how to care for her, since I'll be learning that for the bookstore," said Jemma, in a rush.

"Well, I have no further to look than your radiant face to know how happy you are. This is great news. I hadn't known how much you wanted to work in town, but I hoped that you might want to eventually get some sort of employment around here. I am so proud of you for taking the initiative. It is a very good idea," said her grandmother. "Though I had rather thought you might have waited until things got back to something like normal."

Jemma saw the lines of concern cross her grandmother's brow. "You know how much I love it here. But I just can't sit still. It is wonderful to help out and learn from you, but I was realizing that I needed to be going on to my own next steps, and I wanted to really be a part of the Village, part of things happening there. I love books and love the magic of Folio.

"I was just worried that she would either think I was overqualified because of my museum work or underqualified because I hadn't worked in a bookstore before. I am so relieved that she thought I would be a good fit," said Jemma, continuing with her spell tracing. She concentrated on the work, finding herself oddly both energized and calmed by it.

As she bent over one section, she felt stronger inside, and as she turned to work on some more complex patterns, filled with vines and flowers and intertwined fern fronds, she felt braver and somehow more alert. "What is this that I'm feeling?" asked Jemma, turning toward her grandmother.

"Ah, the spells. Are you feeling strong?"

"Yes."

"Brave? Extra alert?"

"Yes! You don't mean…"

"You've guessed it. As you trace over the spells, all of which are positive and enhance the safety and security of our home here, you will gain the creature components of those things. Strength, bravery, awareness. Also, probably because of your fae, elf, and dragon mix, a great deal of the deeper nature strengths. Deep earth awareness, possibly heightened eyesight and other senses. You'll find out over time."

"Well, I didn't expect this. This is so great," said Jemma, focusing ever more intently on the spellwork.

"I forgot to mention, though, that we must take regular breaks. This is all very powerful, and it can be rather overwhelming, especially if, like you, it is your first work, or if, like me, it has been a while. If I were a better housekeeper, I would be refreshing the spells every six months to a year," said her grandmother.

"Ah. I think I see what you mean," said Jemma, as she felt the room spin a bit. She reached her free hand out to steady herself on a non-spell-covered area of the wall.

"Okay, just hold on a moment. Hand me the brush," said her grandmother, rushing over as Jemma was reeling. "Here, let's get you outside. Fresh air will help."

Outside, Jemma breathed fully and deeply, and shook her head to clear it. She shivered and flicked energy off her hands. Small eddies of dust in the courtyard resulted. She laughed, then went to sit on the low stone wall surrounding the inner garden and flagstoned area just outside the kitchen. "Wow, I didn't expect that. And, like, every one of my senses seems more, well, more there somehow."

"That's all very normal. And more evidence of your development as a young mage," said Grandma Annalyn. "Non-magical people would just find the scent unpleasant. Mages experience all of it, and are strengthened. Those gains will ebb and flow, but..."

"Wait, I hear the scrying stone, I think," said Jemma. "Just that tiny ping, but I can hear it all the way out here." Jemma was back up and heading inside toward the scrying stone. "Let's go see."

Jemma and Grandma Annalyn gazed together at the stone. "Look! Up at the Institute, I think, yes, I think that's Dr. Azule's security team. And they're taking over. See?" Jemma felt a jolt of hope and a glimmer of confidence. It felt so good to be able to see so clearly in the scrying stone. And the best part was seeing this positive scene.

"I hope you're right," said Grandma Annalyn, looking closely. "Yes—these are our forces. Those," she said, pointing to a group of people, "are the rogue forces. And they are ...yes, falling back. Dispersing."

"Good news for our side!" said Jemma, feeling jubilant. Maybe the worst part of this horrible time is over, she thought. She leaned over and hugged her grandmother, feeling reassured and relieved.

Dr. Maximus Constantin

"Hey, Maximus, how goes it?" said the sinewy, young would-be mage, sniggering and glancing toward the others, looking around the room.

"Don't call me Maximus," he snapped, annoyed already at the way the morning began, what with the scruffy young, tough, hacker mages slouched around the once-pristine boardroom of Everland Bay Institute, which he opened up for this meeting. Despite all his hard work cloaking the building with invisibility security that would ensure only his group could enter, he received little respect from the group.

As the young mages greeted his bark with shoulder-shrugs, he knew he was losing, no, scratch that, he knew he had already lost his audience. Before the meeting started. Where were his other team members? His, what were they, really? He thought of them as his partners, but they thought of themselves, he now reflected briefly, as his superiors, since they were the funders of this takeover. He glanced for the umpteenth time at the door, willing it to fill with his partners, who were led by none other than his annoying younger brother, Augustus—Gus—now an overbearing adult. He glimpsed movement in the doorway. Finally.

His brother strode through the door. "Maximus, everyone."

A contagion of tittering crackled around the room. Max glared at his brother and at the young mages. "Gus, good to see you," he said, knowing his brother, loathed the nickname Gus. Turnabout is fair play, he thought.

"Apologies for my tardiness," his brother continued. "And please," he said, looking around the room. "Do call me Augustus. I was detained by the nearly unpassable roads. The others turned back and are rather unhappy. What a disaster you have managed to create here. I am not pleased."

The large man sat down, fussing with his perfectly tailored suit, brushing aside an invisible-to-others speck of dust from the armrest of his chair. He looked up and gazed at the young toughs, who looked a bit more alert as they squirmed their way into upright postures. He looked straight at his brother. "Perhaps you can enlighten me?"

Maximus, who strongly preferred the name Max, which he acquired in his early fellowship mage years and loved the tough-guy quality it had, was not about to give up the upper hand to his brother. Nor was he going to let his anxiety show, even though it was now ratcheting up at an alarming rate. He could practically feel his blood pressure jumping up, up, up, just the way his doctor said was unhealthy. This was not the way things were supposed to go.

He knew that this group, like most, didn't know the two were brothers, so he kept the fact hidden. He and his brother both felt that keeping this secret gave them advantages from time to time. "As you know, I was wrapping up what should have been an easy and successful change of leadership. Your team members here," he waved dismissively at the elaborately tattooed team of ruffians, "were supposed to act as ambassadors of the new young magehood, blending high-tech with youthful savvy." He couldn't help but notice a continued lack of attention from the group.

He pressed on. "The plan was that we were going to continue to gently persuade my Everland Bay Institute colleagues that this was the best and inevitable future of this crumbling institution. Remember? Sounds of rustling fabric, papers shuffling, arose as the young mages squirmed. Max noticed that a paper airplane escaped one young hand and headed out the door.

"Okay, children, calm down," continued Max, snatching yet another paper airplane out of the air while not breaking eye contact with the young toughs. "You need this background information." Max crushed the paper airplane slowly and placed it on the table. Eyebrows raised in surprised unison at this feat, and the young mages sat up straight and became still. Max suppressed an inward smile.

"We were even going to keep on a few of the old guard to teach a few courses for the sake of tradition, nostalgia, and continuity, while we increased the teaching staff of the high-tech, hacker-mage groups. The takeover was going to happen very quietly over the next several years. Years, remember?"

"Oh, come on. We didn't plan on decades of delay. Slow and steady, yes. Glacial, no," said Gus.

"Listen, will you?" snapped Max, standing up and pacing the room. "I almost completely persuaded the Everland Bay old guard that this would simply be a slight change of curriculum to keep up with the times, maybe bring in a nice new income stream, some additional funding from Halcyon Corporation." He drew a breath, trying to bring his blood pressure down. "And you know the rest. Dr. Azule was being sworn in as next director in an entirely routine and unremarkable ceremony, and the clown-car crew here," he glanced at the scruffy mages, "decided to go off-script and ad-lib a minor, no, make that major, insurrection. Complete with a little explosion or two, fire, destruction, and a death," said Max.

"Just the one," muttered Gus, with a small shrug.

"Yes. Just the one, as you put it. But not approved. Not on the agenda. This might be a good time to remind us all that deaths are not a good way to endear us to the conventional world. Consult your PR manual whenever you have time for a refresher."

"Yes, thank you, I forgot what an expert you were," said his brother, sneering a bit.

Max glowered, vowing not to let Gus get under his skin. "Right. Now. I know you know all this information. And you know that none of this was agreed upon. The wretched mess that resulted couldn't have been more different from the plans we all signed off on. And you decided, conveniently enough, to pop out after the first few moments, and stay away throughout the rest of the episode. You simply opted out, as you put it that morning, leaving me with the resultant mess. A pattern for you, yes? You are the one, I believe, who should be doing some explaining. And perhaps your friends here might help you with that," said Max, settling back into his chair.

Silence fell. He felt more confident as he listened to himself. *I sound pretty good, I think,* he said to himself. He could get things back on track. He knew it. Then, maybe, retire. This was all too much work. *And really, what exactly am I holding back for? I'm Dr. Max, for all the gods' sakes. This is just my annoying brother I'm dealing with, and his now-absent cronies, as well as these surly young mages. I have not lost my edge, dammit. Though I have, in fact, lost this battle.* He had worked himself up into an exuberant anger. He could feel his pulse pounding at his temples.

At that very moment, one of the young mages made a critical error, one that would probably, Max reflected, be regretted deeply by the mage. The young tough's lip curled up in a particularly disrespectful manner as he sneered at Dr. Max, and said, "Oh, come on, *Maximus*, it was just a little, you know, tour of the premises. Tore a few things up, just a bit. No harm d—-"

The young mage was stilled mid-utterance. Before he could finish the word, "done," he was. Done. First, completely paralyzed. Then, as a wave of horror and disbelief registered on the faces of all of those around the table, with the notable exception of Dr. Max and his well-dressed money-mage sibling, the young mage began to dissolve. The last thing everyone saw was the look of terror and pain that crossed the young face.

The others gasped, losing their composure entirely. They glanced, eyes wide and mouths agape, at the two older men, at each other, and back. Max saw the glances, smiled inwardly, and knew they must be utterly confused as well as horrified. None of their slouchy disdain was evident now. They were all on high alert. He felt a surge of satisfaction. Maybe retirement could wait. *This is rather more fun than I remembered,* he thought.

"Max. Knock it off," snapped his brother.

"Just giving him a slap on the wrist," said Max, wanting to prolong the moment. He knew that the young mages were inexperienced with this kind of deep magic and probably had no idea, right then, that he, too, was in considerable pain. Not as much as the dissolved mage, of course, but significant. Magic had a price. This was an expensive, flashy use of it. But worth it, he thought, his pain unnoticeable to those who didn't know him well. He knew that his brother likely noticed the beads of sweat glistening across his forehead, but he didn't really care; they were well aware of each other's abilities and had been since they were boys.

With a brisk wave-shaped flourish of Max's hand, the irreverent young mage began to form again. The greenish-grayish cloud of miasma, greasy smoke, and ash began to come together at first slowly, slowly, then in a rush, with a small *whoosh*, the body came back together. Max preferred to do this from the toes up. More dramatic. At the end of the restoration, the youthful mage's hair emerged rather mussed up, a bit sooty, and gray in patches. One complicated knot-spell tattoo had been rearranged and was sparking a little. After their initial gasps, all were completely silent as they took in the spectacle.

Max glanced around the room, turned to his brother, raised an eyebrow. "There now. Let's do a reset, shall we? I believe you were about to bring me up to date on this botched insurrection and your disappearance. And you were rather tardy today, dragging in here late, and without your other colleagues. But perhaps you are not as important to them as you seem to believe. Now. Do go ahead."

His brother scowled, walked over to the expansive windows that overlooked the entire property, and began. "I didn't want to get into classified details here, but in addition to being delayed by the roads, I was detained by meetings with the Halcyon Board of Directors. There is really no need to go into paroxysms of handwringing over the dustup, Max. We will move on from the scuffle, I think. It is true that things got a bit out of hand.

"I left a little early because there was really no need to be there any longer," continued Gus. "Of course, I knew how competent you are, so I assumed that you would make sure no unrecoverable damage would occur. I don't mind ruffling a few Everland Bay Old Guard feathers, but I know you do. So. Now. No need to dwell on a few bad choices by some of our more enthusiastic young folks," he said, lifting an eyebrow with the slightest of smiles at the stunned young mages.

"What we need to do now is take things from here. I really hoped you would have managed to clear things up a bit, Maximus, with this crew or any others you could hire. But as it happens, Halcyon leadership is not troubled by the state of the grounds. You should be grateful they are not as particular as I am," he said.

"Particular?" said Max. "In what way is nearly destroying this place particular? In what way is this sloppy approach particular?" Max was nearly shouting while he gripped the armrests of his chair as if to hold himself in place.

"Well, perhaps it is subjective," said Gus. "I still see myself as quite discerning. To continue, Halycon sees the messy current situation as a perfect opportunity for their renovation plans, in fact. They can simply raze a number of the remaining buildings and build anew in the style they prefer. They have a strong attachment to the Castle and some of the stone buildings, for reasons I cannot comprehend. All that ancient, moldering stonework."

"Which is part of the huge draw for Halcyon, you know-nothing," said Max. "Gives them a sense of propriety and history to be part of some great institution. Would you prefer that it was all rubble?"

Gus took time to glance away for a moment, fuss with the papers on the conference table in front of him. "Yes, yes. Indeed, they are very sentimental about it all, as are you, I see. What it means in practical terms is that they will allow those buildings to stand, as I understand it. I have been working closely with them to approve plans. I didn't realize quite how disrupted the grounds were until coming back in person today, but it is of little concern for them and their equipment."

"What are you talking about?" asked Max. "They have an enormous amount of work ahead, not to mention the legality issue. They don't own this land, remember? And they can't just plant a little Halcyon pennant and say that they are kings of the hill. This is a nightmare, all around."

"Right. All taken care of, dear Max. We, well, they, are planning to treat the grounds with a solution that will make things a little easier to raze. It will probably get even messier than it already is. We will need to stay away for a while as the work is done. All the legal documents will be drawn up then. More on that in a moment.

"And regarding the next steps in practical terms," continued Gus, "There are only a few of us here anyway, the group here, the security guards who are stationed in the teaching hall, you, and me. The rest of the crowds that day, as you know, were holoforms. We are a skeleton crew, but if we don't want to become skeletons in truth, we need to get moving. We will need to depart after this meeting; I have arranged for us all to base out of Halcyon's regional headquarters for a while. We will each return to our own places to live. No need to occupy this place or plan to live here anytime soon."

"Easy for you to say," snapped Max. "I live here, remember? Or I did, before this disgraceful and unnecessary onslaught. I am going to make a small change to your grand plan. I will be staying here. I will move from the central area, where construction is going on, to one of the cottages up in the hills here. That will allow me to, you know, supervise your team and keep an eye on things in general."

"You surprise me, Max. That is actually a good idea. Consider it done. Moving on, all will come together in the rebuilding, and a select few will have the opportunity to have places to live here. We can rethink this at that point, but if you can stand the noise and mess in the meantime, I have no problem with your staying in one of those cottages."

"Great, thanks for your abundant kindness," Max said, feeling extremely annoyed that his brother had again managed to weasel the discussion around into having the upper hand.

"What wouldn't I do for you?"

"Uh, hey," said one of the younger mages, waving a hand.

Max and his brother were both startled out of their bickering.

"So, like, how long will all this take and what's next for, like, us?"

"Right," said Max's brother. "Halcyon says they need about three months. We believe this will all work very well, of course; the Old Guard of Everland Bay will think we have decamped and, predictably, they will try to take it back under the assumption that it is theirs and that all they need to do is tidy things up and just keep going the way they were.

"By the way," he continued, "We've decided that the best way forward is to just claim the land post-skirmish. Halcyon has worked with the authorities to condemn it as hazardous and give it over to Halcyon along with a grant for cleanup and rebuilding of historic sites. They are getting the property condemnation fast-tracked, now that they have images of the destruction.

"They never come out to actually inspect and the wording was really rather creative. Also, you will be securing funds from Groslier Bank and Trust. They are based in the Verandalands, so don't have a personal connection to this area, which also works in our favor. They have agreed in principle to give us substantial loans for rebuilding and transformation, as we called it, I believe."

"Clever, I must admit," said Max, mostly feeling a need to stop the monologue. "I still object, but it is rather savvy of you." Max did feel a grudging admiration. He and his brother were more alike than he ever wanted to admit, and he knew he was going to have to get in line eventually. Might as well be now. *Won't show all my cards yet,* he thought, *but I can still wrangle some power out of this deal.*

"Thanks, Maximus—Max. You are every bit as savvy as I, as we both know, and I know you're eventually going to have some fun with all of this. You'll love this bit," Gus said, sounding to Max much more like he used to, when they were younger. "We told them we would be transforming a known, decrepit pagan center into a redemptive center for the upbringing of true believers. Predictably, they were thrilled.

Nothing could be farther from the truth, of course, but Halcyon is willing to do what it must to secure additional funds."

Gus walked over to the windows and turned to face everyone. "All you have to do is work with their outside loan person. I'll give you the contact information. He is expecting to be working with you. Your future salary is part of what you'll be securing, so I wish you special good luck. In the meantime, though, as I was saying, your colleagues will be no doubt scurrying up here to clean things up and, you know, save the day. The ground and building solvents will make it impossible for them to actually do that, though they may have to find out the hard way by falling down a hole or into a new swamp first," he said, smiling.

"Thanks ever so much. I still resent the mess, but I will, as usual, get all the hard work done," said Max, though now he was allowing a small smile to show up on his face.

"Excellent," said Gus. "And don't forget that the dangerous instability of the grounds, not to mention the odor, should keep them away while our team does its work. Halcyon has a crew that is basically in place, ready to go. Our young mages here will be helping as well, lending tech magic assistance to the demolition crew. Meanwhile, your colleagues will think the place is irreparably damaged and will probably set up various meetings and committees to protest things, which will give us all the time we need to get all the work done.

"Now. As to the plan you outlined a moment ago," Gus continued, "consider it reworked. Halcyon isn't interested in continuing to turtle along, making infinitesimal changes at a glacial pace as you dash about ineffectually, hoping to avoid offending your dear Everland Bay colleagues. Things weren't moving quickly enough for Halcyon, Max. They are really rather pleased with these young, energetic mages, if I am not mistaken."

Max gritted his teeth as the young mages settled back into self-satisfied slouches and his brother raised his eyebrows with a "who, me?" look of innocence.

"One more thing. This little team is all yours, now," he said, rising and heading toward the door, "and they are our future," Gus finished as he left. "I'll be in touch soon with more."

Max watched him go and looked around the room. All the young mages were staring back at him, grim-faced. And while they were not as straight-spined as they were throughout the conversation with his brother, they retained their wariness, given the recent demonstration of Max's still-keen ability. "All right. First, you are on your own for housing. Must be off campus. No place for you here. Second, we are in this together. I was your age once; I know how it is to be young and strong and wanting to make things happen. So. Let's do just that. You," he said, pointing at the four across from him. "Get ready to help direct the Halcyon construction crew. Don't let them take down any but the smallest buildings. Leave all the stone ones intact. I will be in touch as needed.

"And you." He paused, thinking, as he looked at the last of the youthful mages. The one he had dissolved temporarily and reassembled. The tattoo was no longer sparking but was still upside down. It was a once-imposing and intricate knot that was an always-on spell tattoo. It was too torn up for Max to decipher it, but it was likely a spell for protection and warrior-level strength. Now it just looked frayed, shabby. Untied. The formerly bold, elegant knotwork was moving a little; small, inked tendrils writhed, some lifting off the skin and waving like sea creatures, seemingly looking to find a way back to the original form, but not knowing how to recreate the pattern and thereby, the spell.

The patches of gray in the young mage's hair were continuing to expand and move around his scalp. It was difficult to watch, even for Max. "You can follow the gentleman. If you hurry, you can catch up to him," Max said.

There. No need to keep that one anywhere close. Not only would he have rather good reason to resent me, thought Max, he is probably rather jumbled and unlikely to be terribly reliable.

"This part of our meeting is at an end, gentlemen," he said, thinking that he'd never met a less gentlemanly group. "Now. We have work to do." Max moved with the quickness of a much younger mage, snapping on gloves and opening a small case at his side. He tossed intricately carved blow darts to each of the mages, who flinched, then laughed, catching the devastating weapons. These, Max knew that they understood, were illegal magecraft weapons, capable of delivering doses of Halycon-mixed agents to the targets. Max knew it was a bit extreme, but he was no longer a part of the Old Guard at Everland Bay. He didn't need to care anymore, really. When they hit their targets, the result was a slight convulsion, then rapid neurodeterioration that left the targets mentally compromised and addicted. A perfect chemical weapon, Max always thought.

Max snapped out orders as he strode out of the room, heading toward the grounds, talking with the head of the gryphon mercenary troops through his device. "We're on the ground. You know what to do."

The grounds were erupting with small explosions; debris and dirt exploded up out of the earth, scouring the once-beautiful lawns into a hellscape. For the first time in a while, Max threw his shoulders back and allowed himself a grin.

Chapter Nine
Annalyn

Annalyn walked down into the Village, enjoying the first hints of fall as she pulled her flutewood silk shawl a little closer. She heard a faint booming sound in the distance and glanced around. Far away, she could see what looked a little like smoke. Maybe my imagination, she thought, shaking it off with a furrowed brow and going on her way.

The long grasses in the meadow rustled in their newfound dryness; green blades now gold and mottled with the deeper russets and hazelnut tones, ready to fold and kneel into the ground. Small, flying creatures, including charming, walnut-sized pegasi, the miniscule flying horses that are the particular inhabitants of flutewood groves, as well as dragonflies and butterflies, slipped out of the grasses and swirled into the air around her as she walked. She held a hand aloft and watched as a tiny gold-green horse landed for a moment, then flicked tail and wings and flitted off again, spiraling away with the breeze. The loud, festive fuchsias and lemon-bar-yellows of spring and summer had melted down into the soil, making way for the darker, somber ambers, russets, and plums of sturdy autumn plants. Above, leaves were deepening into a rich gold, and the spectacular iridescent bronze of the flutewood tree was beginning to show.

Such a lovely tree it is, she thought, stooping down to pick up one of the leaves that dropped a little early. For Annalyn, these first leaves fall were always a cause of celebration. She could never resist collecting them. Turning over the metallic bronze beauty in her hand, taking care not to hold it along its sharp edges, she admired it fully. A very small sculpture, she thought. No wonder, she mused, for the umpteenth time in her life, so many people came here during the fall.

Here, these trees sparkled like nowhere else on the planet. Of course, various groups had been trying to extract the metal from the trees, with little luck but occasional destruction, over the years.

Annalyn was part of the Fae Friends of the Flutewood for many years, though she was not terribly active. Flutewood, though famed for I ts beautiful leaves in the fall, was equally known for the wood itself, used since the beginning of time by the fae and elves for their flutes and some of their other woodwinds. When cut, carved, and polished, the wood transformed into a burnished bronze-colored metal over time, so the wood was prized the world over. Most of the known professional flutists, whether in human circles, mixed, or entirely magic, tried to get their hands on one as soon as they could afford it.

Some were passed down over the centuries. There were several examples of particularly beautiful and notable ones in the Everland Bay Village Museum. Some of Annalyn's favorite lore about the flutewood tree included the magical quality of even the leaves and twigs; if left to dry naturally, some, the old tales say, could work strong magic when in the hands of just the right mage. Children often picked up twigs and surprised their unsuspecting parents when small rearrangements, explosions, and mischief happened at home.

Annalyn shook her head, smiling at herself for becoming so lost in thought. I suppose I am trying to postpone the inevitable, she thought, as she walked more briskly into the village café. "Charmed, I'm Sure" was the full name, though everyone just called it "Charmed."

Looking around the simply furnished café, she barely noticed the glowing bird's-eye maple throughout or the cream-colored ceramic ware. The berry and slate-colored napkins, she knew, were made by the local seamstress and laundered now into the softness that many years works upon good cloth. She placed one in her lap, smoothing it reflexively, and looked up to see a frowning Giselle Azule striding across the room. "What is it?" asked Annalyn, immediately alarmed.

"No time to talk right now—I have been down here in the Village for a meeting but am just now hearing from security. I need to get back up to the Institute grounds. Immediately," said Giselle.

"What? I thought everything was under control," said Annalyn, motioning to the barista that they would be leaving, pointing to the pantry.

"So did I. Let's portal to your place now and to the operations room we set up earlier. I've got Fletcher on the way now, and Jing. I can head up to the Institute from there," said Giselle.

"We'll take the pantry portal," said Annalyn, steering Giselle in the right direction.

"We were sure we had it done," Giselle said, heading to the back of the café. "Almost. We were *this* close to getting the Institute back under control. The rogue and dark-arts mages were routed by our teams, and the last we were able to discern, they were off the property, we thought. But I am hearing now that there have been explosions, gunfire. Have to go and check it myself. I'll meet security there right after we get to your place and get briefed."

Annalyn bowed her head for a moment, closing her eyes, remembering the sounds she had heard earlier. She took a deep breath. How can this be happening?

"I heard some of that just as I was walking down here, I think. I was hoping I was hearing wrong. And just when we thought things were getting back on track." She felt so weary of it all.

But her deeper store of resilience and experience stirred within as a slight glimmer of hope. *I have been through worse*, she thought, thinking of her daughter. Thinking of other difficulties she had overcome in the past. *We can do this*, she thought. Not at all sure how. But we will get there. She squared her shoulders, looked Giselle in the eye. "We can get this turned around."

The two walked over to the pantry, not generally open to the public, but they grew up with the proprietor and had longstanding portal privileges there. With a quick glance around, taking in the still mostly quiet café, they went inside, where the bountiful pantry was lined floor to ceiling with shelves of flour, sugar, and more—all the ingredients one needed to run a busy café. Annalyn barely registered the pegs hung with colorful aprons and tea towels lining one wall. She kept going, and just past the stack of folded linen napkins, a small door was visible.

To anyone unfamiliar with the magical world, it looked exactly like an old-fashioned laundry chute. A small, square, walnut door, simply finished, with a clear crystal knob, was set into a frame in the wall. Annalyn opened it and dove in. Immediately, Giselle followed along after her. Nearly instantaneously, they were back in the kitchen at Borderlands. Fletcher was there already, headphones on, fingers flying on keyboards in front of the screens arrayed on the long table.

"I'm going to have to tell our friend at Charmed that she could use a bit of dusting help," said Annalyn absently, as she brushed off dust and cobwebs. "One day I will learn to not be the first in the portal!"

"Least of our worries, but you're right," Giselle said with a flicker of a smile. "Okay. Now. We are back here to plan, but we really need the Village with us."

"Agreed. They have so little real security at the cafe, though. I didn't want every word or even our meeting to be so easy to observe." Analyn glanced around her kitchen and felt a tiny moment of calm, the kind that always came to her at home.

"So, to work," said Giselle. "Fletcher, what are you seeing and hearing?"

"Bad news; they're up there and starting to surround the buildings again." Fletcher leaned into the screen, fingers hovering over one and enlarging the image with a spreading movement. "Can't tell yet if they're inside, should hear in a moment," he said, nodding at Annalyn and Giselle.

"Tell them I'm heading in," said Giselle.

"And I'm going along," said Annalyn.

"Fletcher, keep an eye on things here and keep me constantly updated. I'll update as often as I can. I am calling in the good gryphons, and the military pegasi," said Giselle.

Fletcher whistled. "Brilliant. Okay, I'm hearing that there are rogue gryphons on the other side—be extra careful. Also hearing that Jing and the others are waiting for your signal."

"Just now in touch. Jing is on her way," said Giselle, a-whirl as she transformed her travel clothes into a military-grade version elaborately embroidered with nearly invisible travel and battle spells. The fabric was a midnight blue so dark and rare it could mesmerize those nearby.

"She should be here momentarily," she continued. "The others are heading up there ahead of us." A huge shadow overcame the back stone courtyard and Jing's full-sized form filled the window.

Annalyn rummaged for a moment in the mud room, grabbed her ribbon reins, waved her hands quickly over her own garments, turning them a darkened charcoal overlayed with protection and precision spells. Out they went to meet Jing. "I'll ride in front, you can be right behind to stay better in touch with Fletcher and all," said Annalyn. "We'll have to go bareback; no time to get a saddle."

Giselle and Annalyn climbed up with ease; Jing had scaled down to the size of a birthday-party pony, ducked into the ribbon reins proffered by Annalyn, and as she lifted off, scaled up again. Wings extended, Jing soared, heading straight to the Institute.

Black, oily smoke billowed up and engulfed them as they came near. "I can't see! Jing, can you see to land?"

"Visibility is nearly zero," said Jing. "I think I can land, though."

"Try to land in the back near my office," said Giselle.

Jing flew as directed. Annalyn could feel her eyes streaming with tears as the soot and smoke continued to envelop them all. They came to a shuddering landing, Annalyn and Giselle slipping off Jing.

"We can see the center courtyard from my office; should be able to see what is going on from there," said Giselle. The two made it to the old stone building, and Annalyn opened the door.

They dashed up the stairs and into Giselle's office, running toward the floor-to-ceiling windows. "I can barely see a thing. Wait—there are our gryphons. We can meet them on the field. Annalyn, you can do scaling work, yes?"

"Of course."

"Do the map and follow me out. I'm hoping that no one will think to search you," said Giselle.

Annalyn was in motion as soon as Giselle said "scaling work," knowing how important the map was, and turning all her attention to task before her. She stood before the map, which was more like a little diorama of Everland Bay Institute and the grounds. It was about three feet by three feet, and the highest little trees and buildings were a few inches high. She leaned over the map for just a moment. She could see the buildings that they were in, the smoke billowing up all around, the grounds churning, bulldozers grinding along across the scene. She placed her hands on two of the corners, breathed in deeply, and closed her eyes. The sound of an industrial-sized engine filled the room suddenly and, just as quickly, was silent. The map had gone entirely flat, and Annalyn held it there, as if to keep it in place, eyes open now in concentration. "Spider silk? With mycelia? Do you have any in here?"

"Yes, here," said Giselle, opening the top desk drawer. "Shall I apply it?"

"In the center," said Annalyn, breathing hard. She waited as Giselle unraveled the spider silk skein and pressed it into the center. The silk and the attached mycelia, which was present, though invisible to the naked eye, would both soften and strengthen the map as it was in its arrested state. "Okay, good. One, two, and three," she counted. The moment she felt a slight softness in the map, she and folded it up as if it were a scarf, tucking it into her pocket.

"Done."

The two dashed back downstairs and into the courtyard. Devastation was all around them and as Annalyn and Giselle walked front, the soil gave way here and there, causing them to stumble. "Toxic dissolution, I think," said Giselle, steadying herself. She held a silk kerchief to her nose and mouth.

One of the gryphons came up to Giselle. "Director Azule, ma'am," he said, saluting. "We have to get you two out of here. It is not safe."

"I must see for myself," said Giselle, breaking into an almost-run, heading into the open courtyard.

Annalyn was beside her, trying to blink her sight clear. She was barely able to see. Some of the buildings were scarred by fire, some were starting to sink into the morass. The ground felt slippery, and it was hard to keep her balance. She faltered, started to fall, and barely caught herself, heading back under the eaves of the closest building.

Suddenly, one of the wooden eaves came down in flames, grazing Annalyn's arm and slamming into the ground. Giselle turned and ran over to Annalyn. "I'm all right," said Annalyn, holding her arm, hunching over slightly.

"We have to turn back," said Giselle. "Jing!"

Almost before she finished speaking the name, Jing flew straight toward them, pulling up sharply and executing a hurried landing while simultaneously scaling down to her smaller size, just right for the two to climb up. "Ready—quick!" said Jing.

Annalyn eyed Jing's back and realized that she'd never make it up. "My arm. I can't climb up."

"We'll get you up there," said Giselle. "Here. Jing can get a little smaller and, there. Now hold on to her neck with your good arm and I'll be right behind you."

"Ready," said Annalyn. She was wobbly still, but leaned onto Jing's neck, allowing herself to rest in the warmth, trying to regain some of her strength.

"To Borderlands," said Jing, gaining altitude and flying out of the billowing smoke and away.

Annalyn rewrapped the reins around her good hand, wincing at the pain in her shoulder. She leaned into Jing's neck and squinted her eyes against the wind and soot. After a few moments, they had cleared the billowing smoke and debris. Annalyn untangled her right hand, reached up and wiped her eyes. Her head and shoulder were throbbing, and her eyes refused to stay clear, though now, they were filling with tears.

"What a horror," she said, raising her voice and turning her head to glimpse Giselle.

Giselle nodded in reply, mouth set in a straight line. "Too hard to talk up here," she said, raising her voice. "We'll regroup when we land."

Annalyn focused on staying in place. As the treetops surrounding her home came into view, she prepared to land, readying herself. The ground came up quickly and in one smooth motion, Jing pulled up, scaling down to the right size so that Annalyn and Giselle could easily dismount. Annalyn felt herself falter and was grateful for Giselle's steadying hand.

"We were lucky to get out of there without more damage. That burning eave could have done a lot more harm," said Annalyn, slipping the reins off the now-small dragon with her good arm, tucking them into her pocket. She and Giselle fell into step, walking toward the side door and stopping for a moment before going in. "I'm not sure what I expected to see, but somehow I didn't expect it to be such a battle scene."

"Nor did I," said Giselle. "And now we have to redouble our efforts to take control." She turned back toward Jing. "I know this is rough on you, too. Do you think you have enough strength for one more recon flyover?"

"Of course," Jing said, raising and lowering her wings, stretching them out as she scaled back up. "Until later."

Giselle waved Jing off, continuing into the kitchen at Borderlands with Annalyn. Fletcher opened the door for them. "Are you okay? I can call a medic," he said, as he simultaneously called a medic, without waiting for a reply.

"I'll be fine, I am sure," said Annalyn, holding her arm close as she navigated the closest path to a chair.

Giselle stepped to her side to guide her to the chair and get her settled. "Try not to move too much," she said.

Annalyn felt so annoyed, even as she felt the pain course through her. Why did this have to happen? she thought. With her good arm, she reached to pull the shawl away from the gash.

"Careful!" said Giselle, rushing to fold the shawl down.

"Let me keep it close—it has been protecting me and working some healing. The medics will be happy about that," said Annalyn, with a wince.

Medics arrived and barely knocked before sweeping into the room, medical capes a-whirl. They encircled Annalyn and checked vitals, started gently swabbing the wound, checking her quickly all over.

"Yes, ma'am," said one medic. "That shawl did you a lot of good. Lucky you had it with you. I'm just going to remove it from the wound site—it can stay with you, on your lap. "

Giselle and the others withdrew as Annalyn was being checked. She felt fine, really, she thought. "No need for so much fuss," said Annalyn.

"No ma'am. No fussing here," said one of the medics, with a shadow of a smile.

The third waved a flat medical scan-wand over and around her, accelerating the healing and checking for other problems. She nodded briskly, stepped back, glanced at the chief medic.

"Ma'am, you are very lucky. That cape has protected you from serious harm. Please avoid using that arm too much; the bandage will help constrain movement and will speed the healing. Please apply a clean, fresh shawl daily. You can alternate them, washing one each day. If you don't have extras, you can fold one in half so that the fresh side is always against the wound. May we take this one with us? We'd like to analyze it for toxins, deposits of any kind."

"Certainly, please go ahead. And I do have extras, so I'll be fine with alternating them. But I do want that one returned so that I can repair it," said Annalyn, feeling a little saddened by the rips and burns in the beautiful shawl. "And of course, I will do as you say."

"Please be in touch if there is an increase in pain or if anything looks or feels worse than it does now."

Annalyn nodded her agreement and closed her eyes briefly. She could feel the beginning of weariness settling in.

Fletcher escorted the medical team out and turned back to Giselle and Annalyn.

Annalyn took a deep breath. "I'm going to be fine. Let's get back on topic here. Giselle, can you fill Fletcher in?"

"It was a disaster. Our gryphons and security are trying to hold on, but the grounds looked utterly devastated," said Giselle, sitting down at the table. "And here we thought we had just gotten things back in order. It seems as if none of our work held, and the rogue mages undermined everything and may have assured the final destruction with the rotting compounds or whatever it is that they have spread all over the grounds." She bowed her head into her hands as she sat at the kitchen table.

Fletcher's shoulders sagged. "We lost our connection right after you got there but I figured things had gone badly. What about the map?"

Annalyn started to reach into her pouch and winced. Giselle reached over, drew it out of the pouch, and handed it to Fletcher. "Go ahead and get this set up," said Giselle. "Just set it on that table and unfold it. The map will do the rest."

Fletcher set the map down on the large map table in the corner and unfolded the small square. He jumped back as the map immediately went into action, unfolding in a blur, moving this way and that, and with a slight ripple and flourish, settled itself. The topographical features rose up out of the map and it stood at the ready, giving them a real-time look at Everland Bay Institute and grounds. "Whoa," he said. "I have only seen it in your office, Dr. Azule. I have never seen it reanimate itself. Pretty interesting."

"Yes, these are very helpful," said Giselle, peering over the map. "There are the gryphons! They are holding the rogue mages for the moment, but now the sooty smoke is billowing up—once again it is hard to see anything."

"We've got to get this outside—this smoke could be toxic!" said Annalyn.

"We'll all get it out of here," said Giselle, nodding toward Fletcher, who leaped into action.

Giselle and Fletcher wrestled the map outside and placed it on the stone courtyard. Annalyn followed. The smoke began to dissipate in the breeze.

"And just like this ravaged map, the Institute seems to be in total disarray," said Annalyn. "But I was thinking about other possibilities as I was walking down to the Village earlier. We have not been working at all with our other beings, really, in this effort. The fungal net. Or the trees, for example," she said, taking the flutewood leaf out of her pocket and setting it on the table between them.

"Flutewood trees? Mushrooms? Oh, Annalyn, really, I don't understand you sometimes," said Giselle, shaking her head.

"Hear me out. In addition to our more conventionally cognitive creatures, I think it is worth working with some of the more deeply rooted locals—the fungi and flutewood trees, for example."

"I don't see how this is a reasonable avenue. They are extensive, and the flutewood are beautiful and surrounded by mystery and lore, but what can they do right now? We have a complete and utter disaster on our hands, and even now more of the grounds and buildings may be succumbing to the devastation. All of this is in real time. Right now. This is no time for new approaches, especially with trees, of all things. Or fungi. They cannot take up arms, or speak, or move, or..." said Giselle, stopping with a catch in her voice.

"I know it sounds crazy. But I need you to listen. They do speak. They even sort of move, all of them, in their own way. Those trees. I was walking through the grove that is between here and the Village and realizing how powerful they are. Stories about talking trees and moving trees, especially flutewoods, are not just children's tales, you know. And the wood is more than just a strange wood that transforms into metal."

"We have been picking up high activity in the soil and flutewoods but hadn't connected these dots. This could explain what we're hearing," said Fletcher, brow furrowed, glancing at his screens in the makeshift operations room he had set up.

"The fae and elfin folk, and mixed folk like me," continued Annalyn, "have known for generations that the fungal and tree communications networks are very powerful, as are their healing and restoration networks.

"They are actively working all the time, repairing, restoring, communicating. From deep within their roots, to the fungal network, the mycelial network, that extends from every tiny filament to the tops of their famous leafy crowns, they work, communicate, listen," she said, tapping a fingertip for each quality as she spoke. Her shawl slipped a little, and she winced, rearranged it with her good arm.

"They can also take action, in a way. And there is a forest of the flutewoods up the hill at the Institute, connected by a line of linked trees and groves all the way through here and well into the Village," said Annalyn. "The flutewood and fungal network is strong. Unbroken. It may even be possible that they are resistant to the toxins that are attacking the rest of the Institute."

"So," said Giselle, still frowning. "The flutewoods are part of the landscape, but also part of the communications system, security system, armory, etc. Perhaps they are far more than just beautiful wood for expensive musical instruments, you are saying. And the fungi are more than just something to sauté for dinner," she said, looking across at Annalyn with the shadow of a smile.

"Yes," said Annalyn, nodding. "And they love, and desperately need, their homeland. Their home soil. Plus, their communications network through both the canopy and the soil may give us a lot of information, if they choose to communicate with us. And they may be able to let us know what is happening, virtually instantaneously. Also, not only may they be able to resist the toxins, but they may also be able to reverse the harmful properties of the solvents that the rogue mages are applying," she finished, thinking things through as she spoke.

She touched the leaf she placed on the table. It glowed and shimmered, metallic and iridescent. "I can feel it vibrating," said Annalyn. "I wonder if it hears us." She passed the leaf over to Giselle. The leaf seemed to glow more brightly, as if in answer.

"You are so wise," Giselle said, holding the glowing leaf aloft. "We should have been working with the flutewood groves all this time. How did you know about all of this? Can you speak with them now? Are we too late?" Giselle rose from the table.

Annalyn nodded. "I've been part of that world for a while—Friends of the Flutewood, also Society for the Protection of Interwoven Networks: SPIN." She started toward the back door, grabbed her straw hat. "Great groups. Doing so much good. Let's go over to the closest visible family; a small grove lives just over the hill here," said Annalyn, as the two strode out to the meadow.

"Fletcher, can you get this map over to my office while we check out the grove? If it's still too smoky, you can place it outside on the stone bench. We should be back very soon," said Giselle.

Annalyn followed Giselle out the door, making sure the shawl stayed in place. Her pain was beginning to ebb, and she wanted the healing to continue.

Chapter Ten
Jemma

Jemma sat, alert, in a chair at a corner table at Charmed, watching the door.

"Hey, Jemma, nice to see you," called out the barista. "You missed your grandmother and Dr. Azule by just an hour or so. They left in a hurry, and I never got a chance to bring them anything. What can I get for you?"

"Coffee would be great. And sorry I missed them!" Her pocket faeries had emerged from the small wristlet that was her shape-shifted knitting bag, and were perched on her right shoulder, waiting with her. They were not quite as patient, she noticed; as usual, they were whispering a bit, nervous about what was going on. One flew up to her dragonmark and rubbed it a bit with a tiny sleeve to polish it a little.

She smiled, reached up to soothe them, and felt her spirits lift as Keltie and Jake came in. Jemma continued to look for the one absent member of their usual crew. "Hey, everyone. Where's Fletcher?"

"He's on duty, won't be free until after work," said Jake, pulling out a chair, raising his eyebrows a little at the scraping noise, stashing his backpack next to it on the floor, and settling his lanky frame in one continuous motion.

"What are you hearing about what is going on? It feels as if things are really moving, but we have no information," said Jemma.

"Yeah, it is getting intense. Fletch can't tell me any details yet, but he's in touch with pretty much everyone in charge. And we need to be ready to move quickly, I think," said Jake.

Keltie arranged herself on another chair, sipping on the coffee she had grabbed on the way in and rummaging in her expandable pack, fishing out her mobile scrying lens. She glanced at Jemma. "Wow. You are kind of glowing."

"Faeries. They sometimes like to get my mark all polished now that we're in a place where it is safe. Silly things. Don't mind the glow. It will calm down," said Jemma, reaching up absently to touch her mark, which pulsed a little.

Keltie flashed a smile. "Got it. Okay. Here. Let me just focus this a sec. I am seeing flashes of Dr. Max and a crew of really strange-looking younger folk, maybe mages, up at the Institute. They are furtive and, like, spreading this thick stuff—goopy, like glue, sort of, on buildings and some of the grounds," said Keltie. Jemma could see that even thought it was just a mobile version, it was pretty clear. "Also, "horrible soot. And some creatures of some sort. Gryphons! They are pressing back against the rogue mages. Really hard to see with the smoke."

"I think we might need to gather the rest of the really nimble Village young mages and half- or mixed mages—ones you two trust—and go up there," said Jemma. "We could use more than just the four of us— five including Jing, once we see her again." The faeries squeaked in protest, started to huff a bit. "Sorry, you too."

"What about Director Azule and your grandmother?" asked Keltie, glancing up for a moment then returning to scrying.

Jemma hesitated. "I hate to do this, but I think this may be a time when we ask for forgiveness, not permission. They seem to be so bogged down in committees and meetings of the old guard and the village elders, all of whom are arguing about who should be doing what to make things better, or get things back to normal, or whatever each side thinks is needed. They're not really getting anything done, and meanwhile, we are all sensing that the rogue mages are about to take over. Maybe permanently," said Jemma. "And maybe they already have."

"But what is going on with the gluey stuff? And the fire? It seems as if they are trying to destroy it," said Jake. "But why? Wouldn't they want to save the Institute so that they could use it for themselves?"

"No idea. But I'm sensing something else," said Jemma. "And I think the Institute itself won't allow that. I can sense that it is, like, groaning, trying to shake them off. I think we may be the only ones who can help right now. Jake—any way you can help us get outfitted? I know that none of us has earned enough yet to cover that fancy gear at Heartwood, but maybe your boss will let us pledge our wages to him?"

"I can, if my boss is okay with it," said Jake.

"Keltie, can you get a scrying vista together from here throughout the area, including the Institute?" asked Jemma. "We need to be able to see what is going on, I think, as we get closer. I hope. You are so genius at this."

"Thanks. And yes, I can. But there may be still a gate between the Institute itself and the Village. I don't think anyone can just wander in. We will need the codespell for entry. Jake—does Fletcher have that?" asked Keltie.

"Yeah, but Fletcher is not us, and he does not have authorization to grant it to us, I don't think," said Jake.

"But this is an emergency. And doesn't he work somewhere close to Heartwood? I saw him the other day, coming out of a back door. Maybe he can help us now," said Jemma, feeling tense, urgent. She felt her mark pulse a little. The faeries were picking up her energy, and were stirring, agitated. She reached up again and let them hold on to her fingers.

"Right. I don't think he gets to make the call on that," said Jake. "Let's go to the shop; maybe we can find out more there."

The three waved their devices over the coffee and remaining crumbs before they left; images automatically scanned, and payment made instantaneously as they headed out. "Thanks!" called out the barista, with a wave. They returned the wave and broke into a run toward Heartwood, the magical wilderness gear shop.

Jemma's hair blew all around as the winds blew at all of them; she looked upward to see Jing, all sooty, streaking right at them. Scaling down before their eyes, Jing came to an abrupt landing on the path in front of the three. "I wanted to inform you of my movements and alert you," said Jing. "I must fly back over to the Institute. Much is happening right now, and we are all needed. Our brave mages are hurt and are in danger of losing.

"I know you will be up there as soon as you can be—I will be gathering my people; it is time for us to take to the skies," Jing finished as she lifted off, scales flashing iridescent jewel tones; amethyst, aquamarine, emerald, topaz, and metallic gold.

Jemma gave a small salute and turned back with a frown to the others. "We have to get up there as soon as we can." They all continued their headlong dash.

They used the time to catch up a little. She knew how proud Jake was of having a job at Heartwood but hadn't heard all the details. "So how is it going here, then? And weren't you supposed to be starting your fellowship at the Institute proper?" she asked, panting a little with the effort.

"Yeah, so. I had gotten notice—not so dramatic as you with your dragon transport," he said, his more usual grin coming back in flash, erasing the somber gaze. "Those of us with unbroken lines don't have the same entry difficulties as someone like you, but I still had to apply, and be admitted, approved. All that. I applied because it was the family thing to do, but I didn't really have a super clear idea of what I wanted to research and work on. When everything blew up, I knew there was no telling when I'd be able to start there, if ever.

"So, I just applied at the shop. I knew I needed a job if I wasn't going to be at the Institute, and the shop is the place I really love. We're almost there now. I hung around there all the time, so they knew me. I could never afford much of anything, the gear is so expensive, but I am, you know, such a fan. They decided to take a chance on me. And it turns out that village and regional comms and security base out of their way-back storage area. Their entrance is through a different part of the building, so I didn't know, and Fletcher had never gotten around to telling me. It's pretty cool to be there and know that he's somewhere close.

"You'd never know that it was there, so don't expect to see him. It's just so totally hidden. Also, you know, spellwork. Like those ones you were telling us you were helping refresh at your grandmother's. So, no worries; I'm not breaking any rules by telling you. Anyway, I am loving being there. I'm learning all about how to use everything. Amazing stuff. I think I might even be better off continuing my training at the shop and then staying there than I would have been at the Institute proper. I just fit better here," said Jake, with a shrug, slightly out of breath after their dash to the shop. "Okay. We are gearing up for, well, for just about anything, really. I'll get my boss and see what is possible." He headed up to the store office two steps at a time.

Jemma and Keltie turned toward each other as he departed, talking over each other in their eagerness to get caught up.

"I'm worried," said Keltie, "and I have been meaning to get together with you, but things are happening so quickly, I can barely keep up. I'm so glad I managed to get a job at the Botanical Gardens and Arboretum. I'm learning so much and there is a perfect pool for scrying in an out-of-the-way corner. Not mobile, of course, but just amazing. So perfectly dark and still. I've been checking in on events and was just about to get everyone together. Things are looking bad up there. Really bad. I am worried. Hoping we're doing this in time."

"I'm worried, too. Terrified, really," Jemma said. "Things seemed to be okay there for a while, and it looked as if everything was going to go back to normal. Grandmother and Dr. Azule were smiling more and more and the meetings in the Village seemed to be producing at least good ideas and a sense of hope. I was thinking we'd be training together any day, refreshing our skills. Well, I'd at least need that refreshing; you two would probably be fine. Anyway, after a quick refreshing and assessment, I thought we'd be up at the Institute, and just carry on with our original plans. I kept just thinking we'd get back to normal. I have wanted to be there for so, so long."

"I know. And now, I don't think I even know what normal is anymore," said Keltie, shaking her head.

"Truly. But I just was on that track in my mind, you know?" said Jemma.

"You two had your places at the Institute already lined up and ready to begin, and I figured I'd just get more up to speed and be okay, even if it took time. At least I'd be here. I was so excited. It was really my dream come true, even though that sounds a little corny. Then all of this happened. My heart aches for the way Everland Bay was, the Everland Bay Institute my mother and grandmother always hoped I would be a part of."

"I wanted that, too. My version of it, anyway," said Keltie. "All of my brothers and sisters had been here before me. My portal book was on my nightstand since I was about twelve, I think. I mean, I was always going to be here. Learn more about my specialty or maybe specialties, have fun. Then eventually graduate and find my way in the wider magical world. This is just how we do it in my family. Then, poof. All gone," said Keltie, shaking her head.

"I know. It seems so unbelievable," Jemma said. But I've been wondering. Somehow, working together like we are seems important. Feels like something new is beginning. Maybe something better?" she, brow furrowed as she thought things through out loud.

"You say it better than I can, but I'm beginning to sense something like that, too. And right now, we have to get the Institute out from under the rogue mages, because if we don't, they'll not only destroy the Institute proper, they will likely move downhill and try to take over the Village," Keltie said, turning toward the sound of the office door opening.

Jake came out and nodded. "Okay, we're good. Just have to sign off on a loan form. You're both sure you're okay with that?" He looked at Jemma and Keltie.

"Yes. I'll think of this as, I don't know, a student loan or something. I can still sort of get by without much and this is worth it because we may be saving the Bay. I just don't see a way around it. Plus, we are all working, so we will all be continuing to earn at least something, and we'll get through this together, yes?" said Jemma.

"Yes!" Keltie and Jake said, in unison.

Jake went from display to display, selecting a very few items. "Capes," he said. "These are those ones you see in the pro mage competitions and wilderness expert shows," he said. "They fold up, like this." He demonstrated as the gossamer-fine cape folded down to the size of a handkerchief. Then smaller yet. "They are called wedding-ring capes, or shawls, because they are so fine they can be pulled through a ring. Knitted by fae/elfin folk, with a mix of spidersilk and flutewood silk. So, you can stow them in a pocket, then bring them out."

He pulled the square open and snapped it with a flourish, and it floated for a moment, then settled around his shoulders. "They will protect us from pretty much anything, and can moderate the environment, so if it is too hot out, they can cool us, and if it is too cold out, they will keep us warm. Lots of other things, too, like they can be tied up into carrier bags, for keeping and transporting things," he said, as he handed one each to Jemma and Keltie.

Jemma was enchanted as she saw the familiar shawls. The ones she knew from the other side of the equation. "I know these! I've never been to the shop and never knew exactly where these went after they are finished, but these are the ones my grandmother and I make," Jemma said, laughing as the one in her hands started moving. It opened up and wrapped itself around her shoulders. Her resident faeries appeared in a flash, holding the cape aloft, arranging it around Jemma's shoulders, fussing with it in a motherly sort of way.

"Uh, looks like yours *knows* you—you and your faeries," said Keltie, with a wry smile.

"My grandmother probably knitted this one. My faeries recognize it, I think. And I have to confess—I think I may have knitted at least one of yours," said Jemma, coloring a little, then smiling at the faeries who continued to tug a bit at the cape to settle it properly.

"Here comes my boss. He's really great. Like, brilliant and a good man—er—gryphon, too," said Jake. "His family has owned this place forever."

Mr. Gavin Gryzik came out of the back office. He smiled at them all and nodded at Jemma. "I thought you looked a little bit familiar. I know your grandmother very well—she is my best maker, and I'm betting that many in our stock are ones the two of you have made. Lucky to have her work here—she's such a star mage. But I won't disturb you all. Keep going, Jake. I need to take care of the things I mentioned earlier. I'll let you know when I'm ready."

Jake nodded. "Great, thanks, sir. These," he continued, keeping his cape stowed and fussing with the straps of a cross-body bag, "are those gear satchels I've been telling you about ever since you've known me." He looked up, grinning.

"Are these the ones that can supposedly do anything, including become a cavern or a portal, hold gear and food enough for several days in the wilderness? Also cook us a gourmet dinner and accompany it with music?" said Jemma, laughing.

"Well. Pretty much," said Jake, with a chuckle. "No music, though, I'm almost certain. I can ask the manufacturer's rep about that in the future. For real, though, they are, like, anticipation gear bags. So, we stay connected to them and convey our thoughts with the strap in hand, like this." He demonstrated, shrugging the bag over his wide shoulders, and settling it on his right side, grasping the woven mushroom-leather strap firmly. "The mushroom leather is very sensitive, even though it is seasoned and dried; still has its mushroom network thing going on.

"We can command them," he said, demonstrating. "Shelter," he said, with a quick flick and opening of his hand. The satchel became a tent. "Four-creature," and the tent became roomier.

"That's supposed to fit four of us?" Jemma said, peering in.

"Yeah, you know how it goes—those things they call two-creature tents are really only big enough for one. Same for the so-called four-creature version," he said, with a small what-can-you-do shrug.

"Food!" commanded Jemma. She jumped out of the way as a table materialized in front of the tent. It was laden with roasted squash, saffron curry, piles of glistening grapes, miniature mandarins, partially peeled, lemons, sliced and ready, rosemary-roasted fowl, heaps of cherry scones, and star-shaped cookies, sparkling with sugar.

"So, like, food won't be a problem," said Jake, popping a grape into his mouth.

"But be careful. I've played around with it a little. Learned some things the hard way. You have to be really specific about the food, otherwise you'll get the default settings of wherever this is made. Mine comes from a place that serves unbelievably hot food, and I nearly burned my tongue off, tasting it," he said, with a grimace.

"Just tasting it?" said Keltie with eyebrows up as she reached for a scone.

"Okay, well. Inhaling it, really, right? You know me. So, yeah. Big mistake. Be careful tasting any of this, especially that curry over there," he said, waving at the feast. "Next time, ask for whatever you want and order it ultra-mild, until you are sure of the default settings."

Jemma put one finger into a small bowl of the curry, tasted it. "Ouch—you are exactly right," she said, fanning her mouth and reaching for a bit of scone.

"See? Okay, back to more serious duty," Jake said. "Mr. Gryzik, are you ready for us?"

"Yes, come on over," said Mr. Gryzik.

Jake joined him at a glass case, where polished knives in a multitude of shapes and sizes sparkled. Three had been selected and tagged, one for each of them.

Jemma and Keltie looked at each other, eyebrows arching in questions. There was a soft, chiming sound as the outside air crossed the blades inside the case. "Mr. Gryzik insisted on choosing one of these for each of us as gifts, once I told him what was happening."

"Wow. These are legendary," said Keltie in a hushed almost-whisper, taking a moment to admire the hand-tooled scrollwork done in a leaf-and-vine motif around the handle of hers. "My brothers are always coming over here, drooling over these. They are going to be so jealous!"

Mr. Gryzik looked at each of the young mages. All of them murmured hushed thanks. He raised a hand, acknowledging their gratitude and quieting them. "We don't have a lot of time, but I need to fill you in on the basics here." He took Jake's knife and showed them how it worked. "Okay. Stylus. Next, little plunger tip thing here, look!" he said. It produced a tiny spear, handy for piercing small objects. "You can use it as a tiny fork," he said, holding it aloft for a moment. A small, sizzling morsel of something cardamom-scented appeared. He blew on it and popped it into his mouth. "Mmmm." They all laughed. "Also can be used to pierce just about anything," he said, pinning imaginary flying foes.

"But the real strength of these knives is that they can cut through just about anything—fiber, metal, flutewood, spelled wood, stone. The tip and blade, properly maintained, are forged to seek out the spaces between the molecules in any object, and will unbind the chemical ligatures, rendering the object open at a molecular level. Part of the proper maintenance of such knives is that the owner becomes bonded to the knife and meditates with it daily. Silent meditation, either sitting or walking, is usually best. The knives become perfectly entrained with their owners, even able to shape shift as needed and as the particular skills and talents of the mage deepen over time. After a number of years, the three knives will barely resemble each other. They are extremely rare and valuable magical tools, amplifying the magic of the owner if properly conditioned and maintained," he said, looking at each of the young mages.

"No time for the usual bonding ceremony," continued Mr. Gryzik. "But here. We will do a quick version now if you promise to come back later so that I can properly bind you to your knives. With me?"

"Yes. Absolutely. Will do," the three said, one on top of the other.

Jemma felt festive, in a weird sort of way, even though she was in danger, she knew, and so were her friends. So were they all. But it felt, deep down, as if things were really going somewhere now, and she was part of it. It felt scary, and real, and right. She lifted her eyes and met the glance of Mr. Gryzik, who nodded to her. She nodded her assent.

"Okay then," he said. "Knives in dominant hand, folded. Now. Open. That's right. Follow me," he said, as he raised his arm, knife held firmly. "Breathe in. Bring your fist to your heart, blades up. Breathe. Repeat after me: To the Great Power of Love and Light, I open my mind, my heart, my blade. And I follow the light, dispelling the wrong, on the pathway for my life. So it is. And so it shall be. Forevermore," Mr. Gryzik finished. They all dutifully repeated the somber words along with him. Silence ensued.

Jemma felt herself filled with hope and strength and even, maybe, wisdom, she thought. Or something like that. She glanced up at Mr. Gryzik, who held her glance and smiled. "Okay then," she said. "Do we have everything? Jake?"

"Think so. That was awesome, sir."

Mr. Gryzik cleared his throat. "Right. Got all serious there, didn't I? Well. Those are serious knives. They always have that effect on me. Jemma, I believe you are familiar with these—your grandmother has one of the great, old ones."

"Yes! She loves that knife and doesn't let anyone near it," said Jemma.

"Quite right," said Mr. Gryzik. "Okay now, get going! You are needed, I believe. By the Bay itself. Good luck. And Jemma. I knew your mother. She would be so proud of you," Mr. Gryzik said, wiping something from his eye as he turned away. "Don't forget about the power of that mark of yours, though—you might want to learn to modulate the visibility. Could give the enemy an advantage, knowing what it means."

Jemma stared at him, moved and saddened at hearing yet again about her mother and needing to be more mindful of her mark, but unwilling to let herself give in to the emotion.

"Thank you, sir. And will do," she said. Jemma squared her shoulders, set aside the thoughts of her mother for the moment, took a deep breath, waved at Mr. Gryzik, and continued the wave as she nodded to Keltie and Jake, leading them outside. She could feel their excitement, and even though this was a serious time, she felt a sense of happiness and purpose deep within. And she could see, looking at Keltie and Jake, that they felt the same. They all grinned a bit. She knew they had a lot ahead of them, but a moment of glee felt, well, fun. She gave herself a light tap on the side of her eye, patted some cover on her mark, and checked her pocket and her knitting bag, now in its smallest scrunchie size, to make sure the faeries, who had crawled back inside, were okay. "Back to business." She smiled along with Keltie and Jake, however, as they continued on their way together. She felt even closer to them than she had before. How lucky I am, she thought, to have friends to go through this with.

"It's always better when we're together, isn't it?" said Keltie.

Jemma said, "I was just thinking the same thing, or just about!" Jemma felt elated and noticed a slight buzzing in her hand.

"I thought I could hear those thoughts!" said Keltie. "Agreed, though. So good to be together in all of this, however it turns out."

"Hey. Anyone feel that?" said Jake.

"The vibrating? From our knives? I was wondering whether it was just mine," said Jemma, feeling her knife still barely vibrating.

"According to the brochure thingy that comes with those knives, that's a thing that happens when we are all thinking in a useful, coordinated way. Like harmony, but with our thoughts. It lets us know that whatever we are thinking or saying at that moment, it is true and good and right," said Jake.

"I hate to be the downer here, but what happens when we're going in the wrong direction?" said Jemma.

"If I were a mean-spirited person, I would just let us all find out. But I can't do that," he said, smiling. "Seriously, though. We would feel it. I think it, like, sparks or something. We get stung just a little."

"Kind of intimidating," said Keltie.

"Well, let's get on with it. The knives will let us know when we're out of line, but I bet we will know anyway. Back to our plans. Keltie, I was wondering, since you've been working with the botanical gardens, do you think they have any wisdom for us?" asked Jemma.

"Yes, especially a stop at the lab area there if we can get in. Also maybe the library. The librarian and the head botanist should be able to help us," said Keltie, leading the way.

"I've been reading up on the connectivity between the plants and especially the trees," she continued. "The flutewood, which has families—we call them groves—all the way from the Institute through the arboretum and throughout the village, is especially connected, and is connected by fungi, which are then connected with just about everything else. And able to do zillions of things. Well, not zillions, but, you know, a lot, are able to eat just about anything, communicate, heal, send alarms. I think they can help massively with the botanical solvents the rogue mages have apparently been using up there."

"Wow, amazing," said Jake.

Chapter Eleven

As the three arrived, the doors were closing. "Code red, Keltie, we can't have you in here today," said a tall woman in a lab coat, standing squarely in the door and barring the three from entry. "Just think of it as a day off," she said, with a weary smile that overturned itself into a frown.

"But we need to talk with you!" said Keltie.

"No can do. We can talk once this is over."

"No, you don't understand. Our question is probably about your Code Red. Please," Keltie said.

Jemma stepped up, glancing at the woman's name badge. "Dr. Greensleeves, Keltie's right. And she's come up with what could be the solution. Fungi, right, Kelt?"

Dr. Greensleeves paused and left the door open slightly. "Is this something to do with the toxic mess up at the Institute?"

"Yes," the three said, in unison.

"We're all geared up," said Jake, adjusting his rucksack.

Keltie said "You know I've been studying and training intensely in the whole area of fungi and their abilities to do massive cleanup. I've been working with some of the specimens in our collections, all lined up in those galvanized zinc trays. And those fungal things, the mycelial bundles. I think they can be applied now."

"Okay. You've said the magic words," said Dr. Greensleeves, opening the huge, carved oak doors. "Follow me." She turned quickly and headed down the hallway. The three sped in behind her.

Jemma glanced all around and took in the living, pulsing wall of green. She found herself trying to name them as they zipped by, maidenhair, Arthursword fern, rabbit's foot, baby fairy tears, pothos, lemon balm, mint, orchids seemingly levitating, vines without number, emerald, purple, chartreuse. All swaying and bouncing slightly in their wake as they rushed past. The three were hard pressed to keep up with Dr. Greensleeves. Jemma shot a glance at Jake and Keltie, eyebrows raised.

"Hard to keep up here," said Jake, sounding a little out of breath.

"She's very speedy," said Keltie, under her breath. "I think she might be part something else. Not sure what. Just keep following her. She knows what she's doing."

They were following at a trot and came to an abrupt stop, nearly piling into each other as Dr. Greensleeves turned into a corridor down the hall from her office. She ushered them in to a room lined with linens, gloves, mesh coats, stacked with wipes, bio-safe cleansers. "Get in here, quickly. Sinks are there—wash your hands and forearms and put on one of these. Shoe wipes are there and mesh booties are here," she said, pointing. She handed over neatly folded mesh lab coats and booties, pulled quickly from a pile in the small anteroom.

She was a-whirl, helping them on with their coats, handing over the wipes. "Quickly now. We've found it's not necessary to keep perfectly sterile in these outer corridors or my office, Keltie you know all this, but we need to keep things pretty clean. And under wraps. Raise your right hands. Repeat. I swear, on the honor of my mother, to hold all I see here in confidence. Great. I'll have paperwork for you later. For now, you are sworn to secrecy. Good. Let's go," Dr. Greensleeves said, nodding, pivoting, and ushering the three out of the room. She locked the door briskly and turned, walking in her miles-eating stride as she continued to speak.

"We are working on exactly what you mentioned, Keltie." She paused, opened the door to her office, waved them in. "It's one of the reasons we decided to train you in on this area, but we couldn't disclose the most recent news just yet. What we are not clear on yet is how to transport the spores and mycelial bundles up there. Also, we will scale up but now are limited to small-batch work." She waved her hand over her desk and a fine mesh covering shimmered and lifted, floating in midair. A dozen large, metal trays. Must be those zinc ones Keltie mentioned, Jemma thought. All lined with compartmentalized biotrays.

They covered the large, polished oak table. Each was brimming with what looked to Jemma like mossy patches in all the colors of the forest floor. Emerald and peridot, obsidian and amber-toned, too many to count. A wafting cloud of intense green, musty, damp perfume filled the air and it felt as if any moment, a forest would appear around them, pulsing, breathing, alive.

They were arrayed alongside fist-sized bundles of rough burlap-like fabric, sewn into plump rectangles. "Are these the bundles you were talking about?" asked Jemma.

"Mycelial bundles, yes," said Keltie. Dr. Greensleeves nodded.

Dr. Greensleeves continued, gesturing to the revealed trays. "What we've been working on is partly in here. We are cultivating large stores of these fungal spores, as well as large mycelial networks, and have been for years now, knowing that a basic, universal version would be needed at some point. Most of what we are working on is in the annex next door, but this will give you an understanding of what we are doing.

"This universal, multitalented version of our base fungus, just a general oyster variety, can absorb the toxin, calibrate to it, then communicate the information throughout the organism. And to others." She lifted one of the samples. Moving quickly, she lifted it out of its container with a small scalpel and moved it over to a petri dish filled with a viscous, acid-yellow-green sludge. Its sharp and nauseating odor wafted up, assaulting their senses. Jemma and Keltie held tissues over their noses. Jake pulled a face, scrunching up his nose, and rummaged in a pocket for a handkerchief.

"This is an industrial, allegedly forever toxin," Dr. Greensleeves said. Small, nearly invisible filaments began to infiltrate the slimy mess. The toxic sludge began to shrink.

"That will take a little while, but here," said Dr. Greensleeves. "This," she selected a petri dish from the many in front of them, "is an example of what happens." The rancid toxin had disappeared, and the small dish now erupted with a healthy, amber-colored patch of mushrooms, stretching upward, smelling woodsy and inviting and for all the world as if they were ready to be sauteed. They glowed, just a little.

"Wow." Jemma was fascinated. She inhaled deeply, and glanced at Keltie, who was beaming.

"I've only seen photos of this process; have never seen it while it is working. Amazing, yes?" said Keltie.

"Definitely! Why isn't this already up at the Institute? Does Dr. Azule know about this work?"

"Yes. She knows," said Dr. Greensleeves. "We've been working together with her generally. But she's also brand-new as the director so didn't have authority to ramp up the timeline before then. There was no real warning, though, regardless. None of us expected to need it this quickly. So far there hadn't been an active need, and we were still working on the logistics. Hypotheticals.

"We didn't expect to need it right there at the Institute. The attack and ongoing insurrection set us all back, and the dark-magic toxins up there were just discovered. We also can't leave the lab right now because we need to be here to keep the base colonies safe and secure. These are living colonies and we are their keepers. Also, we are warehousing batches of ready-to-go fungi-permeated parcels, which require extra security now."

A knock sounded at the door. "Yes," she said, turning. "Feeding time," said the mesh-suited lab worker.

"Come in and go ahead," she said. "You know Keltie; I've briefed her in. This is Jemma, and this is Jake, now also briefed in and sworn to secrecy."

The lab worker nodded, started the process of feeding each compartment with a glass dropper. "Dr. Greensleeves," said the worker. "I need to move these trays back to the annex; we need to secure everything in one area."

"Certainly; please go ahead," said Dr. Greensleeves.

Dr. Greensleeves continued, speaking quickly as she watched the trays being removed and carried out, leaving just the one she used in her demonstration. "We are all working now frantically on this and haven't been able to spare anyone. We are having trouble finding any couriers; staff shortages abound. We were thinking of mini pegasi transport, despite their erratic flight patterns, but you are saying that you're planning to go up there?"

"Yes, exactly," said Keltie.

Jemma said, "We've all been working together on this. We need to move quickly." Jemma walked over to a window and tried to glimpse any part of the Institute, but it was too far away. "Time is not on our side. We figured that if we could reclaim even some of the ground and maybe keep the rogue mages away, or distract them, or even scare them off, we could help save the Institute." Jemma felt her knife humming a bit in a validating way, even though she felt a little silly saying such a dramatic thing. "And look." She placed her open knife into her hand, palm up. "We have knives that can slice through energy bonds and wraps that can shield us and amplify our strength," she said. Her wrap slipped out of her pack and unfurled, floating around her as it wrapped itself lightly around her shoulders.

"Are those the special knives Gavin has in his shop?" asked Dr. Greensleeves.

"Yes, ma'am," said Jake.

"Okay," Dr. Greensleeves interrupted the demonstration. "Laudable. You're on the right track, but there are only three of you. And I am sorry to say this, but you are too inexperienced. These people, or beings, are killers. Your enthusiasm and gear are impressive, but you need more expertise than youthful high spirits up there."

Jemma's smile faded. She felt herself deflate for a moment, then she squared her shoulders, and as she did so, she felt her dragonmark begin to pulse. She looked up sharply and said, "But how can this be? No one else is taking this on and the destruction up at the Institute is probably continuing right this moment. We have to do something!"

"I know this isn't welcome news," Dr. Greensleeves said, moving in the wake of the lab worker who had finished. With practiced efficiency, she draped the remaining small tray with a fine mesh covering. She fastened the lid onto the incandescent green mass in the petri dish and handed it to a lab worker who stood ready. "Please label this and put it with the other samples. Thanks," she said as the worker departed.

She looked stern as she met Jemma's eyes. "I am completely aware of the urgency, Ms. Avalon. But you are untrained and inexperienced. You'd be likely to get injured or detained—abducted, really—and then where would we all be?"

In the wake of the lab worker's departure the door stood open. They all turned as they heard a dry shuffling sound coming down the hall. It grew louder. Dr. Greensleeves walked toward the office door as three small creatures came into the room. Her features brightened as she looked at the small creatures and flashed a smile at Jemma, Keltie, and Jake.

"This might just work. I can let my botanical mage interns go with you. They are very wise in the ways of forest communication. Much wiser than humans, even fae/elf mixed humans, and can be the ones who can work tree, leaf, flower, and fungi magic to get the green things to work in our favor. Then there is nothing the rogue mages can do. Or at least, they'll be able to do a lot less. The rogue mages cannot communicate with the green things and fungi, because those beings only open to caring, loving beings and energies. This is Leaf, Frond, and Twig," she said with a flourishing wave as the diminutive, green, and very energetic three joined the group with a great deal of leaf-waving and rustling. Jemma found herself staring as she tried to grasp what and whom she was seeing. The mage's arms and legs were fashioned from twigs, hands and feet were assembled from leaves. An entirely different order of being.

"Oh, thank you," Keltie chimed in. "These interns are just amazing. I've been working some with them and learning so much from these three. The green beings, plants, and trees will be able to work with us now, since we'll be able to really talk with them through Leaf, Frond, and Twig. We will be able to work quickly together."

"Can they carry the fungal batches?" asked Jemma.

"That's the best news of all," said Dr. Greensleeves. "They will be even better at that than you two; they will be able to read the ground and talk to all the green things and know exactly where to inoculate with spores and tuck in the burlap bags filled with active mycelia clumps."

The botany intern mages nodded and chattered. Jemma watched them in wonder. She did not understand their language but sensed their exuberant enthusiasm. What a place this is, she thought, shaking her head a little as they all turned to go get loaded up with the parcels.

Chapter Twelve
Agni

"Yes. Right. The funds will be there, but you must sign off on the use clause," said Agni, pacing in his office. He glanced at his desk, grimacing as he saw the familiar photo on his desk of Jemma, Elise, and himself on a happy day now long in the past. Why do I even keep it there? he thought. Too painful. He reached over, turning the photo facedown as he listened to the voice at the end of the line. He wondered what Jemma was up to and when he might hear from her again. The loud voice of his client, Dr. Max, brought him back from his brief reverie.

"I can't believe this is standard. No one has this kind of clause anymore," said Dr. Max, on the other end.

"It is, and we do," snapped Agni. He ran a finger around his collar and started pacing. "Right. Look at page 103, note 47: 'Use for good purposes only, use in compliance with local regulations, and so forth,'" he said, reading the boilerplate language aloud from the printed contract, though he knew it nearly by heart.

"Leftie nonsense from decades ago, I believe?" said Dr. Max.

"Yes, sure, tree-hugging language, I get it. Just standard, though. This went through your legal people at some early stage, yes? That's what I was told. Halcyon should have no problem with this language at this late date." Agni began to feel annoyed.

This is just routine language, he thought. Surely these people had done normal business before. Must have signed countless similar contracts. Yes, there were ethics clauses still around. And this was the final agreement. They'd been working on this for months. He rolled his eyes, glanced at the clock.

"Perhaps we should consider release. You are apparently unwilling to be flexible," said Max.

"What? No! No, I can't authorize your release from our contract." Agni's pacing speed increased, and he just wanted to end the call. This was nuts. He looked at his hand, noticed he was flexing in and out of a fist. *Breathe, Agni, breathe.*

"Listen, my friend," said Dr. Max. "It sounds like you are not up to speed with our direction. I'm told you are changing policy. Our other potential funders made changes ages ago. We're just sticking with you for tradition's sake. My higher ups are sentimental, you know?"

Agni took another deep breath. What policy change? He redirected. "You know, I think we can send this back over to the contract people if your team is asking for different language. I can't freelance it," said Agni. "Right. That, we can do. It'll be over to Legal right after we end this call, and our two teams can let us know when things are ready to roll. On a more pleasant note, I hear Halcyon has some terrific plans for the redevelopment you're working on, yes?" Agni was buying time. He had grown heated, quite literally, and was wiping his brow as he continued pacing and trying to steer the conversation away from the standoff.

"Yes, good. And true. Matter of fact, we're already over there, getting things, well. Getting things underway," said Dr. Max.

"Wait just a moment here. What do you mean, you're underway already?" said Agni. "That can't be. You'll get arrested. Oh, I see. Just surveying? Yeah, I know this is a done deal, but this is not the way we do things. This is most irregular!"

This guy is really overbearing, Agni thought. One more thing to wrangle with Legal. What's his hurry? I wonder if the grounds he is talking about are ones near where Elise did her schooling. Up at

Everland Bay Institute. Probably near there, from the way this guy described it. But clearly not the same place, since he said it was a tumbled down ruin, acquired through an old mage family. That it hadn't been in active use of any sort for decades. Completely barren, uninhabited. Who knows, maybe it'll make the whole area a bit nicer, if the surrounding properties, like Everland Bay Institute, decided to spruce up. Always seemed a little shabby, not so elegant as the more modern properties he preferred.

"Okay, right. Listen, let's just go back to having Legal handle it. I'll mention all of this to them, and we'll get everything taken care of officially. Should hear very soon. Thank you for your time, Dr. Max," Agni said, ending the call with a frown and turning back to his files.

He searched through his documents, picking up one after another, shaking them out to see if he could find a map that showed both properties. Couldn't find anything. Odd, he thought. He'd have to ask Jemma about it when he talked with her next. She had been in such a rush. But oh, how he missed her. Funny, he had even thought about moving over there, to that tiny nothing village, for a while, just to be near her. No need, now that things were back to normal at work. I'm getting too sentimental in my old age, he thought. Maybe I can get her to move back here for at least part of the year. Aren't younger people moving around a lot anyway these days? Maybe if she could be with her grandmother for part of the year and near him for part of the year, she could be happy.

He turned aside from those thoughts as he walked out of his office. He was on his way to a lunch meeting with his boss and was looking forward to it. Things had gotten shaky there for a while, when he was worried that people noticed his dragonmark. He willed himself to keep his hand away from it now, making sure he did not give himself away. The person who had been vocal about it was fired. That person was just a gossip, thank heavens, and was long overdue to be sacked. Turns out the person was spreading rumors about other key executives, too.

This one had an affair, the disgruntled chatterer said, and that one was a known traitor to the company, and Agni was a known dragonmixed mutant. Agni overheard the scuttlebutt in the break room recently and knew he was home free. Just an unhappy lower-level person who hadn't been promoted. Mutant stung a bit, he reflected, but he believed he was back to golden-boy status, and he knew he was bringing in gold for the firm, which generally dissolved any worry in his higher-ups.

He headed out and stepped into the obsidian-black car waiting for him. He felt his dragonmark pulse a little, as he always did when he thought of gold. Such a nice, warm feeling. Secure. Stable. Powerful. So, off to lunch.

"Metropolitan," he said to the driver, who nodded and expertly maneuvered the car into the traffic sweeping past.

He glanced out the window at the elegant cityscape—eighteenth- and nineteenth-century stone and marble façades, Palladian windows, elaborate ironwork grilles here and there. Parts of it looked just a bit like Paris, he thought, shaking off the conversation with Dr. Max. He found himself in a festive mood as he anticipated a good conversation with his boss. Promotion, probably. More stock, likely. Not possible to even think about leaving the firm, he thought. What do they call it? Golden handcuffs. An apt term, though he always thought of that term as it applied to others. He got out of the car, headed into the club. He was here because he wanted to be, not because he had to be, he told himself fiercely.

He nodded to the maître d' and followed him down the soft, silent Persian-carpeted, mahogany-paneled hallway. A chair was pulled out for him, and the thick, cream-colored napkin was snapped out of its folded fan form and draped across his lap. He always enjoyed being in the elegant private dining room in the Metropolitan Club—the private city club his boss preferred for important meetings. Agni had been there many times before. He barely registered the gleaming silver, sparkling crystal, and the impeccable tailoring and formality of the waiter. His boss entered. Agni looked up with a confident smile, partly stood and reached out to shake hands. His boss barely shook his, and

Agni's smile flattened into a thin line as he read his boss's slightly furrowed brow. "What is it?"

"Agni. You tell me."

Agni was caught off-guard. What on earth? He again willed his hand from straying to his mark and tucked his hand under his leg as a further precaution. He wracked his mind, thinking of the deals he was working on, ready to go over the one with this Max guy. He'd expected to get a laugh out of the news that these guys were starting their work. He had some questions about it and the good use clause, but nothing too much out of the ordinary. Nothing that would make his boss look like the world was coming to an end.

"I don't understand," Agni said.

"Right. Exactly, I'm afraid. I'm slightly delayed because I just got off a client call. One of yours—Halcyon."

"Yes, I was just talking with one of their people. In fact, I was going to ask about—" Agni started.

His boss interrupted. "Their guy must have called our legal people the instant you ended the call. Because I just heard about that call, one in which you apparently made rather a nuisance of yourself, pressing for that good-use clause. And questioning their early arrival for a survey. Correct?"

"Yes, that's right. As usual. Just the boilerplate good-use clause, and—"

"Agni. That clause is giving us troubles. Right along with the old truth clauses, which we are now working around," said his boss.

"Working around?" said Agni, his voice rising. "I don't understand. Truth and good use are how we set ourselves apart, they are in our identity statements, mission statements, all that."

He found himself and his dragonmark heating up a little. He felt a little queasy. Off-balance. This was not going well at all. He twisted the napkin in his lap, willing himself to remain calm. Appetizers came; his boss had ordered ahi tuna medallions over seaweed for both of them, willing healthy perfection on everyone, thought Agni. He could feel his heart racing and his palms beginning to sweat.

"Those clauses are becoming rather cumbersome to too many of our customers," his boss said. "Good use is too subjective, they say, too wishy-washy. Really inconvenient. Good use for whom? And truth clauses are just old-fashioned for no reason. No longer really relevant. They need to go the way of environmental protection rubbish clauses. None of those things are helpful to the kinds of clients we want. Clients like," he paused, nodded to the waiter, who left the room and closed the door. "Halcyon."

He raised his voice a few decibels. "They don't need us to be nursemaids, telling them what they should be doing or thinking or developing. They just need our funds. And there are plenty of other, much larger, higher-profile-banking institutions who are happy to give them those funds exactly the way they want them. With no restrictions. So. We have been losing accounts, Agni. Mostly the ones in your portfolio," his boss said, looking down for a moment at his plate.

Agni was stunned, scrambling inside, trying to think of what to say. "But I …"

"No arguments. Halcyon is who we want, and they are much too important to lose. You are good but you are not bigger than they are. So. You will need to call and tell this Max person that you have been recently briefed on a change in regulations. No good-use clauses to worry about anymore." He reached over and sipped a light nectar-colored wine. "Really, this should make all of our lives easier, yes?"

"No! That goes against everything we've always said to our clients. How can we do this?" said Agni, reeling inside. He sipped his water, forcibly refraining from gulping it. No wine today; needed to keep all of his wits about him. He blotted his lips, restraining himself from also mopping his now-sweaty forehead.

"Agni." His boss's voice grew deeper as he drew in a breath and frowned at him. Stopped the conversation to savor a small bite of the wafer-thin tuna nestled in its emerald seaweed-salad bed on the gold-trimmed plate. Finally, what seemed to Agni like an eon later, his boss continued. "Not your call. Our key clients will never miss those paragraphs. They have been giving us grief about them for ages. You haven't been paying attention. They don't have to sign clauses like these with anyone else. And they can develop whatever they want to.

"Wake up, Agni. The future of that property, what is it called? Everland Bay or something fanciful like that? "

Agni felt sick. Dizzy, stunned. He could hardly think –how can this be? Everland Bay is *Elise's* cherished place, and theirs when they were younger. And, God. Jemma's. Where is she now?

As if from a distance, he could hear his boss.

"The future of Everland Bay is the Halcyon Corporation, Agni. And whatever they want to use it for. If they want to tear up the grounds and take down antique, useless buildings, that's their call. Not ours. We bring the funds. Got that? We are at the risk of becoming irrelevant to the larger corporations, don't you see? This opens up our competitive edge again."

"That can't be. I've been meeting routinely with my people. Until this recent blip, there's been nothing out of the ordinary. We still define the competitive edge," said Agni, scrambling inside. He had to make his case to his boss. Hadn't been in touch as much as he should have been. This Halcyon thing had to be just a fluke. He could still make this right, surely. He tried to assemble his thoughts.

"Not negotiable, Agni. My team has been working on this for a little while, you know. So. I'm thinking," his boss said, blotting the completely impeccable visage once again.

"Change of plans. Maybe we should just let you go back and make that call now. We can meet for lunch another time; I really don't mind dining on my own. Can always use a little time on my own, you know? I'm sure your call will go well. And I'm sure Halcyon will be singing your praises once everything is all settled." With a brief smile that got nowhere near his eyes, he turned back to his plate. He nodded and the door opened, admitting the busboy, who materialized to refill his water glass.

Agni felt stunned. "But wait, we were just going over…"

"Agni, we're done here."

Dismissed, Agni got up, nodded to his boss, and left the room. Back down the hallway and down past the landing, he pushed though the elegant, carved doors, not waiting for the doorman, who frowned at the abrupt departure. Down the marble steps he hurried, turning to walk toward his office. He wished he could fly but was not dragon enough to do that. And while it seemed counterintuitive to walk, the narrow streets made for traffic gridlock; it was faster on foot.

He ruminated as he walked, using the time to sort things through as he digested the bombshell his boss just exploded in his mind. The cream and gray stone and marble buildings from centuries past, when those old-fashioned good-use clauses really meant something, now loomed over each narrow street. He fairly flew by, navigating the twisting, uneven sidewalks.

His mind was awhirl. Here it was. The end. And all that he had hoped was just rumor was true. Everland Bay was going to be destroyed, right along with his job. And, far worse, he knew that Jemma was in danger.

He had worked so very hard to hide his true dragon nature. Allowing only the parts that were useful to his banking colleagues to show through. His uncanny ability to bring in larger and larger clients. Funds. Masses of contemporary gold. He still had an old-fashioned longing for real gold coins and bars (and did keep a tiny trove of rare, antique gold coins locked in a cabinet at home), but no matter, funds were funds and gold it was, regardless of the actual form. And most importantly to the firm, he brought in all these funds whenever he made a deal. And he slipped under the radar of the Verandalands norms, partly because he was very careful, but partly because they didn't want to see anything that might get in the way of all that powerful money. Wealth. Funds. Assets. Power. He loved all those terms, and so did his bosses. But now he could sense the ethical part of himself, long buried.

He slowed his frantic pace, forced himself to breathe as he continued the long walk back to his office. It gave him time to think. He knew things had to change.

For Agni really was part dragon, despite everything he did to conceal his identity. And no matter how hard he tried over his many years of being alive, or how much the dragon DNA got watered down over the centuries, the part of his dragon self that he could not evade was the fact that dragons were truthful. His human self, of course, could lie easily. He preferred to call it "being flexible" and "adapting to the current norms." But the human-dragon mix was an uncomfortable one. Concealing his identity was a bit of a gray area, so it sometimes caused him digestive problems, but he never had to directly answer about who he was, since no one in Verandalands wanted to believe that dragonmixed folk still, or ever, existed. And he kept a large supply of medication available to quell his stomach's rumbling. But being completely truthful in matters that came to direct questions or statements was a near-necessity for him.

He, as someone so filled with dragon blood and dragon DNA, had real difficulty lying. And on top of it all, he had experienced true love. Love for Elise, love for Jemma. Inside, down deep, he was a good soul. His working with bad sorts, therefore, and the lying that came with it, felt worse and worse over time. He glanced at the trees that formed the cathedral-like corridors along the antique streets. Slowed his pace a little further, reached up and loosened his russet-and-gold silk tie.

Dragons, in all the past millennia, were so powerful that they did not need to lie the way their human friends did. They were brash and could be difficult, but they were always honest. And over the years, over the millennia, they came to understand that the best way to live was to do good and to be honest, as simple as it sounded. It just felt better, all the way around.

It wouldn't kill him outright to keep up his shady life, but it would feel more miserable. His levels of pain would increase. His thoughts turned back to Jemma as he continued his walk. *I'm already starting to lose her*, he thought.

His thoughts turned to his last, explosive meeting with her, and he played back the look of hurt and disdain he saw on her face. *I just can't let this happen*, he thought. *My relationship with Jemma would be in jeopardy, and we could become estranged. And now she's at huge risk, just by being near Everland Bay.*

Agni ground his teeth in frustration as he walked, pounding the pavement with his stride, picking up speed again as he stormed through the city and continued to think things through.

It was likely, he knew, though not completely documented, that these were the reasons dragons and humans fell out so long ago. Dragons always looked at the longer horizon, matched the current problem against the tenets of doing good and honesty. This meant for bigger and bigger disagreements with humans, and they eventually agreed to avoid outright mixing.

But that was the official agreement. Humans and dragons still fell in love, and Agni's line was one of the results.

Breathe, breathe, he thought, striding along with those words echoing in his head like a cadence, or a command. He knew his anger could derail him right now, and that he could not afford a misstep. He had to somehow change things in his life. He would not be able to go through with this rewording of the funding contracts, no matter what Legal came up with, for it would break him. He had to get out of there and help Jemma and Annalyn.

He walked on. Despite the urgency, he could feel a tiny shift toward a calm inside as he reconsidered his way of being. He felt his shoulders relax a little and paused to close his eyes for a moment. He had to do better. He had to live up more to his dragon self. No longer just skirting the edges of it, hoping his living-under-the-radar life would be worth the pain it caused him.

Passing through the Dupont Circle area, he walked across the gray concrete Q St. Bridge, protected at either end by bronze bison, into the quiet edge of Georgetown, glancing across the treetops for a moment and noticing the deep coppers, golds, and maroons of autumn on display. He passed Jemma's condo building, eyes flicking up to his left at her bay window. He felt a stab of pain and regret. How he wished she was there and that he could go up for a visit. Make things better. The windows were, of course, dark. And who knew when—or if—she'd ever be back?

He got back to his office, breathing heavily after the marathon walk. He glanced around and noticed again the photograph of the three of them, still overturned. He picked it up and felt a pang of grief as he looked at it. His eyes filled and he dashed the tears away with an angry swipe. How he wished he could turn time back to that day. Looking more closely, he saw the radiant smiles of Elise and Jemma in that joyful moment, long ago. Could almost sense the sunshine in the photo, taken on the back porch at Annalyn's.

This time, seeing it strengthened him. And he could see the background, could almost feel the vibrant green land, so beautiful, so strong and calm. His wife's homeland. Her mother's land. Somewhere near Everland Bay Institute and Village. Maybe it was time to make a call to his mother-in-law. He needed to find out more information about Halcyon, and what was really going on. Then he'd make that call.

Chapter Thirteen
Annalyn

Walking together over the property used to always be such an unalloyed delight, Annalyn thought, as she and Giselle hurried over her back acreage. With all the recent upheaval, that simple pleasure lost its peaceful quality, though it did help to just be moving over land that was not torn up. Nevertheless, her property was acting up just a little. "Settle, please!" she said sharply, slightly off balance as the ground was roiling under her feet. The land returned to steadiness as they made their way to the flutewood grove.

Her property was hopelessly irregular and a little rambunctious. The northernmost tip of her lakefront touched a small edge of the outer grounds of Everland Bay Institute, while her southernmost border grazed a small portion of the farthest outskirts of Everland Bay Village. As a result, she had, for many years, thought of her home as the Borderlands. She mostly thought of it as home, however, despite its great size. Annalyn owned many, many acres, and had room enough to create an entire village herself if she ever had a mind to, which she certainly did not.

She enjoyed having the space; it came down to her through her mother, who was the carrier of the elfin and fae lines in the family. This could, from time to time, cause some difficulty, as the land had a mind of its own and the borders sometimes moved around a bit, sometimes changed seasons no matter what the calendar showed. Regardless, and even though things were grim now, she always derived great strength from her land.

"Here. See?" Annalyn caught Giselle's eye and gestured to a large grove of shimmering trees, each more beautiful than the next, it seemed to her. "This is most of my own flutewood grove," she said. An immediate protest erupted as the flutewoods rustled vigorously. "Correction. They are their own creatures, of course, not mine. We live and manage this land together," she said, smiling up at the flutewood in front of them and patting it on its trunk. A susurrant chiming-rustling sound sighed through the leaves.

Turning back to Giselle, she continued, "We've walked here together dozens of times, but never paid particular attention to it for its own sake. As you look down toward the Village and over toward the Institute, though, you can see the smaller groves, families really, of flutewood. And this beautiful chain of trees is just what is visible. Underground, there is an extensive connective tissue of roots and fungi between and among each grove. And probably connected elsewhere, but I don't know much about it. We can use them as a communication method and ask the trees and their fungi to heal the grounds up at the Institute. I hope."

"It will take years, though, won't it? Years we don't have," said Giselle.

"Not necessarily," said Annalyn, turning away from Giselle for a moment. "Yes?"

"I didn't say anything," said Giselle.

"Not you. The trees. Hush a moment," said Annalyn, pressing her palm against smooth bark of the sturdy flutewood in before her. "Yes, I, I heard." Annalyn looked up into the crown of the tree. Thousands of leaves shook, rattled, waved, in chorus, in trills, in a continual, cascade of sound. Like a xylophone mixed with a glass wind chime but made of an uncanny mix of rustling leaves along with crystalline and metallic tones, she thought. "I can hear them, and can translate, a little. They are saying 'We are here, here, here. We are here with you.'"

Giselle sighed. "Very beautiful. But I don't see how that's particularly helpful. Let's consult the map in my office and see what is going on. We are running out of time."

"They have more to say!" said Annalyn, pressed against the great tree now, eyes closed. "Listen: here's what they are saying 'We can guide. We can help. Talk. Move bad ones away. Listen to us.'" Annalyn strained to hear more, but the leaves stopped stirring. Stopped the slow chiming speech. "That's it, I think. For now."

She reached up and gave the tree another little pat and turned back to Giselle. Annalyn glanced around the grove to make sure they were safe and only made out small forms, rabbits everywhere, and the tiny, blue-polka-dotted tinkmunks, like chipmunks only smaller.

The two dashed back to Giselle's temporary office and cottage at Borderlands.

At the cottage, they followed the slight scent of smoke around to the back, looked at the realtime animated map, which was still smoking slightly. Fletcher had set it down out back on a large stone bench. "There," said Giselle, pointing at the miniature schoolbus-yellow lumbering forms, trundling along on the grounds. "Bulldozers. Those mages have gone back to work. And look. They have somehow rigged things to get the bulldozers operating, even though we cut off all energy sources."

Annalyn scrutinized the moving three-dimensional map. "They are tearing down the smaller buildings. This in an outrage! That is Everland Bay's land, not theirs. Where is security?"

"They should be right there. I don't know what happened. You were there with me when we called in the gryphons. And earlier, our security swept the place clear of the rogue mages and all their cronies, or so we thought." Giselle turned to look at Annalyn. She bent over the map. "We can't reach in, you know. The land we are seeing is alive but also untouchable. So we can see but not touch. Rather like scrying, but in three dimensions. This map magic is ancient. The map itself is on a millennium-long loan from early gnomish cartographers. The technology is extremely old and fussy to work with."

"Good thing we managed to get it over here. But I am stunned. The insurrection has continued to metastasize. Here we thought the additional forces we alerted would be able to get things under control," said Annalyn, absorbed in looking at the continuous, frantic activity on the map.

"I'm checking in with security," said Giselle, lifting her device to her ear. "We need more forces. This insurrection has become a full-on invasion. They are taking it all by force. And it looks as if we have run out of time," she said, bowing her head as she waited for security.

Annalyn nodded. "Yes. Yes, it does. And I am terrified to think about Jemma right now."

Jemma

Jemma, Keltie, Jake, Leaf, Frond, and Twig were making their way up the hill as fast as they could to Everland Bay Institute. Jemma skirted her grandmother's place, not wanting to risk getting detained. She would fill her grandmother in later, she said to herself. She felt a small twinge inside but knew they'd be stopped if she didn't just keep going. She knew they were in the right and the Institute needed them. She glanced over to check on her posse, whose idea of fast seemed glacial to her. She tried not to show too much impatience, but she was worried that they would never get this done.

The three botanical mage interns were intent on the ground as they went, scattering a continual stream of fungal spores out the back of their small basket-satchels, pressing an occasional mycelial/fungal burlap packet into likely areas, pausing briefly here and there to put their ears down on the ground, close their eyes, and then speak to the ground. Or to the bark of the flutewood trees, with their leafy hands pressed tightly against the trunks. At least, that's what it looked like to Jemma. She caught Keltie's eye, eyes wide, and gave a slight "I don't know" shrug. Well, they know what they are doing, Jemma said to herself, still fretting that they were slow-moving.

As Jemma watched, Leaf, Frond, and Twig had their heads together, whispering and gesticulating even more intently than before and then stood perfectly still, turning to look at the path behind them. Another being, about seven feet high, brown and green all over, and oddly, rather like a flutewood tree, arrived and joined them. The new botanical being was able to speak in a way that Jemma, Keltie, and Jake could understand.

A deep voice spoke in a low, chiming register. "You can call me Song; Dr. Greensleeves sent me along to work with you. I'm a female flutewood dryad, and I've been with the botanical lab here many years. Longer than my younger colleagues, who are still in training. This threat is too serious to entrust solely to our young ones." She paused as Leaf, Frond, and Twig rustled a little. Jemma thought they seemed a little deflated. "You are wonderful, my dears. My presence here just means that we need all levels of skill. This will be more like when we all gather at work and figure things out together." She glanced up again, and the three sidled over and hugged her at the knees.

Turning back to Jemma, she continued, "I will lead now." Her voice slowed markedly. "Please understand. I need to reserve my energy. Speaking to you with human words is very draining, so I will be mostly silent until necessary. One suggestion; pocket a few of the leaves from my trees; they can be helpful in so many ways," she finished, turning to bend toward the three botanical folk and consult with them. She ruffled their leafy crowns a little and they stirred and rustled a bit, completely restored to their usual good cheer.

Jemma, Keltie, and Jake digested this news as they continued on their way, now with Song leading them. They each picked up a flutewood leaf, tucked it into a pocket. The path became steeper, though still covered in autumn grasses, bronze-and-gold yarrows, and goldenrod. Marled, spotted gray stones, appliquéd with patches of lichens, embedded in the land since the last ice age, were occasionally visible.

As they came to the very edges of the Institute boundary, Jemma looked up and saw the impossibly slanted, churned grounds, now slippery with mud. She caught a glimmer of shredded metal and fiberwork. The old perimeter barrier, now torn. The once-blinding iridescence now pulsed only occasionally. A weak heartbeat, sparking in random spurts.

They stopped for a moment, staring at the devastation. Jemma knew she needed to press on, but she felt her breath catch at the rubble-strewn sight. She willed herself to stay strong, though her stomach dropped, and she felt tears prick as she surveyed the grisly damage. Some of the smaller buildings were partly bulldozed, debris fanning out over the grounds. Ancient stonework had cracked, arched, leaded-glass windows were twisted and shattered, leaving gaping wounds in the once-lovely old buildings.

Jemma felt her heart pounding and she heard gasps from Keltie and Jake as they all beheld the broken land. They crossed the boundary. The tearing, tortured scream of the bulldozers hurt their ears.

"Ouch! Back—be careful! Oh, I—" Jemma said, reeling, as the ground shifted and she reached out to steady herself, grabbing the still-sparking fence. As the energy rocketed through her, she could not speak, could not act.

Keltie rushed to one side and Song and Jake to the other. Song and Jake grounded Jemma and Keltie placed her knife between Jemma's hand and the fencing. The current stopped.

"You okay? Maybe we should go back. Get reinforcements," said Keltie, looking all Jemma all over, along with Song.

"I'll be okay. Just. My hand." Jemma was breathing hard, took faltering steps. No way was she going to get this far and stop, though. She gingerly tested her hand, spreading her fingers wide, then shaking it. There were ragged lines burned into one finger. "Got lucky. Not my dominant hand. And just the one finger burned. Let's keep going. Can't let them win," she said, reaching into her pack with her good hand and fishing out a bandage. "Hang on, I'm just going to put this on," she said, wrapping the stretchy bandage around her finger. "This is supposed to accelerate the healing. Hope it works."

Up the hill, they continued. "Oh, god, so hard to see," Jemma gasped as they got within a few yards of the destruction. She felt tiny in comparison with the enormous bulldozers and the horrific devastation. Tears came unbidden again as she heard the piercing, shearing scream of a tree as it was uprooted, twisted, and savaged by one of the machines. She glanced over and saw answering tears coursing down Song's face.

The crew on the bulldozers didn't notice them, it seemed. Jemma and her posse got within feet of the young mages. One of them glanced her way. He shouted something to the others. Jemma couldn't hear what he was saying. The bulldozers stopped. Silence echoed and clouds of dust billowed up, then were shredded in the breeze.

"Get back, or you'll fall into the grounds," said the mage apparently in charge of the site. "Things are dissolving on our command. Other areas are unstable with the bulldozing. Get out of our way!"

"We're here on official business," said Jemma, chin at a defiant angle.

"Right, little girl. So are we," said the young mage. His eyes scraped over her as he fixed her with a haughty sneer. He held his hands out, palms toward the bulldozers as he yelled at Jemma.

"I'll advise you to move back and out of this area," said Jemma, hoping to distract him as he wielded what she assumed was energy beams. "You are not the legitimate owners. You have no rights here," she continued, buying time, desperately wishing that the soil, which was heaving beneath her feet, would stay steady.

Out of the corner of her eye, Jemma could see Keltie and Jake slipping into the background with Frond, Twig, Leaf, and Song, and fanning out, continuing to press the fungal packets into the soupy grounds, and energizing and strengthening the root systems and the land itself. Flutewoods, though now damaged in places, rustled and swayed despite a marked absence of wind. Jemma saw Song speaking to the nearest flutewood trees. Jemma felt the grounds quieting.

The young rogue mage looked up, startled by the momentary silence and the steadying of the grounds.

Now! thought Jemma, as she took the chance and lunged at him, aiming the knife for what she knew had to be an energy beam coming out from his palm toward the grounds. "Back off!" she said, as sparks flew up, knife blade glancing off the invisible energy beam. "Dammit," she muttered, staggering back. She knew she had been too impatient and had not wielded the knife well.

She moved to a higher position and worked to visualize the outcome they wanted: manicured grounds, all buildings in place as before, grounds stronger and more beautiful than ever, castle sparkling in the sun. While she was focusing, she felt her pocket faeries quietly slipping up out of her wristlet, climbing up her sleeve, and stationing themselves around her collar, placing small hands on her neck to lend strength. "We are here with you, you can do it, we are here," they whispered.

Jemma quickly steadied and re-centered, focusing. Instead of using her knife on any living being, she imagined the pristine scene in her mind covering the current devastation. Grounds immediately shifted, changing into the image in her mind. Green lawns appeared in patches near partially restored stone buildings, deep scarlets and pinks and yellows bloomed in suddenly alive flowers. Even the castle was visible, and a bright blue and gold pennant at the top of a turret unfurled itself, snapping a bit in the breeze, exactly as the scene appeared in her mind.

"Whoa! What? How?" Keltie, Jake, Song, Leaf, Frond, and Twig, all talked over each other as they took in the uncanny scene.

The transformation remained in place, and while it was not entirely real yet, it startled the rogue mages while giving Jemma the information she needed. She stayed focused and calmly placed her blade in between the two scenes, between the rogue mages and the picture of the restored Institute, severing the beam of energy that she could barely make out, emanating from one of the rogue mages. The grounds heaved and she shifted her stance, staying balanced. Bulldozers tipped a little and wobbled, gears grinding to a halt.

Jemma glanced at Keltie and Jake, nodded. "Go!" she said.

"Begone!" Keltie screamed.

"Away!" shouted Jake, as the two surged forward then twisted away in two directions, making feints to the right and left of the young mage, who wound up a fist, ready to hammer someone. Keltie knelt, and the fist passed over her. Jake crouched, grinning and watching.

The mage's eyes widened in surprise as he spun around, looking down at the two. "Out of here, now!" he screamed. Empurpled with rage, he rasped, "You! Have no authority—" Completely off balance, he staggered back and away from Keltie and Jake.

"Now!" said Jemma, rushing in again and angling her knife just beneath the young mage's right boot. She felt a tear as she severed the energy he had been directing toward the ground. He toppled over backward and lost his ability to direct energy. The bulldozers stopped.

"Yessss!" said Jemma, clenching a fist in the momentary victory, shifting back to a ready position.

Keltie called out. "These three," she said, pointing to the botanical intern mages, "say they want to hold on to you and work with you. They are telling me that they can see your mind-pictures, as they call them, and can strengthen them. Can weave everything more securely into root structure and grounds, too."

Frond, Twig, and Leaf made their way over to Jemma and plastered themselves to her boots and lower legs. Song stood nearby and became perfectly still. Jemma felt rooted into place and fear crawled all the way through her thoughts. *What is happening? Will I just be a target now for the rogue mages? This is crazy!*

Then she felt a warmth and a quiet comfort, moving up through the soles of her feet, from the ground itself. "Okay. I'm starting," she said, as she began her visualization again, and imagined all of them in it, calling for the highest good for all in the midst of everything she was projecting. The grounds started shifting again, first explosively, waves of turf roiling and trees rocking and shifting, then quietly, slowly settling back into place.

The land was beginning to solidify, returning to the calm, beautiful green sweeps of grasses and flowers and plants that were there before the bulldozers and toxic solvents had arrived. Gold and purple yarrows and asters erupted from the soil, claiming their places, as if from nowhere. The young mages were silent, panting for a moment as they looked around and watched the land and buildings start to heal. Jemma could see their eyes, wide with fear. The quiet in the air that replaced the ear-splitting sounds of the bulldozers was absolute.

It lasted only a few seconds.

Jemma had been working her magic for a very long stretch, and despite the backup from Leaf, Frond, and Twig, her strength wavered. "I can't hold this!" she yelled. Her arm, first shaking with the strain, snapped back, recoiling, smashing into a branch. A searing, screaming current of pain lanced up Jemma's arm, now lacerated and bleeding. She knew Keltie, Jake, and everyone were doing their best, but the dark magic of the ensorcelled bulldozers and the rogue mage team were gaining. They seemed to have strength far superior to hers.

The moment Jemma's hand hit the branch; raucous cheers erupted on the other side. "All right men, it's all ours. Go!" screamed one of the mages. They leapt into action, gleefully moving into place to retake the land. The bulldozers roared.

Jemma retreated. Keltie rushed to Jemma's side, reached to steady her. The botanical mages moved back. Jake hurried to help Keltie brace Jemma.

"Right," said Jemma. Her arm was throbbing. She felt a sense of terrible dread lodged in her stomach. She also felt annoyed with herself, as she glanced at Jake's pack and was reminded of their other gear. The wraps. Maybe they could help. "Let's try our wraps," she said, reaching back, wincing, to fish out the gossamer fabric.

They all clawed into their packs and drew on their wraps, then shifted their stances to make sure their sides touched. The fibers of the wraps reached toward each other and began to entwine. Immediately, Jemma felt the connection among them, strengthening with every beat of her heart. The slight vibration she felt was warm. Comforting and energizing. She felt a surge of hope boosting her energy, then a sense of calm strength infused her. Song came behind them all. The three linked arms and Song spread her arms wide, able to encompass them easily, weaving energies with Keltie and Jake at the shoulders. Jemma anchored the center, forming a bond with all.

"Keep holding," Jemma said. Yet even as she remained centered and anchored, she found herself beginning to lose hope. She closed her eyes in despair as the bulldozers continued, groaning and screeching as they trundled over the grounds and moved again into the marked buildings. The first small building, partially toppled, continued its fall. It buckled and collapsed. The bright paint of the machines was eerily discordant, the color of summertime and sunshine, incongruous in the searing destruction. The building that was destroyed was one of the first structures at the Institute, built hundreds of years earlier. Jemma's grandmother had showed her a photo of it and told her the story once, years earlier. It was especially magical.

A one-room meeting house, its once-whimsical details, including likenesses of long-ago famous elves, dragons, professors, were mostly missing from the building and what was once a front porch, now a splintered pile of broken boards. One carved gryphon was on its side, panting with exertion. Jemma was horrified as she saw it open one eye, lift its head briefly to look at her, then collapse, stop breathing.

"Don't look," said Jemma. "Too sad. Got to stay focused." Each word was difficult, but she felt the strength of the others helping to keep her standing.

"Right. Trying. Can sense the flow," said Keltie, panting with exertion. "These ones," she said, gesturing to Twig, Frond, and Leaf. "Pulling energy straight up. Sending it to us." She bent down for a moment, hands braced on thighs, catching her breath. "Can't keep it up much longer," she continued. "Song's helping, but it's not enough. We're not gaining ground."

"What else?" said Jake. "We've used up all our tricks. Bulldozers are not stopping."

"Last hope. Surprise attack. Use this energy. Surge together," said Jemma, still trying to catch her breath.

"How's that?" said Jake, as they all stood, still linked.

"On three, charge. Crazy, but they won't expect it. They think it's all over already. Start with the nearest bulldozer driver. And that mage, the one sending energy. Lost his footing earlier. Hope he is still unbalanced. At least a little, anyway. Jake, take him. Keltie, we'll go for the one right there." Jemma saw everyone get in place, ready.

Jemma turned a little, faced the botanical mages. "Vines? Can you get them to wrap around everything? And the fungi to stabilize the soil?" said Jemma, working out the plan. She stopped again to breathe. Pant, really. She could barely catch her breath. She saw everyone nod. She felt an assent from Song.

"Got it," said Jake.

"With you," said Keltie.

"One, two…."

Chapter Fourteen
Annalyn

Back in the great room, Annalyn threw a worried glance at Giselle, who was now looking off through the floor-to-ceiling windows, arms crossed tightly around herself. How she longed to just give her a hug and make the bad news go away. How she wished that were possible. Her device chimed and she felt a small shock, seeing the name, and answered.

"Agni? Agni, what is it?" She saw Giselle look over and raised her eyebrows. "Wait, slow down. Yes. I can get her. She's here, actually," Annalyn said, looking over at Giselle and motioning her over. "Okay, we can both hear you. No. No one else. Go ahead."

"Listen closely," said Agni. "I can probably get only one call out right now. I am on my way to the Institute. I will need to stop and use your place, Annalyn, as a safehouse. I will be contacting Max the moment I hang up here and I will be officially a target as soon as I'm done with that call.

Annalyn strained to hear. "Agni, speak up—it's hard to hear you."

"Okay. Max is backed by Halcyon. They sell spirits—whiskey and the like—but are also into hard drugs. Black market. They run an international crime ring. Plan to use Everland Bay Institute as a dark arts criminal magic headquarters. Don't know everything but they're planning to run the front end as a retreat for ultra-wealthy magical tourism, mixed with ample substance use, intoxicants in liquid and pill and powder, as well as high-end gambling. All of this will fund the new dark-magic headquarters."

"What? This is preposterous. How do you know?" said Annalyn

"I know. They plan to retain the castle and the finer stone buildings for the elite, gut the rest, use some for the crime ring."

"This is obscene—how can this be? They don't even own that land!" interrupted Annalyn.

"Let me finish. Only particular underworld mages will be invited to come at first, and they will be required to pay extremely high fees. Halcyon and their partnering mages are convinced there is a huge market."

"Agni, this is insanity! How can they do this with land they don't even own?" Annalyn pressed one hand to her chest, breathing hard.

"They're trying to get the land re-deeded. Bluffing it through with paperwork and lies. I know. Completely insane. We have to stop them. I was assigned a funding deal with them and was the liaison officer for the Institute dark mages who were working with Halcyon."

"How could you do such a thing?" gasped Annalyn. She could hear rustling and noise in the background. "What are you doing there, Agni? I'm having a hard time hearing you," she said, pacing the floor, turning up the volume so that Giselle could hear.

"Give me a chance. I didn't know. I just now put the pieces together. Getting ready to go—packing, locking up. That's the noise you're hearing."

Agni continued, "I thought they were doing what they planned, according to their proposal. All the cover documentation said it was going to be a beautiful resort for families, exclusive, elegant. They lied.

"Said they came into some legacy land, inherited by one of the principals, but covered in tumbled-down ruins. We rarely do in-person inspections of property these days until the day before closing, relying on images the client sends instead. Then we match to our drone-image database. So, we hadn't had our usual walkthrough yet. Our side also hadn't done the final match. We believed the proposal. Or I did, anyway. They were going to develop the whole property as this resort, and even set aside some land for civic use. Concerts, kid's activities, whatever. Very admirable, all around, so it seemed. Wholesome."

Annalyn glanced at Giselle, and they shared a look, eyebrows up. "Okay, keep going," said Annalyn.

"But they wouldn't sign the usual 'use for good' boilerplate and that got my dragonsense up and running overtime," Agni continued. "I met with my boss, who was upset with me for questioning their refusal to sign. He then told me that they were going to have to remove that clause, as well as the honesty clause, and, well, you know. I can't deal with that.

"Annalyn, I can't do this anymore. It was already wearing on me, going against my dragonself all these years. But I just can't keep going. I am losing my truest self. Too much to go into right now. I couldn't blow my cover right then, but as I walked home, I realized what they were doing. I heard some scuttlebutt around the office and heard more from my boss that day. I put my head in the sand for a long time on this, just hoping that the proposal was the way they were portraying it, a family-friendly magical resort. I even thought I might get Jemma to come back here and work with me, somehow."

"Agni!" Annalyn started to speak. She was pacing, clenching and unclenching her free hand. "Your greed. This is what this is about, you know," she said, feeling an enormous wave of rage and grief.

"You took my daughter away from me and now your *work*," she nearly spat the word out in disgust, "may be hurting Jemma?" She continued pacing the floor. Her heart raced as she felt herself shaking with anger.

"Please. I know. It wasn't like that. I don't expect you to believe me right now, but I am begging you to try to listen to me, even if it is just this one last time. You never have to see me again after this. Please, can you let me try to explain?" Agni said.

Annalyn could hear what sounded like pain in his voice as he pleaded. Although there was part of her that just wanted to hang up in disgust, she sensed that he was telling the truth, and she hoped, desperately, that he might have some answers. "I'm still listening," she said.

"I was thinking that the property might be near Everland Bay Institute. I didn't know it was the exact property. I thought it was adjacent and that it would enhance Everland Bay. I really thought that. I was completely wrong. They are going to destroy everything."

"So," Annalyn said. "What can we do if it's already all over?"

"I can attempt to stall Max. I will call him and say that the deal is not yet happening. That's a lie I can tell and feel good about. That should buy a few hours, maybe a day if we're lucky, just in confusion. I will of course be immediately terminated when my boss finds out. He will reverse all my actions and put things right back on course for immediate work and funding. He wants to be the primary bank for Halcyon."

"Okay. Come straight here. One thing you're wrong about, though. The timing. It's not about to begin—it is happening right now. We will send the word out and do whatever we can from here. We will go and try to reclaim the Institute," said Annalyn.

"No! You don't understand," said Agni. "They will not let you do that. I wanted to warn you, but I think I am too late for anything to be done except to keep you and Jemma and everyone safe. Please keep her safe. Please don't go onto the grounds. I don't doubt for a minute that they will kill anyone who threatens them."

"I do understand," said Annalyn, feeling a surge of heat in her face and a churn in her stomach. "And there is no way I will stay away. I cannot."

Max

"What do you mean, the deal isn't working out?" Max could feel his blood pressure shooting up. He stood up abruptly, scattering papers across the expansive, carved oak desk. He was at the temporary

Halcyon headquarters he'd set up at the Institute to finalize the Everland Bay deal. He paced the floor, striding over to the window, which had an expansive view of the grounds.

This deal must go through, he thought. Everything he worked toward rode on this financing deal. His contact, Agni, said it was a go just days earlier. "No. That is unacceptable. We already have a crew there, taking down buildings, as I told you earlier. I have people on the ground right now—any work stop order might put them in danger!" Max finished, knowing that he really didn't care much about the people there, also that they had started the violent attack themselves, but figuring it sounded pretty good. And it bought him some time to think.

"I am terribly sorry, but we have taken the position that this is not a sound investment for our firm," said Agni.

"Excuse me? How exactly can that be true? You were fawning all over us just last week, begging to finance this deal." Max was livid and feeling cornered. Agni was his guy there. He was the only contact he ever worked with in person on this deal. And since he had been fired after the insurrection, which he privately thought of as the protest, he had to have this deal go through. He had no back-up job.

"Sorry to have to go over your head, but I have no other options. This call is over." Max smashed the button to end the call and smacked his hand against the desk. He could feel his heart racing. *I probably won't make it through this*, he thought. "Get me whoever is above Agni Avalon in that godforsaken bank," he yelled, knowing his assistant had his ear plastered to the door, listening. He leaned against his desk, fuming and waiting for the call to go through.

Annalyn

Annalyn glanced at Giselle as she ended the call. "I'm stunned. But I can't afford to think about it all right now," Annalyn said, as she and

Giselle looked again at the three-dimensional, lifelike map. "He sounded terrified. Oh no! Jemma! There she is!"

She could see a very tiny Jemma, almost unrecognizable at the small scale, with her friends. They were running straight toward the melee.

"Why didn't she come and talk with me? We'll never make it there in time!" said Annalyn.

"Oh, yes, we will, or die trying," said Giselle, grabbing Annalyn's arm. "Portal to my old writer's refuge. Just come with me, now!" said Giselle.

Annalyn followed Giselle into her stairway portal, and barely registered what Giselle was saying, desperately hoping that whatever the idea was, it would work.

Agni

Not going to get there in time, Agni thought, cursing his late-dawning realization of all that was happening. And while his fury at himself and his panic threatened to overwhelm him entirely, some part of him knew that wouldn't help. He reached up to his dragonmark and felt a little stronger, then headed out to try to get to Annalyn and then to find Jemma, locking the door behind him. *Wait, what am I thinking? I need to go straight to the Institute. Jemma may be trying to get there, and I can't, just can't think about what they might do to her.*

Though he was not at all certain it was in good working order, he walked over to the dragon painting in his office and walked straight into his emergency portal.

Chapter Fifteen
Jemma

"Three!" Jemma opened her eyes as they surged forward. She let go of Keltie and Jake's hands and focused straight ahead on the frightening scene. She knew with an icy clarity that this could be her last moment alive. She again began to visualize the beautiful Institute, glorious castle, pristine grounds, happy scholars and others roaming the pathways, even as she also saw before her in real time the tumbling buildings, grounds unsteady, faces of the rogue mages and their forces contorted with rage.

Dust from the bulldozing choked the air around them, and in the midst of the chaos, Jemma lost track of Keltie and Jake.

She stood, unsteady for a moment as she tried to orient herself within the billowing dust and the undulating grounds. She could see one of the rogue mages, clutching some weapon she'd never seen, blowing into it. Just then another mage burst through the gritty dust, charging straight toward her. She reached into her pocket and found the flutewood leaf, holding it in one hand and her knife in the other. Her mind became laser like as she watched to assess the mage in front of her, who attacked, kicking the blade out of her hand and raising another of the curious weapons toward his lips.

"No!" she screamed, lunging with her flutewood hand, slashing, darting, slicing. She summoned all her martial arts training and flew at him. Slashing through his eyelid and down his face, inscribing a downward arc across his body that tore his clothes and carved a bloody line.

He stared at her, transfixed, looking shocked as he crumpled to the ground. His weapon had fallen from his hand. Jemma pocketed it and moved ahead, slashing another mage, this time reaching down and, in an instant, slashing his Achille's heel. He fell in a heap, and as the gritty dust clouds began to clear a little, Jemma could see the looks of terror on the faces of the other rouge mages. She couldn't stop, though, knowing that this was still the last hope she had of saving Everland Bay. But knowing, too, that her strength was again beginning to falter.

High above, a great wind stirred. Jemma glanced up to see the source of the wind. She relaxed for a moment as she recognized her friend. Jing circled high above, roaring; the call hurt Jemma's ears but made her heart soar.

She stopped, exhausted. There is no more inside of me, she thought. Her head bowed as she tried to gather her strength. She pressed her hands to her thighs, bent over, gulping breath. A small gust of wind had come up, further disturbing the dust and grit. She flinched a little, worrying that one of the rogue mages might be ready to attack.

As she stood fully again and turned back to look at the angry mages and their grinding bulldozers, she saw that every one of their faces had turned toward the skies, eyes wide open, mouths agape. Jemma followed their gaze with a quick glance, not wanting to miss a beat if they were merely creating a distraction or were just focusing on the dragon.

And as she craned her neck to follow their gaze upward, she saw the most improbable thing. Flapping winged somethings. Pages ruffling, riffling, flipping. A squadron of—books! In flight. Jing had flown to the rear of a great assembly of flying books? Was that Lula? She instinctively groped for the tiny portal book's usual spot in her pocket and remembered that she left Lula safely, she thought, at home. But Lula was leading the charge of the smallest portal books, flying on point. The skies filled with books, in tight V-formations. The smallest ones peeled off and dove straight toward the rogue mages.

"Portal books—that's my Lula!" said Jemma. "What is …"

"Behind us!" said Jake.

She stole a glance back and nearly stumbled in surprise, for who was behind them but the entire village. Jan, the Folio owner, was festooned with vampire books, which were variously perched along her shoulders and taking off, wheeling, and heading toward the rogue mages. The botanical gardens team moved into place behind Song, Frond, Twig, and Leaf, simultaneously conducting all the living green things—vines, grasses, roots, brambles—to grow up and around every mercenary fighter, every rogue mage, as well as Max and the other grim-looking men, who had emerged from one of the buildings.

The vines were growing lightning-fast over the bulldozers and were covering the grounds. Roots, hyphae, microbes, and countless invisible, living things were holding and stabilizing the soil.

Jemma could see that the dark arts mages, Max, and others were completely immobilized, and that they had no choice but to allow their knives and communications devices to be stripped from them, as the combined Village and Institute security forces swarmed around them.

She turned and saw that Gavin and the rest of the Heartwood crew and tech staff, including Fletcher, were there. Jemma felt a surge of warmth and light as she saw him and all the others. They did it! They were all going to be okay, she thought. She *knew*. She let out the breath she didn't realize she was holding. She felt her heart soar as cheers erupted all around her.

Onward came the museum staff, café owner and staff, and all the good professorial group from Everland Bay. She saw her grandmother and Director Azule, coming up the hill from the old writer's retreat hidden in a shallow valley over the ridge. They were spaced every few feet, steadily marching forward. Those who were able trained beams of high-intensity magelight onto the scene, helping to cleanse and restore the grounds. Behind them came others, the whole village, unrelenting, and overhead Jing continued to fly, along with other dragons and creatures too high to be seen clearly.

Jemma felt her dragonmark pulse steadily, and she turned just as her father came toward her. He came to stand behind her and put his hand lightly on her shoulder. Jemma felt herself flinch a little. She saw his shoulders drop and saw his wry smile, seeming to look for an answering smile, flatten out.

"Dad." She wanted to welcome him but didn't trust him. Why was he here? He only got angry at her for using magic back in Verandalands. She couldn't afford to go over all of that ground again. Not now. She broke away and hugged herself tightly. Her breath was shallow. She turned and looked straight into her father's eyes. She so wanted to be close. But it seemed impossible. "What are you doing here?"

"Jemma, I found out at the last minute that my bank was funding this operation."

"What? How could you do this? You know how important this place is to me. To our family."

Time seemed to stop for a moment, for Jemma. This was worse than she could possibly have imagined. Her father's reply was lost in the noise.

Can't think about any of that right now, she thought. She pushed her father's hand off her shoulder, glanced toward her right. She breathed a little more steadily as she saw that her grandmother was coming up alongside her. Jake moved slightly to allow her grandmother room. Her grandma's warm hand, resting lightly but firmly on her shoulder, felt soothing and calming. Jemma leaned into her a little and felt herself sink into that strength. Silently they connected, all of them. Jemma could feel their support and hoped Keltie and Jake could feel it as well.

Director Azule stood on a small rise, robes swirling some in the breeze around her perfect stillness. Jemma could see her glance sweeping the grounds, the people, assessing the scene. Jemma held her breath as Director Azule spoke to the whole marauding group. "You have no rights to this land or this place. Nor have you ever. You have violated our Institute and our laws. You will not leave here free men and you will pay for all the damage from this violation and all the repercussions therefrom. Your time here is finished," she said with a flourish of her arms.

Dr. Azule turned and nodded to her security team, who stood ready for her signal. They arrested and restrained each mage with wrist and ankle cuffs, secured each bulldozer. They worked with the botanical mages, who allowed the green restraints to sometimes recede, sometimes intertwine with the conventional handcuffs and gear.

Dr. Max was livid, shouting at her father. "We had a deal. You could have made this work. Did you inform on us?" He was silenced by a policewoman.

Jemma wondered why he had some deal with her father. But he wasn't the only one going out with shouts, Jemma saw. None went easily. They lashed out with hands and fists whenever possible, yelling and biting and scratching until the security guards wrestled gags into their mouths, some of them woven of green vines that had stayed ready to assist. The communication devices that were confiscated were immediately sealed in lockboxes that emitted no signals, so they could not be traced.

Watching the scene reminded Jemma of the strange weapon she had pocketed during the battle. She fished it out and held it toward Fletcher. His eyes widened and he nodded, taking it from her and stowing it carefully. She felt a surge of relief.

Jemma, Keltie, Jake, Fletcher, Annalyn all hugged, couldn't stop grinning. Jemma felt her strength soar on wings of hope and joy, now alive inside of her. Tears streamed down her cheeks. She looked at her father, whose cheeks were also wet with tears, and whose dragonmark was blazing.

She felt her heart thaw a bit. Relenting a little, she put her hand in his, and reached again for her grandmother. Standing there together, Jemma held her breath and didn't quite know what to do next. Before she had a chance to collect her thoughts, she saw a small, high-velocity object coming right out of the clouds toward her. She ducked and had barely a moment to even begin to think about what fresh attack she was dealing with.

She felt the small something plummet straight into her pocket, nearly knocking her off balance. Eyes closed and expecting the worst, she let go over her father's and grandmother's hands as she reached for her grandmother's shoulder to brace herself. She gingerly opened her pocket to peer inside. Only then did her shoulders drop as she took a deep breath and began to smile, then grin, as she pulled out Lula, who had managed to dive with pinpoint precision into her pocket. She held Lula aloft and everyone turned to look. She began to laugh, and all joined in, clapping and laughing as Jemma lifted the tiny book up to perch on her shoulder. Lula tipped forward a little, in what looked like a small bow, then tucked herself into Jemma's neck.

Jemma couldn't stop grinning. She looked around and felt a deep sense of connection and tenderness toward everyone around her, feeling elated and just the edge of weariness as the high of the moment began to slip away. She knew that the others were feeling the same; a quiet murmuring rippled around the circle and spread outward as they all stood a little uncertainly, wondering what lay ahead.

Dr. Azule stepped into the center of them all. "It is late, and we are all weary. The security team is in place and there is nothing more for the rest of us to do right now. Your brave actions have saved our Institute and our Village, and we are all in each other's debt forever. Now. Time to go home. To rest. Take care of your wounds and your families. And to those of you whom I've spoken with, we will gather tomorrow."

Jemma brushed her curls away from her brow as a light breeze blew. She caught Keltie's eye, and the two quietly moved toward the side of the crowd, motioning to the others. Jake and Fletcher came over. Song was cradling an exhausted Frond in her arms with Twig and Leaf trailing her, holding hands. Jemma felt too tired to speak, but could feel her strength growing, expanding inside as her heart filled with affection. "I, I love you all, you know." She faltered a little, wiping a tear. They surged around, hugging each other, though wearily. "We love you, too. We will always be a team." Song's low voice chimed quietly, deeply, as she moved away with a wave, taking her charges with her.

Jemma turned to walk back to her grandmother's. She knew she needed to patch things up with Grandma Annalyn but was now completely drained. She waved to Keltie, Jake, and Fletcher and found her grandmother. The two walked back together, arms lightly on each other's backs, allowing a soothing silence to surround them.

Chapter Sixteen

The next morning, Jemma woke up with a start, impossibly tangled in the sheets. No. No rogue mages were attacking her. She shuddered a bit, realizing that she had just been having a bad dream. The worst of this mess was behind her. She went and splashed water on her face, shook out her hair, then carefully wove a small portion into a braid and up over the crown of her head, keeping things a little tidier that way. She looked at her reflection in the mirror and gave herself a wink. Her grandmother had taught her that little braid so long ago. Jemma knew she would like seeing it.

As she stretched and continued getting ready, Jemma peered out of her window. She decided to take an early morning walk, then join her grandmother and the others.

The day was breezy and bright. Jemma was looking forward to the gathering, which would happen later. But she needed time to think a bit on her own. A walk to the lake and back would be just what she needed. She glanced down at her feet and noticed the labyrinth. "Wow, I forgot that was even here," she thought. She crunched over the gravel path that wound out and away from the stone labyrinth, and she touched the now-dried Queen Mab's lace absentmindedly as she walked on.

Memories and images came to mind as she started sorting things out. She felt the breeze on her face and closed her eyes for a moment, grateful for the quiet around her. What a change, she thought, from the time she began, in her old apartment in Washington, D.C., to desperately train to be good enough to qualify for a place at Everland Bay Institute.

Then the complete shock of Jing flying out of the tiny bowl and the dizzying, astonishing flight afterward, which not only meant leaving her museum work and life near her father in Verandalands, but a move to a chaotic Everland Bay Institute under siege. To now. This completely uncertain time. There was no clear path. She glanced at the labyrinth, rolled her eyes inwardly, thinking that her own path was a lot like this—convoluted.

She shook off the gloomy thought, turned, and walked toward the lake, soon finding herself nearing the bluff. The infinite view, aquamarine, spruce green, silver, animated with undulating waves, always soothed her. She walked slowly up the bluff and then started down toward the pebbled beach, feeling the stones under her feet round and smooth as robin's eggs, and some just as blue. She reached down, as ever, and picked up a couple of small, azure stones. Threw one out into the lake. Made a wish. Took a deep breath. She opened her wristlet and her three constant companions flitted up to her shoulders, taking in the view along with her, each holding on to one of her long curls, steadying themselves in the stiff breeze.

She gave in to the calming beauty of the lake, allowing the shoreline waves to quiet her mind. After the completely unexpected and violent insurrection and capture of the Institute, here she was, still alive. And now, making the beginning of a life in the Village. She felt a jumbled mix of unsettledness, gratitude, and relief.

She stopped thinking for a moment, still feeling the breeze on her face. Turning again toward her grandmother's home, she continued. She heard the flutewood grove before she saw it over the rise ahead of her, the autumn-dried leaves chiming in crystal-clear notes. As she passed by one, she patted its trunk, silently thanking it for the gift of its leaf, which had turned the tide of the battle. She picked up another leaf, pocketed it.

Walking through the grove and up the hill, her musing went on. *I never would have known the fun of working in Folio, or really being part of this place,* she thought, *if all this mess hadn't happened. Even the awful parts. I just would have, probably, lived like a guest at Grandma Annalyn's and very likely, would have been in training for a long time, trying again and again for junior fellow status, wondering what to do.*

She thought back to the moments of Jing's arrival in her life as she flew out of the ceramic bowl and took her to Everland Bay. It seemed like ages ago. She smiled a little, remembering those first scary moments.

She picked up her pace as her thoughts continued to roll by. If there hadn't been all of the terror of the upheaval, she never would have had a chance to really be a part of things. Even if she was accepted at some more calm time, she'd be entirely wrapped up with the Institute. Or maybe she would never have left Verandalands at all. But if she hadn't come up in this crazy way, the Village would have felt very different. She reached into the lower branch of another small flutewood on the crest of the hill, and gently tapped a leaf, which chimed quietly in reply.

It would be like a resort or something. A place where you visit and enjoy the time there, but always know you'll be leaving, so never really get to know people. Like when she was little. And the people would somehow exist to mostly just help you buy things—whether it was a book or a frozen custard or a cup of tea, and so there would be, like, a difference. Like you were at a distance from them. They would be a "them," not an "us."

Now, she knew, she was right in the middle of them. One of them herself. They really *were* her people. It felt ever so much better this way, and she never would have thought of that. It felt good to have work to do at Folio, and to also be part of saving Everland Bay, and visualizing it as a beautiful, splendid place. And seeing her visualization and manifestation actually working, even though it still needed improvement, was wonderful. Kind of amazing. Because it wasn't just a practice session. She had used it in real time during a war. And it was also pretty great to have trounced that rogue mage with her own skill at marital arts as well as her wielding of the flutewood leaf. She said another silent thanks to the flutewood clan, and also, a little begrudgingly, to her father, who insisted all those years on martial arts classes.

She reached into her pocket and drew out the remaining robin's-egg-blue stone.

"Levitate, please," she said.

She smiled as it rose upward, bobbing along with her as she walked, hovering two inches above her palm before she closed her fingers around it and tucked it away again in her pocket. Her small magics, like this one, had begun to work even back in Verandalands, and she had been gaining in ability in her training sessions there, all those months ago, with Jake and Rhiona. But this new surge of strength and the beginnings of prowess were probably the result of needing it so much. And working in harmony with Keltie and Jake and the others.

It didn't matter whose magic was doing what. What mattered was putting all their skills together to accomplish a huge thing, even if it seemed impossible.

She glanced up, scanning the hills and seeing the familiar outlines of her grandmother's home. Her home, too.

"Jemma!" called her grandmother, who she could see way up on top of the hill, calling out the kitchen window.

"Right here!" She waved a hand high, clearing out her thoughts as she hurried up the buttercream-colored Lannon-stone walk, and into the side door. She felt her throat constrict a little as she saw her grandmother there, warmed by the sunbeams that slanted into the kitchen. Something mouthwatering and spicy had recently been in the oven. Magical chocolate ginger cake, no doubt, her grandmother's favorite. The kettle was a-boil. She sensed, more than saw, these details, as she rushed to hug her grandmother. Inside, she felt a small pang, knowing that her grandmother might be disappointed that she struck out on her own, instead of checking in, asking for permission. The thing she was too tired to go into the night before. Time to begin to talk about it now, she knew.

"My darling girl," said her grandmother.

Jemma was wrapped in her grandmother's arms. She took a deep breath. "I was going to tell you all about going up ourselves, you know. We…" Jemma started, her voice partly muffled by her grandmother's soft sweater.

"I know. Or I hoped. But hush now, there will be time for all of that. We will talk through all that needs to be said. For now, all that matters is that you are safe, and whole, and here," said her grandmother.

They stood back from each other, taking in every detail. She saw her grandmother wiping away a tear and felt her own tears starting. In a near-whisper, she said, "For a minute, I didn't think we would make it."

"I didn't think so, either. I can barely think of it even now, with you right in front of me," said her grandmother, hugging Jemma close again.

Jemma felt a wash of relief and the outgoing tide feeling of a terror escaped.

As her grandmother turned and put the elf-painted teacups in order, festooned with cornflower-blue roses, pink rosebuds, and beribboned green-and-gold vines held in place by tiny painted dragons. Passed down, woman to woman, fae, elf, human, Jemma knew, from time out of mind. She noticed her grandmother's hands, shaking just a tiny bit. She felt a stab of regret, knowing what pain she had probably caused. *We will talk this all through,* Jemma thought, *when we have more time.*

"There will be plenty of time for talking more later," said her grandmother, echoing Jemma's thoughts. Jemma could feel herself relax completely, knowing all was right.

"Jake! Keltie! And is that…" said Jemma, turning toward the banging at the door.

"Fletcher!" said Jake.

Jemma's eyes and smile went wide as the three tumbled in, high-fiving and laughing and hugging. A ripple of laughter trilled around the very top shelves near the ceiling, as the tiniest of faeries erupted in a contagion of delight.

Lula's cousin, her grandmother's mini-portal book, flew around the room. Lula flew out of Jemma's pocket and joined her, causing more glee as they zoomed around the room.

"It's a bit like having parakeets on the loose, yes?" Jemma's grandmother said, flapping her hand at the antics of the books, and smiling at the chaos in her usually quiet kitchen.

Jemma noticed someone else coming into the room as Dr. Azule walked through the door. And then, was that Jing? Yes! Jing scaled down to her safe-for-inside size. Jemma watched as Jing sized down a bit more, so that she could sit comfortably on the counter. The now-tiny dragon's tail snapped a bit, and her emerald, gold, and amethyst scales seemed particularly jewellike today. Jemma felt an answering fizzy feeling in her dragonmark and reached up to touch it, then walked over to Jing and gave her a little caress. Jing leaned against Jemma by way of a dragony hug and curled her tail around Jemma's wrist for a moment or two. She leaned down and kissed her on the top of her scaly head, and petted her a bit, tucking a finger under one wing, feeling the warm dragondown there.

Then Jemma felt something else, a different sort of tingling in her dragonmark and an uneasy mix inside that she could not quite name, and somehow, she knew her father must be here somewhere, too. She looked over at her grandmother. "My father? Where is he? Is he still here somewhere?"

"Yes, he is here. Or rather, very nearby. He has been staying out in the other guest cottage since the moment he came here to find you. The one down the path there. We had to allow him to stay after he joined us—he was there, you'll remember, as we all walked up together. After Dr. Azule and I had portaled over. But we know he might be a security risk, so we have taken the precaution of putting a guard there until we have a chance to understand how safe it is to have him with us. He will join us a little later if it seems wise."

Jemma swallowed hard and felt both relief and sadness; she knew that it made sense to keep him apart but wished that it wasn't necessary. She headed for the kitchen and started to wipe down the counters and put things to rights, trying to stay calm. She felt a spark of anger chasing her sadness. How she wished that he had been with her all the way along, as in, all her life, and how she wished that he was not so set on staying in banking in the Verandalands. This thread of thought followed a familiar and painful pathway in her mind; she wished that he had never taken them to Verandalands. Perhaps her mother… but for the moment, Jemma stopped the next thoughts.

Right now, she knew, she needed and wanted to cling to the parts of this day that were good and strong and hopeful. And there were many. She squared her shoulders, glanced at her grandmother, whose loving glance told her that she probably guessed her thoughts, and, putting down the dishcloth, she turned to her friends, feeling a little stronger again. "I think, if I am not mistaken, that there is a magical chocolate ginger cake in our future," she said.

"Indeed, there is!" said her grandmother, who turned to the counter and began to slice the heaven-scented cake. "I always have the ingredients on hand, just in case." She arranged the sweet, crumbly slices on a favorite serving platter, trimmed with tiny hand-painted roses and gold ribbons held aloft forever by miniscule pegasi.

"Dr. Azule, for you," said Jemma, with a slight curtsy and a smile.

Dr. Azule reached for the cake with a smile. "Thank you, my dear. Annalyn, this looks as delicious as ever." She looked around the room. "I can hardly believe you are all here, all safe, all well," she said, glancing down for a moment.

Jemma handed a slice of cake to Keltie and said, "I was so focused on the rogue mages that I barely looked at you, but I could feel your energy."

"Yes, I was sending it to you, and adding a web of spells everywhere I could think of. Just weaving in more and more, adding strength to our side," said Keltie.

Jake jumped in, fork poised in one hand, before he began devouring the treat. "Me, too. It seemed right to stand together and send energy, and I kept thought-elixirs going through the soil, sensing my way toward the botanical mages' energy lines, and blending with what they and the fungi were doing. They are amazing, you know," he said. "This cake is also amazing." He grinned, tucking in.

Fletcher added a somber note, glancing around the room, setting aside the cake. "Yesterday was one of the toughest days I've ever lived through. I wasn't sure we were going to make it."

Jemma turned toward him, noticing the worry that creased his forehead. She felt the answering quiet of the room. "When those rogue mages just kept rolling with their bulldozers, tearing up the ground and starting on the smaller buildings, I thought we were done for. That it was all over, and we lost. The roots themselves were screaming out from the torn ground, twisted and shredded. What were you hearing on your end?" she asked.

Fletcher turned toward Dr. Azule. "Some of it is classified; Dr. Azule will be briefing those of us in security a little later and I'll be able to say more then."

"You may tell everyone the highlights," said Dr. Azule. "I know you are aware of what to keep for our conversation."

"The rogue mages are part of a large network of organized magical crime. Dr. Max, who was one of our professors until he was fired after the insurrection, had been encouraging them for years, penetrating the board at Everland Bay Institute and radicalizing some of his colleagues."

Fletcher took a deep breath before he continued. "This is hard to wrap my mind around still, really. But anyway, Dr. Max was convinced that a move toward what's known as urban tech magic was the way to go, to keep Everland Bay current and fashionable among the avant-garde magery worldwide. Problem is, that kind of magic is deeply tainted by organized-crime magic. Those bulldozers, for example, are not normal bulldozers that are seen in the human-majority lands. They are clever constructs, woven of a base of nonmagical engineering, techwork, and illusion. It is not that bulldozers are a problem, specifically, but they are able to wreak havoc more quickly than hand magic or hand tools during the right conditions, which they had. We'll have to figure out how to break those down later, by the way.

"They relied on stealth, surprise, fear, and confusion on our side to exaggerate the illusion of their invincibility. The destruction was swift. When the resulting gashes and wounds in the landscape were then seeded with poison and rot, as they were doing, the rot took the ground very quickly. Their willingness to use weapons that could cause permanent harm is one of the flags we know to look for when we are doing surveillance," he said. "They may be using banned toxins; we'll have to keep an eye out as we comb the grounds. The weapon you found, Jemma, is likely one of the delivery systems."

Jemma shuddered. "But how did he get such a foothold?"

"Dr. Max is one of those men who is a toxic mix of golden boy and bully. Has been all the way through his time here. Others underestimated him. Kept making excuses for him."

Dr. Azule broke in, nodding. "I'm afraid Fletcher is right. Those of us on the Council kept giving him chances, kept hoping for better from him."

Fletcher waited for a moment, then continued. "It was bad. He kept breaking rules and hurting people and creatures and was not stopped. Because he was a bully and really harming others, people shied away from confronting him. At the same time, in his earlier days, he was a brilliant magician. Innovative as well as aggressive. He pushed for more authority. He also hid the vicious, destructive elements of his darkening magic. Hid his torture of small creatures, for example." Fletcher glanced at Dr. Azule.

Dr. Azule nodded. "There is more to all of this; I cannot go into much of it. We began to reign him in. He had supporters, though, who were very well respected, and we were committed to being fair. We did, however, underestimate him, and his supporters, in the end. And we were too late to stop him." Dr. Azule stood up, paced the floor.

"We thought he acceded to our demands," she continued. "Which included dissociating from any dark mages or magic, and coming back to a standard, classic approach to magic. He agreed. He even signed legal documents stating his agreement. We did not count on his duplicity. His lying. And many in the Council just couldn't believe he wanted to harm us. They continually said that he would 'pivot' back to a reasonable, mature, wise self now that he had signed the agreement."

She turned and faced everyone, paused for a moment. "We questioned him at length last night. And we found out that he long ago decided he would master this new world of magic himself. He loved the power and believed his path was the way to get it. He took it upon himself to approach legitimate human-run large banks, like your father's, Jemma, as well as dark-money funders in the shadow world of organized magic crime, which also intersected with the worst of human organized crime. You've all heard of Halcyon. The company, the substance. It now is a stratospherically wealthy organization that is thoroughly criminal at its roots. They decided to make Everland Bay Institute their base of magical operations. We did not know the full breadth of their hold here until the insurrection and attempted takeover. Thanks to all of you, we have been spared. I believe this is why Jemma was summoned by Everland Bay itself. And why you were brought back early, Jake. Those of us who were in charge here were not seeing what was right in front of us. The three of you—Jemma, Jake, Keltie, with a strong assist from Fletcher—probably saved us all. Now, come gather around the map," said Dr. Azule.

They did so and marveled at the Institute and landscape all around it. The grounds were beginning to heal.

"Look! Mushrooms!" said Keltie. Sure enough, tiny rows and groupings of mushrooms were just visible, all along the seams that had been lined with mycelial packets. Some of them were glowing a bit. A murmur of awe circled the room.

Chapter Seventeen

A few moments later, Jemma was startled to see a familiar figure out the window. She glanced at her grandmother. "My father is here."

Jemma's father knocked on the kitchen door but didn't wait for an invitation as he strode through the door and joined them all. There was a silence.

"Is it true? That you were funding them?" Jemma started, standing up and facing him. Her heart raced and she felt herself turning red. She had hoped that things had begun to get better with her father, but this news just made everything a hundred times worse. She was breathing hard, furious. She felt as if she'd been punched in the stomach.

"Jemma, honey," her father started. "It isn't so simple. I need to explain."

A lifetime of pain and anger boiled up and out of her as she stood facing her father. "Explain what? How could you be part of this? I thought you were doing work that was normal. Legitimate. You always told me about the importance of banking—how it helps everyone, not just wealthy people. You always told me how honorable your work was. How it would be such a good field for me." Jemma shook her head in disgust.

She stalked away, toward the windows. "And I was hoping, maybe, when I saw you coming to join us yesterday, that you were truly part of us. That you were on our side. *My* side. How could you do this to us?

To me?" Jemma said, shaking with fury. She turned back and saw her father's expression change as his initial smile cratered into a frown.

He bristled. His eyes flashed, and his chin went up as he turned toward them all. "I was hoping for a welcome." Silence greeted his words.

Jemma noticed her grandmother and Dr. Azule glaring at her father. His bravado evaporated under their harsh stares.

He sat down heavily, hung his head. "But I am afraid that you are right, though not completely. I am ashamed. I have been lying to myself for a long time. And to you, and to your mother before that. But not consciously. I was so convinced. You and I have had some of this conversation before. I was hoping and hoping that I could balance my dragon self, which can't abide the bank in Verandalands and finds it unethical, with my human self, which feels so strong and powerful and justified as I bring in more and more wealth. I find the human part of me wanting to prove that my motives are good and therefore justified, and just make you accept my wishes," he said.

"Like you've been doing all these years," said Jemma, walking back a few paces, turning to confront him.

She saw him tense up as he glared again, briefly, at her. Then the light in his eyes went out a little. He bowed his head. "Yes," he said.

There was a long silence. Jemma was so tired. Tired of the struggle with her father. Painfully aware, as ever, of missing her mother. "What changed?" she asked.

"There was a lot that I didn't know."

"How could you not? And how much more have you known all along? Maybe Mom would still be alive today if you hadn't taken us down to live in that awful, practically nonmagical world. Where we were both bullied and shamed. At the end, I was in danger!" Jemma put her hands in her hair, feeling desperate. "Did you know that? How could you want me to stay there? How could you do that? How—" Jemma stopped, hardly believing she had said all of that, feeling suddenly nauseous.

"Please." He raised his hand, palm out, in a stopping motion.

All the others were completely silent, looking down and away from Jemma and her father. Jemma sensed the unease but was livid and didn't feel like downplaying her anger. She glanced over at her grandmother, who nodded at her, and who motioned to the others to move into the next room.

Jemma spun away and stalked over to the windows again. Shaky inside from voicing the forbidden topic. Her mother's death. Their greatest grief. And the dangers of being in Verandalands. It was as if she touched a rail of pure electricity.

"Just try to hear me out," her father said. "I never meant to cause harm. And this recent project—I did not know that they wanted to take down the place. I just realized it all yesterday, after a critical meeting. The moment I put it all together, I called your grandmother and rushed up here to try to help." He went over all the details and the timeline of when he knew the true danger of what his bank was doing.

Jemma listened from her place at the windows, staring out over the forest and fields, hearing his words as she was fuming, still breathing hard, trying come to grips with her thoughts and emotions.

"Will we ever be safe around you? Will I ever be able to…" Jemma could not finish.

"Trust me?" said her father.

Jemma nodded.

"I hope that one day you will find a way. I know that for me, things have already changed completely, as if a spell was broken after all these years. I have no interest or desire to go back to that life of evasion, of half-truths, of painful appeasement of my bosses at the bank, of hiding and hoping no one notices my dragonself, my dragonmark," he said, reaching up to the corner of his eye, briefly touching the iridescent mark.

Jemma reached up in unison, touched her mark as well. She also felt tears and closed her eyes briefly.

"The most painful part for me is that after losing your mother, I have now lost you," he said, putting his head in his hands. "Nothing seems important anymore."

Jemma looked at him, then left the room, unable to speak. Unable to continue the celebration.

Walking outside and down beyond the meadow, Jemma found herself again heading toward the lakeshore. The tall grasses gave way to sand dunes, undulating ribbons of long sand-and-soil ridges, which then gave way further into the bluffs surrounding Lake Michigan. The breeze blew her hair away from her face as she looked at the shifting grays and blues of the water below. Whitecaps rode the crests and seemed to echo her roiling emotions.

Her father was behind her, running to catch up. "Jemma." His hair blew in the wind, and he stopped, panting a little.

She looked at him. "Did you really not know? Did you really think Everland Bay would be safe?"

He put his hands lightly on her shoulders, returning her gaze. "I swear it. I heard rumors that the development was nearby. Never that it was the exact property. The documents I was given to work with all said it was a ruined parcel of land, abandoned long ago. Known to be in this area somewhere, but this region is large," he said, sweeping one arm out and around, indicating the vast landscape. "Some of the old magical estates have been left uncared for, though it is rare. I wanted to trust my bosses, our clients, their documents.

"And that was my great mistake—I knew that they were unsavory. But I thought they were simply typical, aggressive developers. I had no idea about the criminal aspects. Zero. I hadn't been able, or willing, to connect the dots until just yesterday." He paused. He looked down. "Can you ever forgive me?"

Jemma looked at her father and again at the lake, trying to absorb its raw energy, as the breeze picked up and the waves surged and roared. The wind tore at her, and she wrapped her arms around herself, feeling lost and alone. She turned away and jammed her hands in her pockets, flinching as she felt a leathery, square shape and heard a squeak—Lula!

"Oh, Lula!" She stroked Lula's cover and found a smile forming in spite of herself at this creature's sweetness. She also felt the leather, metallic flutewood leaf that was still in her pocket, grateful that she had not sliced her hand on it. It reminded her that she was part of Everland Bay, and all of the people and magic there, including her own. She glanced at her father.

"I can try," she said at last.

"Good enough," said her father. He started to reach for her shoulder again but before he could get there, Lula hopped over to him, perching on his hand, and tilting toward him, as if to inquire about something.

He glanced at Lula, and Jemma saw the ghost of a smile on his face. Eyebrows raised, he asked, "Can I take this as a good omen?"

Jemma nodded and found herself unable to hold back first a small smile, then her tears. She reached for her father, who hugged her tightly as Lula fluttered up and dove back into Jemma's pocket.

"I've missed you," he said.

She wiped her eyes with the back of her hand. "I've missed you too, Dad."

They took their time walking back, slowly navigating the shifting sands, the shore grasses, then the ground as it grew firmer underfoot and gave way again to the bluffs crowned with grasses, scrub bushes, and forest. Dragonflies and pegasi were startled out of the bushes and flew out and around them, breaking the somber mood. Jemma ducked away from a particularly aggressive one, who nipped at her right ear. She brushed it away. "Shoo! Such pests. Cute, but can be pesky."

"Never did get used to those," said her father, with a smile, ducking and waving the miniature flying horses away.

***

They walked into the side door of her grandmother's. The others had all gone, leaving just Grandma Annalyn and Dr. Azule.

Silence enfolded them as they entered the main room and sat down.

Jemma looked toward the two women. She could sense their strength, and she could see that they were waiting for her lead. A part of her wished that they would just take over now. Say all the right things and make all the right decisions. But another part of her felt strong enough to continue.

"We've been talking. I don't know what is next. I don't know how to feel. I am still pretty stunned, and sad, and angry. And more than a little confused," said Jemma, glancing over at her father. "But I also know that I love my father. And I am very like him, as a part-dragon being. I don't know what to do with that, but I think I want to learn with him."

Jemma's father reached over and patted her shoulder lightly, reached up and touched her dragonmark, which glowed in response. "Oh, honey. I do love you so. I cannot bring your mother back, though every part of me wishes each day that I could. But I want to do everything I can to be a good father to you, even though I know I'm very late on this. I have burned every bridge to Verandalands and the bank. That world is gone for me. I don't know what is next or what is possible. I will ask here, or at someplace in the greater magic-friendly lands, whether they are interested in my skills. I hope to start over. What's most important, though, is that I am hoping to have a chance to start over with you."

Jemma moved away a little, regarded him, then hugged him again. Her grandmother and Dr. Azule smiled.

Silence greeted his words and continued to bring peace to the room. Jemma looked at her grandma, who was looking right back at her, her eyebrows raised as if in a question. Jemma gave her a barely perceptible nod, and the smallest of smiles.

"Well, now. I think we have even more celebrating to do here," said Grandma Annalyn with a nod. "And Agni, I believe you have earned a little of my chocolate ginger cake."

"Only if it's the magical variety," he said.

Laughter and relief rippled around the room. Jemma felt her heart fill as a sense of hope arose deep inside. She found herself smiling widely at her grandmother.

"What other kind is there?" said Jemma, taking a filled plate from her grandmother and ceremoniously handing the spicy cake to her father.

Later, after more laughter, a little more recapturing all that went into the day of the battle, and a bit more cake, they began to tidy up.

Jemma's father stacked dishes in the kitchen, rolled up his sleeves, and began to wash the delicate China. Incongruous in a faded, pink-flowered apron, he grinned as he washed every last dish. He took off the apron, wiped his hand across his brow with mock exhaustion, hugged Jemma and her grandmother. He turned to go. Dr. Azule called out to him, "Agni, I am staying at my place on the grounds here, just a little before the guest cottage—care to walk with me?"

Jemma watched them leave and was grateful for the time alone with her grandmother. She was surprised to see the sun beginning to go down.

"The day has gone by so quickly. And it's just the two of us now. I know you'll probably be thinking about looking for your own place eventually, but I am so glad this is still home for us both," said her grandma.

"I wouldn't want to be anywhere else right now," said Jemma.

The two finished straightening the room. Jemma looked around, comforted by the familiar pillows, colorful throws and shawls, muted now after years of sun-fading and use. They each found a well-loved wrap and curled up in favorite chairs. Jemma felt the familiar comfort of the shawl; this one, she realized as she pulled it around her shoulders, was one that her grandmother had knitted long ago. She could feel it connecting to her energy, soothing her. The faeries sensed it too, she knew, as they slipped out of her wristlet and tucked themselves into its warm folds. She smiled, glanced at the end table, and reached for the Storybook. "Can you tell me a story?"

Her grandmother came over, kissed Jemma on the forehead, took the Storybook, and began. "Long before anyone remembers, long before our grandmothers were grandmothers, there was a very special place for mages young and old to gain deep wisdom."

Jemma reached for her knitting, breathing deeply and feeling a deep quiet within as the familiar words wove their story and the dark settled softly in the woods and fields around them, slowly erasing all the features of the landscape.

The End

About the Author

Lynne Shaner has been captivated by fantasy, myth, and fairytales since childhood, when her mother first read *Charlotte's Web* and *The Wind in the Willows* to her. She lives in a village in Wisconsin, close enough to Lake Michigan to walk to the shoreline every day. Shelves overflowing with books line her home, and there is always a knitting project on her needles. She lives with her husband, and Merlin, her small, adorable pup. When not writing, she can be found reading and knitting in her garden, when she grows herbs and flowers and story ideas. This is her first novel.

Note from Lynne Shaner

Word-of-mouth is crucial for any author to succeed. If you enjoyed *Journey to Everland Bay*, please leave a review online—anywhere you are able. Even if it's just a sentence or two. It would make all the difference and would be very much appreciated.

Thanks!
Lynne Shaner

We hope you enjoyed reading this title from:

www.blackrosewriting.com

Subscribe to our mailing list – *The Rosevine* – and receive **FREE** books, daily
deals, and stay current with news about upcoming
releases and our hottest authors.
Scan the QR code below to sign up.

Already a subscriber? Please accept a sincere thank you for being a fan of
Black Rose Writing authors.

View other Black Rose Writing titles at
www.blackrosewriting.com/books and use promo code
PRINT to receive a **20% discount** when purchasing.